The Arriviste

The Arriviste

James Wallenstein

milkweed
editions

The characters and events in this book are fictitious. Any similarity to real persons, living or dead, is coincidental and not intended by the author.

Published 2011 by Milkweed Editions
Printed in Canada
Cover design by Jason Heuer Design
Interior design by Ann Sudmeier
The text of this book is set in Dante MT Pro.
11 12 13 14 15   5 4 3 2 1

First Edition

Please turn to the back of this book for a list of the sustaining funders of Milkweed Editions.

Library of Congress Cataloging-in-Publication Data

Wallenstein, James, 1963–
    The arriviste / James Wallenstein. — 1st ed.
      p.   cm.
    ISBN 978-1-57131-084-2 (pbk. : alk. paper)
    1. Investment bankers—Fiction. 2. Avarice—Fiction. I. Title.
    PS3623.A445A89 2011
    813'.6—dc22

                          2010046012

This book is printed on acid-free paper.

To Christina

The Arriviste

part one

chapter one

If by 1970 I had started to slip, it wasn't by much. To make more
of the decline would be easy: exaggeration resonates in candor.
My income had fallen, though not to any depth. That would
have required a spectacular reversal, and, contrary impulses
notwithstanding, I seem to avoid spectacular actions of any
kind. I still had plenty of money in 1970, more than my neighbors could reasonably hope to come by, yet not so much anymore that I could forget them. My lawn was no longer quite big
enough nor my hedges high enough.

In the little while since he had moved in, the man next
door and I had had several distant encounters, tentative nods
and waves from both sides of the property line. You'd have
thought we were marooned soldiers uncertain whether our
countries were still at war. Things between us might have
begun and ended there, our curiosity satisfied by what we
could see of each other—the broad, swarthy, well-groomed,
well-dressed young businessman on the move I took him for
and the deliberate, disheveled, abstracted, middle-aged professional he might have taken me for—and what we could infer
from what we had seen—on my part, that his bearing was a bit

too ethnic and his stride too hurried for an organization man; on his, well, it is hard for me to say how I came off from that distance, whether it was my eyeglasses or the hitch in my step or the rattle of change in my pocket that caught his notice. But something did catch it.

I'd see him arrive home from the train station after work, a chrome-trimmed black-and-white LeSabre coming up the driveway, his wife beside him in front—she'd shut the door on her side of the car so quietly that you couldn't be sure the latch had caught. He himself wasn't so quiet. He'd all but slam the door on his side off its hinges, and his voice would follow her up the flagstone path into the house. *When* he followed her in, that is. More than once he turned instead toward the hedge on the border, toward me.

I thought at first that he was checking his flower beds, but he hardly looked at them. Something else took hold of him, re-straining the swagger that came with doing well enough to get where he had gotten. Eyes narrowed and lips pursed, he'd turn and look my way. There was confinement in that look. He's discovered landlock, I thought. Not the fact of it—he must have known that all along—but the feeling. My way lay the Sound, and so the sea. To reach it he'd have had to go through me.

I abandoned the third-floor window, crossed to another, and parted the curtain to reveal the bay—a green sliver in sum-mer, in winter a mighty chevron.

Our first meeting, which I thought nothing of at the time, seems now—twelve years later—to begin a story I have yet to escape. And the memory of this first meeting is framed within our second, on a late summer afternoon when he dropped in. His timing was bad.

I was at my desk, supposedly looking over some documents

but really staring through the windowpanes in the grip of some bewildering emotion. I had returned from upstate, where my wife, Joyce, and I would go in August to see my mother. Joyce hadn't come this time. I'd thought her absence might be welcome, but it made my mother, Lenore—which my older brother, Mickey, and I had long ago corrupted to Leon without letting on to her—suspicious and even more vinegarish than usual. It seemed that I was only just back when Mickey insisted on sailing across for a visit. The change in my circumstances, he said, had made him want to see whether I was holding my own.

"The change in my circumstances," "holding my own": the phrases were typical Mickey—bluff, evasive in the service of a politeness more abrasive than most rudeness. When it came to me that they were the same words I had used some weeks earlier to break the news of the change to him, the irony of their phony delicacy provoked me. Whether he'd meant to throw them back at me or had parroted them made no difference.

I had been served notice of this change in my circumstances on the Triborough Bridge in June. Joyce and I were on our way to meet another couple for a play. We were late. Joyce had made us late. It was her habit. Lateness seemed to excite her, to turn a ride into a race, an outing into an adventure. If it hadn't meant keeping our friends waiting, I wouldn't have minded. But we *were* keeping them waiting, and I did mind.

"We're only a few minutes behind," she said in that deep, diaphragmatic, merry voice of hers, a voice that gave some people the idea that she was brassy. "You act like the sky is falling whenever we're a few minutes behind schedule."

I held my tongue through stop-and-go traffic. The guardrail had just been painted green.

"We can always eat after the show," she continued, her eyes

on me. She turned back and stared straight ahead. "So you're bent on ruining another evening, are you?" she asked. It was as though she was daring me to ruin it and, beyond being curious to see whether I would, wasn't herself concerned.

"Don't be ridiculous," I said. "It's all in your mind. I haven't said a word." I wasn't about to have the punctuality argument again.

"You don't have to say anything. It's in the set of your jaw and your grip on the wheel." She might have been discussing a picture.

Light from the city reflected off an iron crossbeam suspended from a crane—skyscrapers were going up in the outer boroughs. "I'm sick of hearing you analyze my behavior," I said, "sick of your thinking you know what's going through my mind."

"Okay then, what are you thinking about?"

"I wasn't thinking about anything."

"You can't think about nothing."

"Just watch me."

"Money, Neil? That's where your mind goes when it's in neutral. When other men twitch in their sleep they're supposed to be running from something. You're kicking figures around."

As it happened, I did have a worry right then. A pension fund that lost several million on a questionable long-term debenture that Weissmer, Schiff, Marne—the small investment-banking firm I was a partner in—had unloaded on them was suing for face value plus compensation. Although I had been trying to reduce my in-house counselor's role, I was also planning to withdraw my interest from the partnership and had a particular stake in limiting the damage. But I wasn't about to let her in on it. She'd only say it was my fault.

"I could be thinking about the rebuilding." A hurricane had torn a section of roof off a house Mickey and I kept in the hills above Puerto de Habòno. "If I don't keep my eyes open, we might end up with a tin shack."

She kept shifting positions. She never could get comfortable in a bucket seat. "I see," she said. "Your obligations may make it impossible for you to be an amiable companion tonight."

"That's right. They can do that."

"And lateness has nothing to do with it."

"I don't think it does."

She might have started to answer, but we had come to that part of the bridge approach where the road's surface changes from asphalt to metal grid and the hum of the wheels drowned her out. It seemed I had carried my point—a rare victory, tainted by the sulfurous odor rising from the river.

I sped up when I saw that a taxi driver was about to cut me off. He tried to do it anyway, and I blew my horn.

"I think I'll go for a while," she announced when we were back on asphalt.

"Go? Go where?"

"Go, you know, away."

"On a trip? Sure, I guess. Have you thought of taking Vicky?" I was speaking of our daughter.

"Vicky's a big girl. She's about to take her own trip." Seagram's Seven cascaded into a highball glass on a neon billboard. "And I'm not taking a trip."

"What do you mean?"

I didn't see it. The bridge, its silver cables and beams and rivets; the river, the wavelets rolling northward; the sky, a low arrow of haze extending from LaGuardia to the Bronx—none of these would let me see it.

"You know what I mean, Neil."

"I don't, I'm afraid."

"I mean, leave home."

"Leave home?" I thought of her dark eyes and a dimple that appeared at a corner of her mouth when she smirked, fondly or contemptuously—identical yet unmistakable expressions. I thought of the inward curl of her hair above her shoulders, the slenderness of her arms, on which the articulation of the muscles around the wrists and of the wrist bones themselves would have been seen as exaggerated had they been sculpted. I thought of how when she was excited she opened and closed her hands as though clicking castanets. Her hands were doing that now.

"You mean, me."

She stared straight ahead.

"You mean me, don't you," I repeated. It had grown warm inside the car. I lowered the window.

Some genius a couple of cars ahead had missed the change basket at the toll and gotten out to hunt for his dime.

"Why?"

Another genius behind us leaned on his horn.

"Put that window up. It's freezing."

I put it up halfway. "Why?"

"Oh, come on, Neil. How many laughs have we had lately?"

"Laughs? I seem to've lost count. Sorry."

"Well, it's not for lack of fingers."

The FDR Drive was clear for a change. The feeling that at any moment traffic might back up kept me from making up much time, though.

"And since when have you been counting?"

"Since when? Oh, I don't know. Sometime after Peter." She meant our son, who had died at eleven in 1961.

"Are you telling me that for nearly ten years—"

"I don't know if it's been ten years, Neil."

"I said 'nearly.'"

"Let's just say it's been a long time."

She wasn't going to let it go on any longer. Next morning, after what might have been a pleasant night out, she left. She seemed to have condensed all the air in the house into her suitcases.

"This is how it happens," I heard myself say aloud. There wasn't air enough to say more.

But my happiness had never been my brother's worry. His expressions of concern were the merest pretense. I tried to discourage him from visiting by insisting that Joyce would be back. He came anyway. "Always looking for an excuse to spend time on the boat," he told me. It was clear before long that he was working up to something.

"Well, there aren't any obvious signs of chaos anyway," he said, dropping his heavy frame on a lounge in the sunroom. His mouth hung open and the points of his incisors glinted in the light coming through the window. "No change in the atmosphere in here."

"The atmosphere? The dehumidifier runs without a woman's touch."

"But what about you?"

"I'm all right."

"Are you? You're looking gaunt, frankly. I don't guess you're putting away your three square. And you're dressed like an undertaker, not that anybody would take you for one. Undertakers are always well shaved, and you've missed a whole patch along your jaw. Looks like an outline of the state of Maryland. And what's that, a sore on your lip? I hope you haven't gone out and caught the clap. Slide those down this way, will you?" He pointed to a bowl of nuts and a nutcracker on a lacquered tray in the center of the coffee table between us. It was no nearer to

me than to him, but he'd have had to sit up to reach it. No one
had touched the bowl since his last visit. To everyone else it
was an ornament, but Mickey was a great one for nut cracking.
Pecans, Brazil nuts, macadamias, hazel nuts: he'd crack them
all. Eating them was an afterthought—he'd half grimace at
the taste of them. They seemed to make him cough. I slid him
the tray.

There was a silence while he took a walnut and ran it over
his palm. I yawned, but he didn't seem to notice. "These things
can cost quite a bit," he said, "quite a bit." I thought he meant
the nuts. "Half your assets and a good chunk of your pretax
income, if she shoots the moon. You'll need to make it up."

"With Joyce?"

"Well, sure, that'd be best, of course. . . ." He took up the
nutcracker and squeezed the shell of a Brazil nut till he was red
in the face. He turned it and had at the other seam, but it still
wouldn't open. "Stubborn little cunt," he muttered. "Only, that
isn't what I had in mind."

"No?"

"I was thinking that the expense—alimony, property division, et cetera—might make you hungrier than you've been."

It hadn't taken him long to show his cards—he'd hardly
made it through a quarter of the bowl. Our fraternity rested
less on a common fund of childhood memories than on a stable
of profitable partnerships-at-will we had formed, in coal and
natural gas initially, later in building and manufactures as well.
Mickey had a talent for structuring deals along heads-we-win-
tails-you-lose lines, and roughed-up entrepreneurs were forever suing our joint holding company, McNeil Bros. Ltd. These
suits had always been dropped or dismissed, until, about a year
before, a ruling had gone against us and opened the gates to
other claims.

"Just wanted to see how I was holding up, did you?"

"That's right—trying to keep you afloat."

"Isn't the litigation wearing you down?"

"Why should a few hardship cases wear me down when the law is on our side and there are opportunities wherever I look?" A piece of almond that had attached itself to his lower lip bobbed as he spoke. He felt it there and tried to lick it off between phrases, but it stuck.

"You'll have to seize them without me."

"But can you still afford to be on the sidelines?"

"It's no time for me to take chances." This was only half true. If I didn't keep ponies or host shooting parties or race my own cars, I still had about as much as I wanted. I could identify the pinched feeling etched on the multitude of new faces around me, but I hadn't known it myself. And as long as I minded my own business and remained wary of Mickey's prospects, this was how it would stay.

Mickey wouldn't hear of it. Every building site we drove past—and they were everywhere: you couldn't tell whether the shopping malls were going up around the new houses or houses around the malls or whether both were there for the sake of the roads that led to them—provided an occasion for a harangue on the favorable climate. He kept at me until I agreed to look over documents he'd happened to bring with him. It was these that I was pretending to grapple with upstairs when my neighbor dropped in to thank me for the favor I'd done him when we first met.

He didn't seem to remember that I hadn't done the favor willingly. Or if he did remember, he didn't care.

A record playing in the living room (a scratchy string quartet I'd stopped listening to in the search for the pack of cigarettes

I was beginning to suspect I'd again left by the pool), the tones of Vicky's phone voice merging from upstairs with the line of the viola, our scaredy-cat mastiff Frances sprawling across the newspapers that were scattered at the foot of an Eames otto-man in the library, ice cubes melting in a tray on the kitchen counter: such was the scene when he stuck his head through the screen door and said "Hello?"

Frances went through her routine, the folds wrinkling be-tween her eyes as a sense of alarm penetrated her anvil skull. She rushed for the door, pulled up short, and barked once per-plexedly before hiding herself behind the couch. "Come in," I answered.

"Big dog," he said, staying put.

"Big pussycat."

He entered and extended his hand to me, a straightforward offer after many cautious salutations. "I'm Bud."

He didn't look up close as I'd imagined he would. Black, Vitalis-sheathed hair pushed back and to the side, broad brow barely creased but heavily freckled, eyebrows tapering into arrows that pointed at his pulsing temples when he frowned, hooded eyes, a nose that was big without being long or wide and suggested the bowl of an upside-down tobacco pipe, an upper lip that didn't fit evenly into the lower. His face was an odd fit, a motley composite hard to take in all at once, hard to take in and hard to pin down because he was always in motion; he talked with his hands, listened with his brow, agreed or dis-agreed by touch. No wonder that my brush with his memory comes as a clap on the shoulder.

"Bud?" I asked. "As in . . . ?"

"As in Schullberg, Adler, Hackett, Rommel."

"Rommel?"

He clapped me on the shoulder. "Jumpy, huh? Just seeing if

you were listening. I often get away with that. My last name's Younger, by the way."

Younger than whom? I thought, and nearly said.

"I moved in next door a few months ago. You've seen me coming and going, haven't you? I know I've seen you."

"Well, sure," I said, finally taking his hand. "Neil Fox. Pleased to meet you."

His wife had taken his five-year-old daughter, who was running a high fever, to the hospital. It was just a precaution, he explained; there was no real danger. Still he wanted to borrow a car to go see them.

He had put me on the spot. I owned three cars, but only my pleasure car was in its bay, an Alfa Romeo runabout in that red that only the Italians seem to be able to get—vermilion luster with crimson depth—or that looks the way it does only beneath their enamel. I had lent the car out before, and it hadn't come back in the same shape. Even good drivers were prone to struggle with its tricky clutch. Who knew what a father racing off to save his daughter might do to it? The simplest thing would have been to drive him there myself. The fact that I'd put a few scotches under my belt wouldn't have stopped me, except that I'd recently been pulled over and couldn't risk its happening again.

"You see, I'm due somewhere."

"You wouldn't have to take me. I could borrow a car." He absentmindedly swept a few bits of ice from the countertop into the sink. "Your wife—you're married, aren't you?"

"Yes."

"Doesn't she drive?"

"She's away."

He nodded in the direction of our three-port garage. "And you haven't got another car?"

"Normally, yes, but just now they're out of commission."

"Maybe you'd have time to drop me there beforehand?"

"I'm afraid not. You see yourself that I'm not dressed to go out."

"How long will that take?"

"A taxi would be here sooner, I'm sure."

"A taxi, here? It'd take forever."

"I'm sorry, if it was any other time . . ." Any other car, I meant.

My refusal staggered him. That is, the look he gave me before he turned to go—part wince and part sneer—staggered me.

"Hold on a minute," I said, following him out the door. "Can you handle a sports car?"

"I used to sell them for a living, practically."

I decided to go with him. At least this way I'd be able to assess the damage to the car if not to control it and, after some coffee, drive back myself. "Be with you in a minute," I told him and went upstairs to run a razor across my face and change my clothes.

He was waiting by the car when I came down. "Were you able to change your appointment?"

"No trouble at all."

He did know how to handle the roadster, handled it so well that—despite the usual difficulty getting into reverse—I enjoyed the ride, a rare occurrence as a passenger in my own car.

I wasn't the only one enjoying myself. He seemed to be taking us on a tour of the neighborhood.

"If it's the hospital you want," I said as we made our second lap around the local streets, "there are more direct routes."

"There's a shortcut to the Expressway. You go behind the park up there."

"Take a right up here. It'll put you on the access road."

"But I'm telling you, we can go parallel to it."

There was no such shortcut but I let him drive on. It had been a while since I'd taken any notice of the hilly streets named for fallen stands of trees or of the specimens that survived along the edges: locusts along The Locusts, birches along The Birches, dogwoods along The Dogwoods, hemlocks along The Hemlocks.

When the crash of '29 threatened to ruin the masters of the estate of Dunsinane—its hillside chateau commanding the harbor, stables, polo grounds, and dairy—they sold their woods to a builder who put up the genteel houses he christened "Dunsinane Gardens." Now, a generation later, the professional men who had been its pioneer settlers were moving on or dying off and their successors, far from being the sort that the masters of the manor might have known, weren't even the sort whose names they could have heard without alarm.

My place in this succession was unusual. I had come later than the first generation but earlier than the second. My house was higher than the others, my grounds larger.

But not by as much as they had been. Bud's land had until recently belonged to me. Selling off an acre of the property had seemed like a perfectly good idea. The builder was trustworthy and the price was right. Besides, I hadn't figured on staying. The prospect of looking at what had once been mine didn't concern me.

"Lucky for you we're in a hurry," Bud said as we were beginning our third lap. "Otherwise I'd find that shortcut."

We turned off the residential streets and onto an empty boulevard over which traffic lights hulked from braided cable. The lights had four and five and even six different lenses that flashed the alert or blinked for prudence or pointed to new roadside oases: to a turquoise and orange ice cream parlor-cum-motor lodge, to a transmission service endorsed by a former middle-weight champ—or onto the highway itself.

I haven't sensed anyone's inner clock ticking so loudly at a red light as Bud's. Trivialities already consumed enough of life, I could hear him thinking, without this automated bureaucracy adding to the sum. And being behind the wheel of a machine that strained at idle as much as he himself did must have made him even edgier. When it stopped, that car didn't sit so much as crouch like a sprinter on the starting block. The lights went our way and we flew down the boulevard past the motel and the rest, up the highway ramp, and over a buckle in the road that stirred the memory of a wreck I'd been in some years earlier. "Let's get there in one piece!" I exclaimed.

He didn't answer. He gave no sign that he'd even heard me. He saw daylight and went full throttle. The space closed up and he hit the brakes. He had to, though he didn't have to slam them. The tires screeched.

"Take it easy!"

"How can so many people be heading for the city at eight on a weeknight?" he muttered. "Where do they all come from, the bottom of Lake Ronkonkoma?"

He veered to the right and, finding the service road at a standstill too, eased the car onto the shoulder and sped up. Everyone honked as we passed, and I started to protest that this was making us conspicuous.

"If you don't like being conspicuous," he asked in an off-the-cuff manner that distanced him from the question, "what are you doing with a car like this?"

I didn't answer. The present held all the embarrassment I could contemplate. Our race down the shoulder of the road drew more honks and killing glances. I slunk lower in my seat and, withdrawing from conversation with my go-go neighbor, studied a cotton-ball cloud to the west.

I'd have liked to turn around the moment I dropped him off but thought I'd better take a few minutes to sober up. The walk from the parking lot might have been longer than the drive. I picked up a cup of coffee in the cafeteria and made my way to the emergency room.

It was hot. Nixon and Rockefeller stared down from the wall like hawks waiting for someone worth diving for. Two men wondered whether the air conditioning was out or off; the subject changed to annuities. I lit a cigarette. In less time than it took me to smoke it the Naugahyde seat was sticking to my bottom. I switched places and, waiting for the new seat to stick, leafed through a discarded afternoon paper that was hardly different from the morning edition. Volatility was in short supply.

Bud came in as I was getting up to leave.

"Lizzy's fine," he said, shaking my hand. "Stick around for a moment and you'll meet my wife."

"I'd better be on my way." I thought I'd been imposed upon enough for one afternoon.

But on the way back I found myself ruing my departure. What had become of my spontaneity, my sense of event? I waved the feeling away—the driver beside me seemed to think I was making some sort of hand signal and slowed down. I went home to the ice tray I'd left out on the kitchen counter. The cubes had all melted in their boxes. Melting ice, that too was an event.

As he had when he'd come to borrow the car, he rapped on the doorjamb, pulled open the screen door, and shouted "Hello?" like a city kid calling from the street to a friend in an upstairs tenement. An open door meant an open house to him, and when no one answered, he let himself through the side gate and into the yard. From the window beside my desk, I saw him,

a package in hand, going down the path in back to the swimming pool, where Mickey was fulfilling his daily quota of laps
and lengths.

The weather had begun to turn, summer to retreat: every
day the sunlight blanketing the water's wobbly surface did less
to warm its depths. Soon fallen leaves would clog the skimmers,
stilling their flaps and blocking the light, and darkness would
rise from the bottom as in a lake. It would be time to close
the valves, shut the pump and filter down, and drain the pool.
The approach of winter always weighed on Mickey, who'd be
determined to get in as many workouts as he could before it
got cold. Though not a fluid swimmer, he was dogged. Even
from my window I could see that he was in his own world, a
trance of hums and slaps, of hurried breaths and clumsy strokes
and kicks. Bud put the package down beside a chaise and stood
waiting to be noticed at the edge of the pool. Running out of
patience, he grabbed Mickey's wrist as he was coming to the end
of a lap. It must have startled the hell out of my brother. I could
almost hear the heart that had been throbbing from exertion
knocking inside him from fright.

Bud's nerve in grabbing a stranger surprised me, until I realized that he had mistaken Mickey for me. We weren't much
alike as brothers go, but from certain vantages we were alike
enough. This was an uncomfortable realization, though not
because I had a low opinion of Mickey's looks. They were fine,
certainly better than my own. But in other matters I was in the
habit of thinking of myself in contrast to Mickey. Bud's mistake
made me wonder whether there weren't other points of resemblance that my eagerness to note the differences had made me
overlook—the set of our shoulders, perhaps, the shapes of our
skulls, the proportions of our limbs.

Mickey unglued the goggles from his eye sockets. Bud
recognized his mistake and began to retreat up the path. But

instead of continuing his workout, Mickey leaned against the side, boosted himself out of the water, and toweled off. Bud remembered the package he had left behind and came back for it. He and Mickey exchanged more words, which led to Mickey's offering him a seat or to his helping himself to one.

I couldn't make out what they were saying. Their voices refracted off the water and scattered. I thought of Bud's curiosity about me or my house or something that was out my way and grew uneasy. I thought next of Mickey's pretense of interest in my well being and was uneasier still. I imagined Mickey blithering on about me and Joyce, asking my neighbor what he knew about it. Their looks and gestures were directed toward the house. They almost had to be talking about me. Who or what else did they have in common? But evidently I was in no hurry to break in on them. I stayed in my chair for a while before going downstairs.

I found them lounging on their chaises as though it was seventy-five degrees and not fifty-seven, sunlight falling through the bare spots in the branches onto Mickey, who in his gold-colored robe resembled a leopard after a good feed. Reclining in that bulky, half-open robe with his body hairs spilling between the lapels, he seemed too large for the chaise's pallet. The broad chest and big gut merged to form a trapezoid in which it was hard to tell where the muscle ended and the gristle began. It took a leap of faith to believe that somewhere beneath that mass a skeleton was buried. Considering all that they had to support, his legs were scrawny and his skin pale for a regular swimmer's.

"It's out of my patch," Mickey was saying, "but I do know a thing or two about it."

"How are you, Neil," Bud said.

Mickey's right shoulder was twitching. In uneasy moments, his head was prone to twist and his shoulder to bob against it so hard occasionally that he had to clench his jaw to keep from biting his tongue. The anticonvulsive serums that he had been dosed with in childhood filled our medicine chest. The spoon often had to be jammed down his throat. He'd been right to resist. If they weren't harmful, the elixirs were unnecessary. The tic was seldom so severe that he wasn't able to shake it off, as he did now.

He turned to me and raised his hand to shade his eyes. "Bud was just telling me about something of his, ah . . . what did you say it was, Bud, a process?"

"I'd put it more in the realm of a concept."

"A concept?" I asked.

"It's a straightforward thing," said Bud. "It's hard to believe that it hasn't been thought of."

"Probably has," I ventured.

"All great concepts have a disarming simplicity," added Mickey.

"I see," I said. "It's one of the great concepts."

"We're looking forward to hearing all about it." Mickey smoothed back his hair as if smoothing over my hostility. "We have an insatiable curiosity about new ideas. Comes with the territory. I gather, Neil, that packaging comes into play. That's right, Bud, isn't it?"

"Sounds intriguing," I broke in. "But you know, Bud, my brother is leaving tomorrow and we have a lot of ground to cover."

"Of course," he answered. "I'm running late myself. I'd only meant to drop by to give you this." He handed me the parcel he'd brought and fixed me with a look hinting that before I came downstairs my brother had been talking about me after all.

"See you again," I said as he was leaving.

"Count on it, fella."

When he was out of earshot, or when Mickey thought he was, Mickey turned to me. "We were having a nice chat till you came along," he said. "What in hell have you got against him?"

I looked at the box Bud had left for me. Its shape promised a bottle of King's Ransom, the scotch du jour. It was tasty stuff, I had to admit. Few other gifts could have made me regret my unfriendliness more. "What have I got against him? Not much. Which is why I wanted to get rid of him. He doesn't want to get mixed up with us."

"He's the one who brought it up. And why shouldn't he have? He's got an idea he believes in. He's casting around for backing. If it seems worth looking into, then I think we should look into it. It's the way things are done, Neil. I'm not sure why you need to be reminded of that. You seem to think there's something unsavory in what we do."

"You do see, don't you, why I wouldn't want my brother to start doing business with my neighbor."

"I don't see it, I'm afraid."

"Because if you start, *I'll* end up doing business with him."

"And what'd be the matter with that? You don't like the idea of the sweet smell of success coming from next door?"

"It's the other smell I don't like, the sour one. Imagine living next door to that."

"It's all sour as far as you're concerned. You've become so mistrustful that you wouldn't know a fair proposition if it stood on its hind legs and sang for you."

I unwrapped the box and found a note from Bud thanking me for taking him to the hospital. There was also an invitation to a party. The thought of it nearly ruined my pleasure in the anticipation of the gift. It isn't that I disliked parties. But the prospect of rubbing elbows with a clutch of boisterous strivers seemed, well—it seemed the very opposite of whatever it was to sip at the King's Ransom in the peace of my own living room. At least the party was a long way off. I'd have plenty of time to come up with a plausible excuse. But what did I care whether it was plausible? In fact, it'd be better if he didn't believe it. He'd know not to invite me again.

I had just hung up the phone in the foyer one afternoon and was thinking about the things I needed. A housekeeper, for one—our latest, a Holy Roller who as far as I could see spent most of her day in a rocker singing hymns, had decided that it would be unseemly for her to stay in the house with a bachelor. I needed another station wagon. And after calling around to car dealerships and discovering that orders for wagons were backlogged, I was thinking that I needed a personal secretary. Joyce's attention to romantic intangibles might have slackened over the years, but on practical matters it had never flagged.

The phone rang again. I let it ring—a splotch of sunlight streaming through a transom onto a corner of the wall had caught my notice, a hydra-headed blue and orange shadow that twirled, disappeared, and returned in a different spot—till it occurred to me that one of the car dealers might have found something. But it was no car dealer. It was Joyce.

There were greetings and pleasantries, and I heard the old warmth in her voice, the intimate or at any rate exclusive tone she used when she was away and anticipating our reunion. But when the formalities were done, she remembered herself. Her voice closed up and she was all business: the things she wanted and needed and didn't want and didn't need and had forgotten to mention.

I didn't say much myself, and was careful not to contradict her. But however I agreed on every item, there were more on her list, and more, their recitation like the construction of our estrangement's barrier. Finally I broke in to ask her how she was really, and after pretending not to know what I meant, she declared that she was "thriving under the new dispensation." I was all over it.

"Thriving under the new dispensation? Where'd you get that one? Don't tell me you've taken up with a clergyman."

"Watch it, Neil. I don't have to put up with your sarcasm anymore."

We hung up, and I found myself staring at that shadow. It was awfully busy, its spheres and specks bobbing and spinning. Too busy for my liking, evidently—I was running my hand over it like a cat trying to pin it down with a paw. When the shadow disappeared, it seemed that I had succeeded—till it was back again, as irrepressible as the meaning behind Joyce's stilted phrase.

Though I must have come across Bud in the following weeks, I can't say that I noticed him. Only a memory of him in his garden comes to mind: a stray lock dangles over his brow while he digs holes into which his daughter places the bulbs lying in burlap beside her. But this might well come from another time. Having been vandalized by sentiment, the dates on such images are generally illegible.

I didn't see him, and then I saw him all the time—mornings inbound, evenings outbound. In the station house or on the platform or inside a train car, I'd see him and he me. We'd say hello and go back to our newspapers. A hint of embarrassment at my earlier rudeness to him lingered. Winding my way down the slalom-course of the newspaper's columns I'd remind myself to make amends without really intending to do so. But I wasn't about to invite him over. The idea of entertaining anyone, let alone him, was impossible. Joyce's absence would make it too awkward. That I ultimately met the obligation was only thanks to Vicky—thanks, that is, to her wild backhand.

In her girlhood Vicky had been a natural at tennis, strokes smooth and balance steady from the moment she'd picked up a racquet. I encouraged her and got fast results, victories in local tournaments, and a regional ranking. But before long the round of camps and clinics and coaches was taking her away from us. Joyce was for weaning her off competition. I had another idea. I had played seriously myself and didn't see why Vicky and I shouldn't work out together. I decided to build a court for her at home.

And I did build it, over Joyce's objection and despite some hostile geology: the ground was less stable than I'd been led to expect, the bedrock higher, the drainage faster, the water table deeper; a silver-colored copper beech that in the original plans had been left alone had had to come down. I let Joyce choose the barrier between the court and the surrounding ground. She rejected them all: clubhouse, fence, hedges, ditch, terraces, a stone wall. Nothing would do. The clay court we ended up with was easy on the feet and the eyes too, but it punished you for missing. Other than the brick ledges I had the builder sneak in, there were no backstops. The ball could fly or roll—or fly and roll—where it would. What we had, thanks to Joyce, was a court for experts. This was okay, my partners qualified. And Vicky could hit a spot and hit it again. You'd have had trouble pitching it from ten feet as accurately as she could put it there from the other side.

But that was Vicky at twelve. Thirteen was something else. She put her racquet down right on schedule and for the next four years hardly picked it up. It was all I could do to drag her out there. If not for visitors using it from time to time, the court would have gone to waste.

Now seventeen, Vicky had come home from a summer cycling trip with an appreciation for physical fitness. All that pedaling had done her good. She had decided to go out for her school tennis team. She would train in the afternoons and on weekends for as long as the fall weather would let her. Was I willing to help? Of course I was willing. If my legs weren't what they had been, my eyes were still good.

It was a far-fetched plan. Tennis was serious business at her school; no one joined the team as a senior. Her real motive was for us to take up where we had left off five years earlier, to revive a broken home. But I was too enthusiastic to see it then. The plan was a portal to a fuller salvation—turn the clock back on one mischance and you turn it back on all the rest.

That evening we sat on the porch watching the last of the fireflies on the lawn, and drank to our future success. She would play on her school team in the spring, and next year in college. Had I been able to guess at the stray forehands and backhands to come, I'd have had her go out for baseball instead.

A check that I had left Vicky miraculously reconstituted itself on her return from the village as racquets, balls, shoes, and what had to be one of the skimpiest tennis dresses a father ever saw on his daughter. It was no more than a bikini, really, with a few beads for a bodice. After an arm-crossing, foot-stomping, teary melodrama, I prevailed on her to take it back.

That afternoon and the next, all through the week, we hit the court, though it'd be more accurate to say of Vicky that she hit everything *but* the court. She sprayed balls everywhere, upending the grooming tools, knocking roses from the vines and leaves from the trees.

She was bound to be rusty, I reminded myself. I might even have taken her wildness as an encouraging sign. But I couldn't take it that way. Her once smooth strokes were now hurried;

her hips and shoulders, whose motion had been instinctively coordinated with her racquet's, now lurched on their own. None of this would in itself have doomed her chances, though. The damning fact wasn't that she was missing her shots. It was that she smiled after she missed them. She hadn't lost just her form. She had lost her drive.

The old Vicky had been intense and exacting. The new Vicky was a hit-and-giggler, as giddy at the sight of an errant ball as at a shooting star. She'd spin around, wave her arms, even laugh, and seeing my frown, cry "C'mon, lighten up, will ya, Dad?" Lighten up! I saw Vicky's campaign as a second chance and myself as at an age where second chances are not to be taken lightly. My humorlessness seems foolish now, or worse.

We kept running low on tennis balls, though our hopper would be full to overflowing when we began. With Vicky swatting them like a sandlot slugger the shortage wasn't surprising. We lost time collecting them, and lost them themselves in the undergrowth and in the salt pond. Then there was Frances. For such a hulking beast, she was avid for tennis balls. But she was no retriever. She'd pick them up, gallop away in triumph, and, slobbering them up, scatter them like giant seeds. We might have had tennis-ball trees everywhere.

Vicky was coming back from a recovery mission, the half-empty hopper swinging on her arm, when she announced that she'd just met our neighbor and invited him over for a game.

"Him?" I pointed Bud's way with my racquet. "When?"

"Oh, sometime, I don't know. I thought you'd be glad to have someone to spell you."

"Gee, thanks. I didn't know he played."

"Maybe he doesn't really. We'll see."

"Maybe he doesn't really? Now Vick, you don't want to waste your time out here. Didn't you ask him how he plays?"

She straightened her racquet strings, which clicked like the tongues of a disapproving chorus. She could infuse our discussions with the feeling that I was interrogating her. Call it an instinct for sullenness. "Sure I asked him, but, you know, how much can you tell from that?"

"Exactly. And what did he say?"

"He said '*un peu.*' You know, 'a little.'"

"He answered you in French?"

She moved from her strings to her barrettes. Refastening her mane was an undertaking. She pulled back a tress and held an open barrette in her teeth. "Uh huh," she said through the clip.

"Why'd he do that?"

"Oh, I don't know. It was in context."

"In context? In what context?"

"In the context of my telling him I'd been in France and him asking me whether I'd picked up any of the language and my saying '*un peu*', which is what you're supposed to say, and so him saying it when we got to talking about playing."

"I see. He was answering in kind. But a little might really mean a *little*. He might have picked up a racquet once or twice in his life. You know, when you're working on your game the way you are, honey, you really shouldn't agree to play with just anyone. A weak partner can bring you down."

"God, Daddy, I was only being friendly. He seemed nice."

"He is nice. But it may be hard to get rid of him for just that reason. I've been in that kind of situation before. It can be awkward. And he does live right there."

We'd planted a dogwood on the first anniversary of Peter's death, put a bench beside it on the third, and planted a rose that turned out to be a climber on the fifth. The rose had clambered over the bench and was taking over the tree. I was looking at it a couple of evenings later, thinking it needed trimming, when the percussion of a tennis ball being steadily exchanged reached me from the court below.

Vicky and I had agreed to take a few days off from training. She needed to get ready to go back to school, she said. They were rainy days anyway—not the misty September rain that drips in slow tears from the leaves, but a gustier variety that shakes down those leaves and sets them hopping like birds in the grass. Though I'm sure that Vicky's excuse for our layoff was honest, I couldn't help suspecting that she was also making me pay for the way I'd spoken to her after she'd invited Bud for a game.

I marched down the overgrown avenue in what was supposedly our apple orchard but was really our apple graveyard. We never managed to harvest the fruit, and the worms gorged themselves on it. As I came over the rise at the top, I pushed an apple aside with my toe and exposed one that was as thick as a slug, with that band in the middle like a cummerbund put on for the meal.

"Daddy!"

The call seemed to come from behind me. I took a few seconds to line it up with the figure of my daughter below on the court, reluctant to believe that the thwack . . . thwack of shots and replies like the call of a bottle-throated bird had been coming from her racquet and Bud's.

"Neil!" he called.

I waved and they started up again. There was some uncertainty in his motion, the mechanical exaggeration in something newly learned, but he had the knack. His shots were square, and even if he'd only recently taken up the game, he and Vicky played it in sympathy.

Darkness was falling on them, pink cloud trails consuming the daylight. They'd soon have to quit, unless they were so attuned that they could play by moonlight. They stopped rallying and approached the net, and I saw that someone was watching them from the bench beside the court—a hunched figure in a dark jacket with a briefcase on his lap. "What next?" I heard myself exclaim.

I turned back up the row of apple trees.

"Come down!" Bud cried.

"Catch up with you later!" I shouted back and continued over the hill.

"Catch up with you later," I had said to Bud, and now, deeper into the week, he was catching up with me or, having come off the court from a second game with Vicky, trying to. But again his timing was off. By catch up with you later, I must have meant something less definite and further off than later this week. He had done no more than accept my daughter's invitation to play tennis and been a good partner to her. I couldn't blame him. I wasn't about to thank him for it either.

In the intervening days, Vicky and I had gone back to practicing together and I had gotten to appreciate her improvement up close. But it didn't bring us together—we didn't click. I wanted to help her to continue her progress, but she wanted me to marvel at it. She not only ignored my corrections, she took offense at them wherever she could find it. What she was after was a yes-man, not a coach. And that was what I became, looking past her flaws and limiting my comments to compliments that couldn't have done her good in the end.

This end was mercifully approaching—the end of school vacation, that is and, a few weeks later, the end of the season. The wind would replace the dirt it had stripped from the foundation with leaves, and a dry thaw would crack the clay. The net would be taken down from the posts, the tape for the lines up from the ground, the pipes that fed the sprinklers drained, the roller and brushes stowed away, our racquets screwed into presses.

It was a matter of chance that I should have come home early from work. I hadn't gone in till noon, but the firm's internal investigation had reached such a pitch that I grew tired of the shouting and knocked off before five. I might have had it in the back of my mind for Vicky and me to squeeze in one last workout.

The auspices were good. At Penn Station I ducked into a train as the doors were shutting. My timing had given me no chance to pick up an afternoon paper, but even this turned out well. The trees were in their autumn beauty. The farther we got from Manhattan—past the markets, depots, sedge-stubbed marshland, and water towers of Woodside and Flushing—the farther east we traveled, the deeper the color of the leaves, the redder, the more golden, the fierier, and the more advanced the season. With the section-ends of the rails clipping beneath us like the second hand of an accidental clock, we seemed to be heading into the future, except that since I was riding backward, I imagined instead that I was backing, counterclockwise, into a lovely past that unfurled itself in retreat from the setting sun. I arrived home renewed.

I went inside, and hearing voices from the back, found Bud, Vicky, and a boy about her age in the living room, racquets, soft drinks, and a briefcase on the coffee table between them. "How are you, fella?" Bud said and stood up. He had a way of engaging you before you'd had a chance to size things up, a forward charm. But I didn't find it charming then. Even from the periphery he was becoming a persistent presence. My domain was shrinking.

"This is my son Daniel," he said. "Danny, shake hands with Mr. Fox." The boy was sitting cross-legged, and the uncrossing seemed to give him some trouble. Bud might have reached over and jerked him up if the coffee table hadn't been in the way. "Get up, Danny! Sorry, Neil. He's got no instincts for the social graces. Brilliant kid, though. Mind like a steel trap."

Bud wasn't kidding about his son's lacking social graces. Still in his overcoat, the boy looked like a seminarian. Darkly sallow, pimply, and shy, he was already taller than his father but stooped away the extra inches, which were just more awkwardness.

He limply shook my hand while gawking past me. I thought that he was staring from shyness at his briefcase till my glance shifted from the coffee table to Vicky's side of the couch. I felt my jaw set and my blood rise. "Excuse us for a moment, will you?" I said. "Vicky, if I may speak with you privately?"

Vicky took her time getting out of her chair. A cobweb dangled from a curtain rod behind her. "Put down your glass," I said to her, "and follow me."

I led her to the maid's room, shut the door, and switched on a light. The wallpaper had horse-and-buggy drawings and was beginning to peel. The bedspread was covered in newspaper, the bolster doubled up for reading against.

"I thought we'd agreed on your returning that . . . that outfit."

"I didn't get a chance. I needed something to wear today. No laundry gets done around here anymore."

"You must have a dozen other things."

"Not for tennis, Daddy."

"And in your mother's closets?"

"Her stuff? You must be kidding."

"I'm not."

As we argued, I advanced toward her and she retreated, not

so far that I was standing over her but near enough to see the goose bumps on her arms—and not only her arms. In the entirety of its width and span, that Italian number wouldn't have covered more than a few dozen goose bumps.

"We've already had this discussion," I said. "We've got guests out there."

"So why are we in here then? Let's go entertain them!" she shouted and did a lewd little shimmy that her slinky top didn't begin to clothe.

"I can't . . . I won't have you—"

"Listen to yourself—you can't even speak! You should see yourself quivering like an old schoolmaster."

"—I'm saying that I won't have you looking like a tart!" And when I heard myself, I even felt like a schoolmaster, a tyrannical schoolmasterly father who thinks it's his duty—his impossible duty—to see his daughter through other eyes than his own. But then I looked at her again in her half-naked ripeness and thought, She doesn't know what she's doing!

"I mean," I continued more quietly, "that you shouldn't provoke—"

"Who, who am I trying to provoke, which member of the family"—she pointed toward the living room—"the bookworm in there? He'd only notice me if I were in a book. His dad? He seems to like you. You think he's hard for his friend's daughter—the man he thinks is his friend. Imagine that!"

"Not them, me. You're trying to provoke me."

She started past me for the door.

"You are not going back out like that!" I said.

She grabbed the doorknob, and I grabbed for her. I wanted her shoulder but instead got her hair, and before I quite realized what I was doing, I yanked her by it, wrenching back her head.

She staggered, and one of her barrettes landed on the twisted bolster.

She went over to get it and sat down on the bed. "Is that what you do?" she asked through tears. "I wonder why she waited so long."

I went back to the living room. They'd had the sense to go, though Bud had found a cardboard coaster and left a note on the back in block letters, with a cursive postscript:

NEIL,
SUPPER TIME. WE'RE OFF.
SEE YOU AT OUR PARTY IF NOT SOONER.
BUD

P.S. Quite a girl you've got. Hits it like a ton of bricks.

That damned party—I still hadn't sent my excuses. After this performance, it was a wonder he still wanted me to come.

I picked up the pen and scribbled on the coaster, "THANKS FOR THE INVITATION. AWAY ON BUSINESS. REGRETS," and walked it down to the mailbox at the top of his driveway.

And what sight greeted my eyes at the bottom? An Alfa roadster not unlike my own, a newer model in a different color—beige, taupe, off white, ecru, who knew what they called it. I knew what I called it, by any color.

chapter two

Sometimes, when Frances was a pup, I would walk down with her for a late paper and a pack of smokes to a stationery shop in the village that stayed open on weekends. It was a nice ritual. The shopkeeper was cordial and the cigarette on the way back tasted especially good. But a shopping center opened, dozens of storefronts on the spine of a hill running almost a mile west to the center of the next town, and the supermarket at our end ran the village shop out of business.

I went out for cigarettes one Friday night. The moisture was licking the panes from below as much as drizzling from above, and the automatic garage-door opener sounded even more like a cement mixer than usual. I fumbled for the lights and wipers on the new station wagon I'd finally managed to come by.

The thought that I wouldn't have walked to the old shop anyway on a cold damp November night couldn't keep me from ruminating on the tendency of good things to yield to bad. My gloom expressed itself in haste—I raced down the driveway. When I saw the car blocking me in at the end, it was almost too late. Only by veering off the gravel and plowing over the shrubs on the margin was I able to avoid a collision. I jumped

out of my car fit to smash the other, an Olds. Then I saw that
that the Olds wasn't the only car blocking me in. It was part of
a long row parked on the edge of my property. I heard voices in
the distance and car doors thudding shut and remembered the
Youngers' party.

I headed straight for Bud's house, too angry to care that I
was betraying my excuse for declining. I wasn't going to be
held captive while his guests used my lawn as their parking lot.

A pair of headlight beams hit a fire hydrant and an elm
trunk before jumping a gap in the rhododendrons and blaz-
ing up the Youngers' driveway. The light couldn't travel far,
though. The driveway was full. Guests milled around, wondering what to do with their cars.

"Norman!" a woman exclaimed to her husband. "It's Nate
and Nikki, for Pete's sake."

"Nancy!" exclaimed the other woman, Nikki presumably.
They kissed, and their perfumes mingled with the scent of holly.
I knew these people, knew their kind. Like creatures to the Ark,
they had come in twos, north on the Meadowbrook, east across
the Whitestone, or west down the Turnpike through Jericho.
They had come in big sedans with heavy doors and heaters that
heated faster than those in their houses and hooked exhaust
pipes whose intoxicating benzene and oxide billows resembled
their own exhalations misting into the frosty dark.

They had come in twos, but they wouldn't stay in twos.
They'd circulate individually and collide fortuitously, seeking each other out only when something could not wait to be
told. One would otherwise know that they were a pair only
because that was how they were known: not as Nate or Nikki
or Norman or Nancy but as Norman and Nikki and Nate and
Nancy. To compensate for their awkwardness, the men would
be glib and the women would let the men's glibness pass for

wit. Everyone would kiss and squeeze and mock everyone else and feel proprietary about everyone else's children. Even though they weren't kids anymore themselves, the old college excitement would have survived their transformation. I knew them, all right.

A man in a beaver hat and cavalryman's coat hurried up the driveway and jumped into the last in the line of cars. There's the dunce who blocked me in, I thought, and started toward him. Before I reached him, he'd backed the car away.

"Guess he's the valet," said Nikki.

"Could be a thief," Nate replied. "Let's see whether he comes back."

"Every time Nate gives his car to a valet, he panics as the guy drives off," Nancy said. "If that guy went to the trouble of coming here and dressing up to steal a car, he wouldn't choose our Pontiac."

"It's a Bonneville," Nate protested.

The valet returned. "So much for that," said Nancy.

The valet gave Norman his keys and left his hand extended for a tip, but the gesture betrayed him. Norman lifted the beaver hat off the valet's head. "Oh, for cryin' out loud!" his wife exclaimed and planted a kiss on Bud's cheek.

"Buddy boy!" Nate cried.

I waited while Bud finished greeting his guests and sent them up the flagstone path to the house. The sounds of their glee trailed behind.

"Bud," I said sharply.

"Who's that?" he said. "It's Neil! You're here after all! How are you, fella? Don't tell me you canceled your trip especially to come."

"I'm afraid not. It was canceled for other reasons. But there's been some kind of misunderstanding here. My driveway's blocked. There are cars on my lawn."

"Space got short. I remembered that you were gone and thought I'd make use of your frontage."

"Well, that's one thing, but the driveway—"

"I couldn't very well block you in when you were out of town, could I?"

"Do I look like I'm out of town?"

"I wouldn't say that, no. I'd say you're here and, with a blocked driveway, won't be going anywhere soon. Join the party!"

Another car pulled up, a Volkswagen. Its suspension was loose, and the beams from its headlamps bounced like spotlights following an acrobat. "I can leave it here?" the driver asked.

"I'll take care of it," Bud said, opening the door for her. She fiddled with a few things before getting out, and I took the opportunity to press my case.

"I'm really very busy," I told him. "I was just running out for some cigarettes. I've got to get back to it."

"Cigarettes? Help yourself—we've probably got one for every match in the place. I'll tell you what. Go inside, have a drink and a smoke." He lowered his voice. "There are women in there practically crying for a man like you. For that matter, here's one *you* can cry for."

The driver got out of her car before I could refuse. Bud introduced himself and me. She looked young in the torchlight, even for this crowd. She was willowy, with long wavy hair and earrings dangling like fobs on chains. "I'm here to meet Lee," she said with a hint of Spanish in her pronunciation.

"Lucky man," Bud said as she started up the path. "Lee," he said to me, "it doesn't ring a bell. She must be at the wrong party. Go on in. Maybe you can be Lee."

"Not tonight. I've got to get some cigarettes and go back to work. Now if you'll move those cars at the head of my driveway."

"Think I know whose car is whose? Go on in and help yourself to all the smokes you can carry. You'll be back at your desk in no time. It'll be a perfect break for you."

What could I do, threaten to have the cars towed? I went ahead, up the path and through the door, where a clamor of voices overwhelmed the sound of wind and rustle behind me.

One of the Younger boys came to take my overcoat. He was freckle-faced, with a mouthful of braces and a cowlick.

"Thanks," I told him, "but I think I'll hold on to it."

"What do you wanna walk around in your coat for? You'll boil!"

"I'm only coming in for a few minutes."

"A few minutes. Then why'd you come at all?" He tugged at my sleeve. "Listen," he continued, "I'm supposed to take everyone's coat."

"Well, you're not taking mine." I tried to make him let go but he held on. Our tug-of-war continued. Heads turned.

The apple really hadn't fallen far from the tree; he too was stubborn. "I see—you want it for yourself. If I give it to you, how will I know you won't make off with it?"

"Make off with it? But I've already got a jacket. It's a Mighty Mac. Wanna see it?"

"Not right now. Maybe some other—"

"—and I've got a bike and a go-cart and we've got two television sets. How many have you got?"

"One."

"Only one? That's too bad. At my friend's house they have three. What kind is it?"

He was leading me through the house, to an upstairs

bedroom where he kept the overcoats. He might have been taking me on a European grand tour, to judge from the decor: French tulle upholstery, Dutch muslin curtains, Flemish oils, German piano, Viennese wind-up clock, Scandinavian fur rug, Venetian cut-glass lamps, Roman *cassone,* Turkish runners— all from as far east as Third Avenue. But then, I wondered, where was England? England's bounty had been excluded. I mulled that over till it struck me that there was something of England in the house. From England the Youngers had borrowed their name.

The pile of coats on the bed was higher than the boy himself. He draped mine over a bedpost and put my gloves and astrakhan on a shelf beside it. "I'll need a chit for that coat."

"A chit? What's that?"

"Be on guard," I said as I left him. "Could be some second-story men in this crowd."

"Second what? You *are* strange."

His reply followed me down the hall and at the top of the staircase—which lacked the grandeur that its wind suggested— gave me pause before my descent.

The crowd at the base of the stairs surged and I bumped a woman whose hair was wrapped in a tall bun. It was a tower, a Babylonian ziggurat. Her earrings were long too, like inverted lampposts, and made the bun seem even taller. She grabbed my wrist and said, "See my eyebrows—would you describe them as melodramatic?"

"The line, she means," a man standing closer to her than he had to explained.

Her eyebrows were ordinary, nothing exceptional about them. Besides, with a hairdo like hers who would notice the eyebrows? "Come on," she said, "be honest."

"I don't find them melodramatic," I said. "Not at all. Dramatic but not melodramatic. They have the perfect amount of drama."

I tried to head toward the bar, but everyone was standing toe to toe, women lifting themselves toward men's ears, men bending toward women's, pendants and neckties swinging. I made progress following an hors d'oeuvres server, her tray a horizontal shield before which the guests had to yield.

Someone grabbed me from behind. I turned and a walleyed woman said, "You're not Stan!" in the accent—part Bronx, part Northumberland—for which people ridicule our island.

"And neither are you."

"Oh, for heaven's sake, I saw Mina there next to you, and I thought you were Stan." She nudged me to the side and leaned toward Mina. "Where's Stan? I thought he was Stan."

"He's too tall to be Stan."

She turned me around. "No, Stan's about the same height."

"As him?"

"Yeah, sure."

"Oh, come on—maybe when he's erect." Mina howled and mussed my hair.

"Are you done with me?" I asked.

A server offering mushroom canapés thrust her tray forward. The mushrooms rocked on their doilies and the guests parted before them. I saw my chance and followed in her wake. Though she didn't lead me all the way to the bar, she got me close enough to push my way in. Nobody seemed to take it amiss, and when I'd gotten a drink I was pushed aside in turn.

I found myself face-to-face with a man wiping what appeared to be pâté from the deep, crumb-collecting corners of his mouth with a balled-up napkin. "I'm reading the most fascinating book," he told me after he'd gotten every last crumb out. "It's called *The Greeks of the Middle Ages*."

"I've read that one too," I said.

His eyes lit up—nothing to do with me, I realized. Something behind me had provoked his glimmer—somebody, that is. "Peek-a-boo," he exclaimed past me, then, lower, "Hello, lovelies."

Another tray was passing behind me. He reached over my shoulder for what was on it, a morsel of gravlax napped in dill, as I discovered from the sauce he dripped on my sport jacket. "Sorry," he said grudgingly, as though he'd been acting out of duty and had had no choice in the matter. "Will ya grab a napkin off that tray for me?" he asked after bolting the hors d'oeuvre. He balled that one up too and had at the spot on my jacket. "As good as new," he said after a few dabs. "Better."

I craned my neck to check the damage.

"New's not all it's cracked up ta be," he added. He inspected the napkin he'd dabbed at me with. "When an item's new, it's anybody's."

"Or nobody's."

"Well, exactly. So you agree." He clapped my shoulder. "That little spot, invisible to the naked eye, is like your signature."

"Yours, you mean."

"It was an accident, for Pete's sake. So much for que sera, sera. Whaddya want me ta do about it?" He took out his wallet and flourished a few twenties at me. "Is this what you're after?"

"Put that away."

"Oh, so *now* it's c'est la vie, eh? A little indelicacy always works wonders with your type."

"My type?"

"Lighten up, pal. Just pulling your leg." His laughter revealed a spanakopita remnant between his teeth. "To the victor goes the spoils," I thought I heard him say. He offered me his hand.

"Excuse me?"

"Hector Spolz," he said. "Pleased to meetch'."

I gave him my name and said "Likewise." He had a deal-closing sort of handshake.

A man appeared beside him. "You know Buddy a long time?" he asked me. He had hound-dog eyes and a mouth set in a frown that seemed to extend to his bow tie. A bushy mustache might have given him a hint of dapperness, but when he sipped his drink it collected froth at the corners and deepened the frown. "I'm Izzy, by the way."

I introduced myself and said, "I met him only recently."

"I hardly know him. Not that I haven't seen him around. Anyhow, with a name like Bud it's easy to feel like you know him, if you know what I mean. Hector knows him."

"Sure I know him," Hector said. "An advanced case of the fidgets."

They started in on Bud. I might have left them to themselves if I'd had anywhere to go. I wasn't so annoyed with my neighbor that I liked the idea of listening to a sourpuss and a sad sack dissect him. But I mustn't have been wholly averse to it—I stayed put. Now that I'd made it to the bar, moving didn't seem worth the trouble. Trays of strong pink cocktails were passing our way.

"The man can't sit still," Hector said. "He's got a new scheme every couple of years. You can't build a business so quick."

"Not a real business," said Izzy.

"To tell you the truth, with those suits of his . . . What is it they go for, two hundred?"

"Two-fifty. Two-fifty, easy." The idea of the figures animated

Izzy. He punctuated his utterance with karate chops, and grew pensive. "That's what quality costs these days."

"Quality nowadays? Don't talk to me about quality. It's only a slogan." This may have been one of Hector's own slogans— his mind was elsewhere, if his eyes were the vanguard.

I turned and saw what he did: the woman who'd come in the Beetle while I was talking to Bud in the driveway. One thing I hadn't seen out there was her smile. It was like a schooner riding high on the water.

We helped ourselves to more cocktails.

"Are these pink squirrels?" I asked, holding up my glass.

"What's surprising," Hector resumed, "is that I'd always thought of him as a bit of a . . . a bit of a . . ."

"A Harry Horseshit?" An impish type with a cauliflower ear and pastel florets printed on his shirt turned around to supply the phrase, and turned back.

"Thank you, Garson," Hector said over his shoulder. "A Harry Horseshit. But a place like this takes real money."

"It's a nice house," Izzy added, "a nice town. Cornwallis decamped here, you know. There's a plaque on the village green."

"*Decamped?* What does that mean? Am I supposed to be impressed? The man camped everywhere."

"It speaks to the age of the place. The village is old, is what's impressive."

"My grandma's old too. Does she impress me?"

"Washington was here too," Izzy interjected. "He came to secure the harbor."

"George Washington, now there was a Harry Horseshit, first class. Couldn't even keep his wig on his head. He was tall, was what he had going for him. That's why they gave him his command."

"What's that, melba toast? Grab me a piece, will you?"

"How did they keep their wigs on their heads? I mean, if the wind came up while they were in battle?"

The group behind Hector disbanded, and Garson slipped into our midst. "Well, something must've worked out for him," he said.

"I'd say so. You don't become the father of the country—"

"For Bud, he means," said Izzy.

"I'm always telling him to develop property. You know what they say about land," Hector said. "But he just shrugs. A sure thing is beneath him. It has to be some new twist or he isn't interested."

"I heard that he made out so well selling lawn furniture on commission that he took home more than his boss. When they tried to give him a haircut, he quit."

"It wasn't lawn furniture, it was lawn sprinklers."

"Sprinklers?" Garson twirled, adding sound effects in imitation of a revolving sprinkler. "You'd have to sell a lot of them to—"

"It was pie in the sky."

"Then where does he get it?"

"My guess," said Hector, "is, it comes from her side."

"The old story. He marries his way onto third base and acts like he hit a triple."

"Now let's not get carried away—I wouldn't exactly call this third base. I'd still rather be where I am. Did I tell you we're—" As if on its own, Hector's hand grabbed a miniature quiche from a passing tray and stuffed it into his mouth before he'd finished his sentence. He chewed frantically, eyes bulging. "I'm always burning my goddamned tongue," he gasped.

We waited dumbly, Garson, Izzy, and I, watching him ingest his quiche, till a laugh, really a series of laughs knocking in bursts like a motor that refuses to turn over, made us turn around. Bud's back was to us, and the heaving of his shoulders hazed the sheen of his gabardine jacket. When his laughter had subsided to the point that the pauses between laughs were longer than the laughs themselves, he must have sensed a vacuum behind him.

"You've been introduced?" he asked, turning from me to Hector and Garson and brushing back a Lionel-Barrymoreish curl.

"The way he was glowering at me," Hector said, "I wasn't sure about giving him my name. I drip a little sauce on his tweed, and he's ready to twist my nuts off." He brandished a plastic-cutlass toothpick. "Good thing I'm armed."

"Don't take it personally. I used to think he was glowering at me too, till I realized it's his regular look!" Bud thumped me on the back.

"We haven't met," Garson said.

Bud hesitated, then said, "Neil Fox, Garson uh . . . Garson . . . ?"

"When your first name's Garson, you don't need a last name," Hector said.

I started to sidle away but Bud grabbed me. "Enjoying yourself, Neil? I did tell you that this was a party, didn't I?"

"I have been enjoying myself, but, you know, it's time for me to be on my way. I told you I had work to do."

"Now? Who're you kidding? A friend with some real chops is about to sit down at the piano."

A woman with Cleopatra eyeliner and a Peter Pan haircut darted between us and put her arms around Bud. "All this talk is hunky-dory," she cried, "but after a while a girl needs to dance." She swung him around.

I saw that it was past midnight and left to get my coat. Back downstairs, I waited for a chance to meet and thank Bud's wife,

Irene. It was the first time I'd been near enough to see the wave of her thick dark hair, the green of her eyes, or the cometary beauty mark splashed high on her cheekbone. This was as near as I'd get. She was in demand. A woman who'd struck a mock silent-movie pose, with one hand on her hip and the other behind her head, was saying, "You would not believe her, you really wouldn't, an absolute diva"; the caterer was apologizing for cracking a lamp; her daughter tugged at her sleeve. I waved, mouthed a thank-you, and headed for the door.

Guests were still trickling in. They looked happy to be inside, and once I was out I saw why. The night had turned frigid, the kind of breathtaking chill that quickly detaches you from your own sensations. I could hardly feel myself walking. I heard the ground crunching underfoot and couldn't be sure that my own steps were the cause. The burning in my fingertips and earlobes seemed far away.

A car's hazard lights flashed against the hydrant at the bottom of the driveway. Someone shouted, "Can you give me a hand?" I fastened the top button of my coat and, going over to him, saw that it was Garson. There was no escaping him. "Oh, it's you," he muttered.

The car was running; his wife had slid behind the wheel. "Listen, we just need a quick shove—I got stuck in the ditch somehow. It doesn't make any sense. If I'd turned the other way, I'd have creased my fender against that tree."

"I left my gloves inside," I told him. "I'll be with you in a minute."

"One good push should do it."

"I'll be back."

"Hey man, thanks a lot. Remember, what goes around comes around. One day you'll be in a fix like this."

I told him again that I'd be right back, but he'd already given up on me and started up the driveway to look for help from someone else.

I really had left my hat and gloves behind, though I might have gone back the next day for them. But if only to keep to my story, I went back in.

It was like going to another party, and not only in that the drinks had been switched from pink to more familiar colors. I'd been pretty well anonymous before: now people I'd met twenty minutes earlier called out to me like old pals. "How's tricks?" they cried, and "Take off your coat and stay awhile, chief." It was the liquor talking in them, of course. But there was some of the same stuff in me, and it listened. I caught myself smiling my social smile in a genuine way, as tickled to see them as they apparently were to see me.

Bud's pianist friend turned out to be Stan. His stubby fingers galloped over the keyboard and his eyes shone with a pixilated gleam. When he played "Everyone Says I Love You" and "Why Am I So Romantic?" and "Alone," my new comrades puffed up their chests, lifted their chins, and sang; I was swept up in the general benevolence and between cascading arpeggios even chimed in myself. The fellow feeling ran so high that you could hardly distinguish your own voice, or anyone else's. Only Bud's, a baritone with plenty of carry, stood out. It was his recital if it was anyone's. And he could sing, though to judge from his exuberance, maybe not quite so well as he thought.

The woman who'd caught Bud's eye and Hector's came out of the bathroom as I was going in. "I don't know this music everyone is singing," she said, presumably to cover her embarrassment.

"It's from before your time," I answered, and went in.

She was in the hallway, more or less where I'd left her, when I came out. Now the embarrassment was mine. "Did you ever catch up with Lee?"

"Lee? Oh, yes, he was here. But then he left." If there was any sign of distress in her smile, I missed it. But I probably missed a good deal. The dangle of her earrings suggested imperceptible tremblings and vibrations.

"You didn't quarrel?"

"No, no. He was just tired. But I have only two weeks here. I'll sleep when I go home."

"And home is where?"

"I come from Montevideo."

"Uruguay?"

"You go Uruguay," a man on his way past us and into the bathroom said.

"Your English is fluent." I listened more closely for the trace of an accent.

"I went to an American school. My father's an army officer. We know lots of Americans. Would you like to dance?" I wondered what she meant by it—she was already half dancing in place on her own, bobbing discretely to a private rhythm. Maybe I was supposed to curtsy every now and then in sympathy.

"You're here on vacation?"

"For vacation, yes. And for the wedding of my half brother."

"He's getting married here?"

"At Valley Forge. He's in an officer's training program." Her motions grew more restless—she hadn't come to explain herself. "You're a good dancer. I can tell."

"And how can you tell?"

"Older men know how to dance."

I knew what she meant, that she didn't like the freestyle dancing that had come into fashion, but I winced all the same.

She smiled. "I didn't mean to say that you're old, I meant that you're debonair, a gentleman." After a minute change in the angle of incidence between her upper lip and lower, her smile became inviting. "I like a man who has a little gray around the temple."

"Nice try."

"I don't understand," she said, though it seemed that she did.

"Never mind," I replied, and introduced myself. When I took my hand off the cover of a phone book I was leaning on, I found that it was clammy.

"I am Cecilia Marta Bernal."

"Unfortunately, Cecilia Marta, there's no music for us to dance to." Stan had stopped playing. "You may not need music, but I do."

As if on cue, someone put a record on, and the music led us to its source in the living room, where the crowd had thinned out enough to give us room to maneuver. It was a slow bossa nova number, not exactly my style, but Cecilia Marta helped me till I caught on, leading with her hips and following with her feet. A few other couples started dancing too, and all indications were that I was enjoying myself.

As we capered here and there, I started to see people I knew over her shoulder. Our up-and-coming county executive, John Nickelson, who'd had his right arm withered by polio and become a collegiate squash champ with his left. My orthopedist, who was chomping on an unlit cigar, and mouthed "How's the knee?" to me across the room. A junior partner in my firm whose deference to me in person led me to suspect that he was a backstabber. A man who always seemed to be on my train no matter what time I took it. A slight, kinky-haired, tightly dressed stranger whom I disliked without knowing why, until a helmet-headed guest moved out of the way and revealed the person to whom he was gamely holding forth to be my wife.

It couldn't be, I thought. Of course I'd mistake anyone who looked even the slightest bit like her. I hardly knew how she looked anymore—I had recalled her image too often not to distort it.

"Is something wrong?" Cecilia asked.

The woman not only had Joyce's face, she had her things too: the bright silk blouse, the dark beads, the darker handbag, the cigarette perched at the base of the V of her fingers. It had to be Joyce.

"It is," I said, and steered Cecilia aside.

As I made my way toward Joyce, I thought I saw her hand on the arm of the man beside her. She was leaning his way, her head cocked close to his, her mouth hardly moving as she spoke to him.

She had straightened up by the time I reached her.

"It's nice to see you," I said, which was understatement and overstatement in equal measure. "I wouldn't have thought you'd venture so close to home."

"And I wouldn't have thought this was your scene."

"It isn't." I glanced at her companion, and thought that I was reading too much into the situation, that she wouldn't possibly take up with him. He was an irrelevance, whatever she might think of him. If his presence meant anything, the humiliation was hers, not mine.

"Or your time of night," she continued. "Isn't it past your bedtime?"

"I'd say you've ceded your authority on that question."

"And good riddance to it. I only meant that I wouldn't have expected—"

"It doesn't exactly sound like you were hoping to run into me."

"Well, let's be honest. It isn't the most comfortable thing in the world."

"And yet you went out of your way to turn up here."

"I hardly went out of my way. I didn't think there was any chance that you'd be here, especially at this hour. Besides, I'm not going to start letting what I do be decided by . . . I'm not going to start sneaking around."

Her weedy friend had been making motions to excuse himself and was drifting away. "Hold on, Jules," she said to him, her sneer becoming a smile before she turned back to me.

"Jules?"

"This has really gone far enough. I came to a party, not an inquisition."

"Cut it out, Joyce, will you?" I said.

"Enjoy your evening, Neil," she answered and moved on.

I'd have gone home to bed if I could, but leaving was beyond me as long as Joyce was there. For twenty years, her words and deeds had been as inevitable as the hours of the day. Then she'd gone, and when I wondered where she was and what she was doing, I had nothing to go on. Joyce, or, rather, the figure of her, went from being entirely familiar to utterly mysterious. Nothing could be confirmed or denied, and so the possibilities were endless. The rest of my life might have been spent guessing at the rest of hers.

And here she was. I could see her, might even have touched her if I'd chosen—though that would be quite another thing. I felt almost giddy at first. The Joyce I'd been imagining didn't correspond to the flesh-and-blood Joyce I was looking at. This had nothing to do with her appearance, or with my memory of it. She looked the same as ever. The green of her eyes, the slenderness of her arms, the half-disdainful, half-amused curl at the corners of her mouth were as I remembered. She wasn't taller or broader or more or less beautiful or imposing. *She* wasn't the trouble. It was all in my mind, where her absence had spawned a surrogate that had taken on a life of its own. And this life had become more real to me than the original.

Why couldn't I take my eyes off this Joyce, the one in the room with me? Maybe I was trying to lay the ghost, to bring the imaginary one back into line with her. Or maybe I was waiting for her to come to me in my dark corner with my replenished tumbler to tell me that her experiment was over and she was ready to come home.

I'm sure she felt my eyes on her. I'd never known her to carry on the way she was now. She was either drawing smoke in or puffing it out, speaking or poised to speak, laughing or poised to laugh. She pulled at Izzy's mustache and mussed the county executive's hair; he mussed hers back. She pretended to pick my orthopedist's pocket, danced a few steps of the cha-cha with the Youngers' little daughter, trotted out her imitation of Rita Hayworth singing "Put the Blame on Mame." It was a tacky performance, and the fact that it was for my exclusive benefit made it worse. If I was implicated in this display, then it was within my rights to put a stop to it.

The time came to exercise those rights. I saw her new friend Jules touch one of the buttons on her blouse—the top button, it was. He mightn't have meant much by it: the fingertip that touched the button extended from a hand that held a glass; they were standing with another couple and might have been discussing Joyce's wardrobe for all I knew or cared. When you see your wife giving herself the appearance of availability, your interest in the finer details is not what it was. That touch had the look of a liberty. It was enough for me.

I closed on them quickly; the crowd was thinner now. Jules hadn't let his hand linger on Joyce's button for long. He was just lifting it as I reached them. It was already a little higher than her neckline when I grabbed it—grabbed his wrist, I mean. He tried to pull free of my grip and jerked his hand back hard. I heard his glass crack as it hit Joyce's mouth.

"Get away from me!" she cried, reeling back and slurring her words. She covered her mouth, but from a slack corner peeking through the space between her index finger and thumb I saw a gleaming white shard and feared that the glass wasn't the only thing that had cracked.

There was quiet, then confusion on as many sides as there were guests left to form, and the stirrings of an indignation that I withstood long enough to see that gleaming shard on Joyce's lip melt to water. "You bastard, you sonofabitch," Jules kept saying, but not so much to me as in some kind of tough-guy parody for the bystanders. He had a coward's gift for advertising his affront. Shifting his weight from one leg to another, cocking his head this way and that—his kinky hair bouncing like the coils of a spring—balling up his fingers and opening them again before he'd closed them far enough to make a fist. I was hoping that he'd take a swing at me, but it didn't take long to see that he wouldn't. The crowd that had gathered knew it too and dispersed, and when Joyce went away, I was about the only one left to hear him muttering. There was nothing for me to do in the end but march off dismally to fetch the hat and gloves that had brought me back to the party in the first place.

On my way to the makeshift coatroom, I bumped into Cecilia again.

"I'm afraid I owe you an apology. That was a terrible way to end a dance."

"It's okay. We all get jealous sometimes." I found the hint of an accent I'd been looking for in her pronunciation of "jealous." She made jealousy sound especially poisonous.

"It's good of you to forgive me. But, you know, it wasn't a question of jealousy."

"Of course not. No one admits to being jealous. It's always more complicated. It's more complicated, yes?"

"Well . . . yes, that's right."

"It was good to meet you."

"I hope you'll give me the pleasure of another dance sometime." It was a quaint phrase, but it fit. She was like that.

"That would be nice."

Charlie Younger had remained at his post, and lay fast asleep beneath a pile of coats on the bed with a cigarette tucked behind his ear. My things had gotten mixed up again in the heap, and while I was fishing them out, an older man waylaid me. He had shaggy eyebrows and a muffler that he had trouble keeping clear of his chin. "I'll tell you something," he said while I searched for my astrakhan. "Know what they say about power? It's a very tricky thing, tricky, tricky, trickee."

"What is?"

"Power."

I don't know what it was—just then my mind was churning: in the pile of coats I'd come across Joyce's mink—but the word *power* sounded strange and unintelligible, like one of those nonsense words you'd hear in an exchange between a cowboy and his Indian guide in a Western.

"Power?"

"Maybe you don't think so. I can see that you just waltzed around to the other side of the desk."

"If you say so."

"That's all it takes as far as you're concerned, isn't it? You just walk to the other side of the desk." I found my coat, and realized as I put it on that I was swaying on my feet. "You think that's all there is to it. Well, it's not like that, not for some of us. Some of us, we start on our way around, and what happens." He was looking me in the eye, trying to get me to look back into his. Behind him, on a silent television, a man in a yellow mackintosh riding a tricycle in fast motion hit a curb and fell over.

"I couldn't tell you."

"I thought you might like to know."

"Okay, what happens?"

"What happens? The desk vanishes. We're on our way around it and it's gone. Paff, into the ether. Just like that, paff."

"No kidding," I said, and pushed my way past him through the door. He might have knocked me over if he'd pushed back. I was suddenly that bleary. I crossed the landing to the head of the stairs and was about to start down when I ran into Bud going the other way. "I'm calling it a night," I said.

"I won't ask what kind of night you're calling it."

"Yeah, well, every party needs at least one good row. They're what people remember."

"Come with me. I want to show you something."

"I'm really all in."

"It won't take a minute," he said.

I was about to refuse when Joyce and Jules rounded a corner below and I remembered that she hadn't collected her coat. I hoped they'd have gone by the time I looked at whatever Bud had to show me.

He led me quickly down the hall—too quickly, to tell the truth; his spryness at this time of night made me feel old and sodden—through the master bedroom to his dressing room. "Have a seat," he said and went over to a bureau facing a window. He took an envelope from the top drawer. Then he looked up and, pointing at the window, said, "See that?" The twigs and branches outside the window were outlined against the scrim. "When the moon's bright, I see this pattern against the shade and say to myself, *it's supposed to be plain.*"

"What is?"

"This, these lines," he said. "Their meaning is supposed to be clear. But it's not. It looks like some kind of Eastern calligraphy on a parchment."

I lit a cigarette, and gave another to him.

"I guess so. But why should it mean anything?"

"Because it's the writing on the wall. And what's the expression? It's as plain as the writing on the wall."

"I don't think—"

"And haven't you ever said, when some inevitable-seeming tragedy occurs, say a man's business goes belly-up—"

Or his wife, I thought.

"—that the poor sap couldn't see the writing on the wall? Well, maybe this is mine, or ours, in some crazy alphabet! What if our future is spelled out right here?"

"Ours?"

"It might foretell success or romance."

"Sure," I said. "Or both."

"Let's not get carried away." His laughter broke out again, but I didn't join in and he couldn't go on alone for long.

"Here," he said, handing me the envelope. "Mickey's already got a copy. He said I shouldn't be surprised if you were slow to warm up to the idea."

"The idea?"

"The one we discussed a little while ago, when Mickey was here. It's my proposal you're holding. The confidentiality agreement's in there too."

The mention of his venture doubled my fatigue. I put down the envelope. "I thought I'd told you that I'm not in the business of backing new enterprises anymore."

"Maybe you're not seeking them out the way you once did, but when something like this comes along and bites you on the ass, I think it might be another story." I was having trouble sitting up in my chair, but Bud's eyes only got wider as he pressed his cause. "I'd think this is one that merits a good hard look anyway. I'd hate to see you kicking yourself later."

We fell silent. The wind came up and the outline of the branches trembled on the scrim.

"Forgive me, Neil. I understand that it's been a long night. We'd never have invited her if we'd known."

The door shut hard downstairs. "You invited her when you'd also invited me?"

"We didn't know who she was."

"What do you mean—how could you not know?"

"She wasn't introduced to us as 'Fox.' We didn't make the connection."

"You weren't given a surname?"

"We were—'Rose.' She was introduced as 'Joyce Rose.'"

"That's her maiden name. So she doesn't even go by 'Fox' anymore." It was an odd surprise. I stood up from it.

"I hope you won't mind my saying so, but I'm sorry for you, Neil. Truly sorry. I could tell ever since I moved in that things haven't been right with you. But they will be again. And I'm not just saying that. These kinds of problems always work themselves out. They have to."

These kinds of problems always work themselves out. They were about the first earnest words I'd heard from Bud, and they could hardly have been staler. They might have infuriated me if I hadn't found comfort in them.

I turned to go. "You don't want to forget this," he said, extending the envelope to me again. "There's no hurry. Look it over when you're ready, if not for your sake then for mine. Mickey says you've got an uncanny business sense."

I took it. Which philosopher is it who remarked on how much easier our lives would be if we could sit still and keep quiet? I'd thought I was doing a better job of it than most, yet here I was about to go over the top of another slide.

I'd outlasted all the other guests. I tried to check my watch but couldn't see the numbers. The moon had gone down; the writing on the wall had faded. It was no longer late.

chapter three

Another diabolical particular: how the timbre of a ringing phone can seem to change in a series of identical rings, how the friendly invitation of the first ring becomes a plea by the fourth and a threat by the sixth, turns brittle by the eighth and menacing by the twelfth. And at six in the morning, the change seems that much harsher.

Early one workday morning a couple of weeks later as I sat over a cup of coffee and watched the season's first snowfall, the phone rang. I let it ring. It had been ringing a lot lately. Weissmer, Schiff, Marne was on the brink of civil war. The adversaries were hurrying to line up their ducks for the meetings that were supposed to straighten things out. These meetings had nothing to do with the suit or its outcome. They were internal political struggles, avoidable if I could avoid the entanglements leading up to them.

The phone rang on and on. I stayed at the breakfast table, watching the snow through a row of slanted windows waft from on high and fall thicker and faster as it approached the ground, veering at all angles toward the objects it would land on, like birds swooping into the trees from below.

Office politics was only half to blame for my refusal to answer the phone. I had decided in the aftermath of the party that maybe Joyce had been right to go, that we might be better off apart. This was a wise decision: the fascination with imagining where she was and what she might be doing at every instant wore off. But when my old sense of her, the one I'd developed in the course of our marriage, began to come back to me, I started to worry. I remembered her impulsiveness, her moodiness, how little it could take to make her pity herself. A cold gust or a headache or a quarrel with Jules might be enough to make her dial her old number. If she caught me in a weak moment of my own, when the sound of her voice was enough to make me think of how we ought to have gotten along, she might ask to come back—or make me want her to ask. Either way, I'd have lost ground.

I poured myself more coffee and the ringing stopped. A half minute later it started again. I was rattled, my resolve spent. I grabbed it.

"I hope I'm not getting you out of bed," Mickey said.

"Like hell you do. You wouldn't have rung the phone off the hook if you'd been worried about waking me up."

"I didn't have to worry about that. It's obvious that you were already up."

"And why is it obvious?"

"Because people are more decent when they're just waking up. The first words out of the mouth of someone who's still muzzy are never 'like hell you do.' Not unless he's a hoodlum."

A water pipe began to knock behind the baseboard. "Is there an emergency? Has Leon finally given up the ghost?"

"Are you kidding? I spoke to her last week, invited her down for the holidays. Know what she said? She said, 'You want me to come to that fetid charnel house?' That's what she said."

"*Fetid*. She loosed that one on the waiter the last time we ate out. There was nothing wrong with the restaurant." I said nothing about charnel house, which didn't strike me as inapt. Mickey's house was one of those late Victorians built against the sun and its devils: all hallways, nooks, back stairs, closets, and pantries under crow-ridden coffee trees and black locusts. I'd driven through storms to avoid staying the night there.

"She also said that Diane was a tramp," he continued. Diane was Mickey's first wife. She was long gone. Not dead, just out of the picture. "You're right on that score, I told her. She meant Jeanette, of course,"—his current wife. "But she's no tramp— not that she hasn't got it in her. Most of them do," he added. "I wonder what she'd say about Joyce if she knew. I take it you haven't told her?"

"You didn't ring the phone off the hook at six in the morning to ruminate on women's inconstancy, did you?"

"There *are* a few things, as a matter of fact. There's Linda's Christmas bonus." Linda kept our books. "I thought I'd give her—"

"I leave it to you."

"But it's your money too."

"Then take the figure you were thinking of and double it."

"Well, that works out perfectly. I thought I'd give her half what you suggested. One must never be middle class about money. Right, Neil?"

"What else?"

"Bisbee's up to his old tricks, trying to dicker with us on the lease extension for our drilling contract. I'm for siccing Monash on him." Monash was a wolf in lawyer's clothing whose services we'd had regular recourse to. "It's time to lower the boom."

"Then lower it, Mickey. But will you please leave me out of

it? You know what you want to do. You ask me for my advice, and then when I give it to you, you do what you want just the same."

"You *are* surly this morning. I was going to ask what you thought about your neighbor's proposal, but I'm not sure I dare."

"Of course you dare."

"Well, then—" The water pipe knocked again. It was as if a mine were being worked behind the plaster. "What in hell's going on there?"

"Just some clatter from the plumbing."

"I thought you might be smacking the receiver against the table."

"I'm afraid that my aggression still comes in more evolved forms. They won't be carting me off to the bin just yet."

"Good. Then you'll be able to make it next week."

"No, I won't." An epic sigh escaped from me. "Make what?"

"That proposal. I thought we'd all get together over a drink." He was practically shouting. I held the receiver away from my ear. "You and I and Bud. Size him up, see if he's for real, et cetera."

"I'm too busy for et cetera, Mickey. You have no idea."

"What's that? Would you speak up, Neil?"

"I haven't even opened the file. I don't know the first thing about his business."

"The usual hocus pocus, charts, graphs, tables . . ." Mickey couldn't be bothered to read business proposals and relied on me to brief him. It was part of his pretense to being duly diligent. Though he disregarded what I told him when it wasn't what he wanted to hear, he couldn't or wouldn't proceed without consulting me, as if by pointing out the risks of a venture I was diminishing them. It wasn't short-term prospects that concerned him anyway. Our interests and those of the businesses we funded weren't always strictly aligned. Their early struggles could be turned to our advantage.

We described ourselves as sleeping partners, declining to mention even to ourselves the more active role we might take in a business's later stages. We were certainly aware of it, yet it went unacknowledged. I don't know what Mickey felt about it: something less than pride, I'm sure, but also less than shame. Whatever this feeling, he didn't let it get in the way of his appraisal of entrepreneurs. It was hopefulness he looked for in them, the hopefulness of the man who's said to himself "If only I can find a way to get started" and who sustains himself by saying so.

This could make the entrepreneur grateful to the investor who'd help him get his start, lead him to accept unfavorable terms that boxed him in but left this investor room to maneuver. By being too accommodating when it comes to what might seem to be technicalities—redemption dates, rates of conversion, events of default—a man who thinks he is finally going to be working for himself may discover that he has traded one boss for another, whose power, if it is less overbearing from day to day, may ultimately be more insidious.

"It looks good to me. Still, I may be missing something in the numbers," Mickey said. "I count on you to tell me."

The snow was letting up, or had stopped. I couldn't tell whether the flakes I saw drifting around were falling from the sky or had blown from the trees.

"There's nothing you really want me to tell you, Mickey. You know it all already."

"I want to know whether his assumptions are sound and his estimates hold water."

"And what if I tell you they don't?"

"I thought you said you hadn't looked at them."

"I haven't. I'm speaking hypothetically."

"Let's not cross that bridge before we have to. My guess is that the man may be on to something." What Mickey meant was that he himself might be on to something. "Which night next week are we on for?"

There was no escaping the meeting. The thought of the pleas I'd have to endure if I refused was enough to secure my capitulation. Mickey and Bud seemed to feel that their connection had to pass through me. Though a party to their dealings, I was also to serve as the witness to them. But what kind of witness? If I was neutral, it was by virtue of being biased against both sides.

Coffee cup in hand, I was headed for the door when the phone rang again. Mickey often called back a second after we had hung up—the thing he'd have forgotten to mention was usually his real reason for calling. Fearing his postscripts, I let it ring.

The scent from a patch of chrysanthemums that clung to life hit me as I went through the door. I crossed a section of the lawn and stopped beside an upside-down wheelbarrow that leaned against a tree stump. A few birds that hadn't had the sense to fly south flitted around it. The air was surprisingly warm and still, and the horizon was the yellow of a guttering match flame. Directly overhead, a whiter light tinged the outline of a cloud, an enormous snow crystal flaking into millions like a giant sloughing its skin. Snowflakes hissed as they melted in my hair.

Frances nosed her way out the storm door and bounded through the thin blanket of snow, kicking up her back legs, and trawling her snout through the powder. I threw snowballs and she tried to fetch them. After a dozen or so, she figured out that I was putting her on and capped off her frisk by barreling straight into me. I barreled back. The bout was brief but furious. I came away with slobber-caked snow melting on my wrists and waist and under the tongues of my brogues.

I marched to the bottom of the driveway, picked up the paper, and dusted off the tube into which it had been rolled. On snowy days, Peter and I had taken this walk for the paper, playing catch on the way back. The tube and paper together made an excellent football, easy for a little boy to grip. As I went back up the path, I saw the moss beside it nearly hidden, the juniper beginning to kneel, the tool-shed ramp like a model of a glacier. The sand trucks were already out on the access road; the flagstones were rumbling.

But from upstairs, through the arched window opposite the medicine-chest mirror, the same patch of lawn looked cheerless, the light a flat gray over the meager snow cover. The tree stump and wheelbarrow were hardly distinguishable from the rocks beside them, and the birds looked smaller than the whiskers I was shaving. I had just come out of the shower and kept having to wipe steam from the glass.

I cleared the mirror once more and saw a man in it, far off in the background, on the lawn beside the stump and the barrow, where I'd been. His image was all of the length of a finger and quickly passed out of the frame. I tried to recall him as soon as he was gone: the tilt of his fedora brim, his camel hair overcoat the color of a giblet-rich gravy—a youthful, prosperous-looking, raffish figure. But how could I have gathered all this from a tiny, fleeting image in a foggy mirror? It wasn't possible. I'd taken myself in, overlaid a daydream on a steamy reflection.

This dismissal was disappointing. The appearance had restored the exhilaration that had come to me with the snowfall. I rinsed the last of the lather from my face, unstopped the drain, wiped the mirror. And I had the sense that if I looked into it hard enough, I might see the barrow wheel spinning in the wind, the sparrows flitting, the stump casting a blue shadow.

I heard a sharp rapping on the front door as I knotted my necktie. A new housekeeper, Magda, had been coming in on weekdays, though she usually arrived after I was gone. Maybe, worrying that the snow would hold her up, she had left earlier than usual. As I trotted down to let her in, I reminded myself to set her straight on a few things. She cleaned in out-of-the-way places, worked miracles on fixtures and moldings, and turned up an old parking permit and backup sets of keys in a trophy cup she'd taken down to polish. But this meticulousness was bound up with a tendency to protest my burgeoning bachelor disorder by piling miscellaneous items in visible locations. I'd come home to cough-drop tins, eyeglass cases, bank books, cigarette packs, tie clips, pocket combs and collar stays heaped like jacks that children play with; to a mountain of books and magazines and newspapers teetering on a coffee table beneath an urn that was no paperweight. The idea that particular record albums belonged in particular record jackets also escaped her: Saint-Saëns would turn up in Mancini, who would turn up in Stravinsky, which should have left Stravinsky on the turntable but didn't. Her method of promoting temperance also rankled. She put liquor bottles on top of the refrigerator. This was no reflex. The refrigerator was tall and Magda was not. She'd have needed the stepladder to get them up there. Sometimes she set them so far back that I needed it myself.

I was glad she'd come early. It would be easier to explain to her in person. I opened the door and felt my face fall.

"What's the matter, fella? Expecting someone better looking?"

Bud brushed the snow off his rich-looking overcoat, stamped his feet on the doormat, and stepped inside. We were standing too near each other. The brim of his fedora nearly grazed my hair. I retreated a little, but not much. "It was you," I muttered.

"Come again?"

"On the lawn. A couple of minutes ago."

"Well, sure. I had to cross it to get here. Actually, I got a call when I started over. I had to go and come back again." His gaze drifted past me as he spoke, toward the top of a credenza where I threw the mail after opening it. A bank statement lay open there, near enough for him to identify but not to read.

"So, what can I do for you?" As I was asking the question, I thought I knew the answer.

"I stopped by to see—"

"I've already spoken to Mickey. I know about the meeting. I'll do my best to be there. But I won't be prepared to discuss anything before then and would like it if you don't ask me about it."

"Ask you about it? Please, Neil." He fingered the crease of his hat. "Do you think I'd come to badger you about that first thing in the morning?"

"Well, now that you put it that way."

"Damn right I wouldn't. I thought you might like a lift to the station. I don't know about your Alfa, but mine doesn't do too well in this stuff."

"I'm all set. I've had another car for a while now."

He rested his hand on my shoulder. "Maybe I'll see you there," he said.

There were packs of schoolkids on every block. Listing under the weight of their book bags, lengthening their strides for speed, they were an occupying force whose hold over the territory lasts as long as the snow does. Some kept to the sidewalk, but others, seeing cars creep along, marched down the middle of the street and hardly gave way when I tooted the horn to inch past them. They played keep-away with snatched lunch boxes and pickup football with a rolled-up newspaper; they ganged up on fat boys and made them eat snow. I could see their vehemence in the shapes of their mouths. But as the snow muffled their cries and the rubber seals around the new car were tight, I felt that they were miles away.

They seemed to sense my remoteness and tried to breach it. They threw snowballs at me from the bus stops. From within the pandemonium of the buses themselves, they pressed their sluglike tongues against the misted rear windows. When that didn't get much of a rise out of me, one boy hiked down his trousers and squashed his buttocks against the window.

Once again, I'd treated Bud badly. What was it about him that provoked me? My animosity was spontaneous, like an older brother's, without the allegiance that underlies an older brother's bullying. It wasn't under my control, I didn't quite mean it. But it was there. It had even struck Mickey, and a thing had to be truly conspicuous before he'd pick up on it.

Bud had insinuated himself into my affairs and found out more about me than I'd have liked him to know. But it was possible that this knowledge also bound me to him. He had become, if not a friend, a felt presence, an observer of my existence in Dunsinane. His intrusions, or the threat of them, helped keep my feet on the ground. With Joyce gone and Vicky away at school, I was spending time on my own. I didn't mind the solitude. But there were moments adrift, spells in which I couldn't be sure whether I was waking or dreaming.

Bud had a knack for taking me out of myself. He'd drop by or call or appear on my visual or mental periphery. His entrances were varied—varied and, the more I thought about them, not the impositions that I'd take them to be. Not always anyway.

I was thinking about them as I sat at a red light on my way to the 7:38. The new station wagon's violet interior was suddenly oppressive, the seat belt was like a halter, the steering column a trap. My throat was dry; a suffocating heat blew from the defroster. I pressed a button to lower the glass—the whine of the motor was like the mewing of a stray cat—stuck my head out the window and drew in the fresh air. The snow had stopped. It was getting colder.

The light turned green. On the mall beside the boulevard, a French pastry shop and a macramé boutique had opened. A Jack LaLanne health spa was on the way. At the pipefitters', a man in a mackinaw spread a tarp over a truck bed. A woman in rubber coveralls scattered melting salt around the entrance of the local animal shelter. Snow covered the prow of a boat bobbing on the inlet.

As I pulled into the station parking lot, I saw Irene on her way out. She stopped and rolled down her window. Tiny creases ran from her cheekbones to the corners of her eyes.

"I'm glad to run into you. I've been wanting to apologize."

"Apologize? What for?" I asked. I knew what for.

"You're right—how clumsy of me! Enough said."

A car pulled up behind me. She leaned toward me, breaking the plane of the open window with the top of her shoulder and the crook of her arm.

"I'd better move along," I said.

She stared straight at me, but there was nothing disarming or intimidating about it. "Our house mustn't seem very warm after a housewarming like that. I hope you'll give it another chance."

I'd have liked to turn around and give it another chance right then. Scintillas of covetousness: our neighbors' wives are the vestals of suburbia. "On the contrary, your house couldn't be more inviting," I told her as I pulled away.

The waiting room was jammed. I got a cup of coffee but had left my copy of the paper at home. The kiosk was sold out. The machines on the platform were empty as well. A faint wind rippled the surface of my coffee. The sky was still low and gray, except where it was pierced by a white light. Its reflection off the rails and lampposts and roofs was sharp, a light that affronted the eyes both with its drabness and its glare. We were all squinting under our hats and fishing in our overcoat pockets for sunglasses we'd left in our Windbreakers.

An outbound train hurtled past. I went to the edge and looked through the glare down the tracks for the inbound. There it was in the distance, the light bouncing off its silver siding. My averted gaze landed on Bud at the bottom of the stairs to the overpass. I saw him in profile, his head wagging, shoulders swaying under his coat, feet twitching inside his wingtips. He was talking to a hatless man who was shielding his eyes from the sun. The hatless man laughed, then snorted.

I was walking down the platform when the train pulled in and idled with its doors closed. A crowd gathered before them. The fog on the windows was so thick that the doors might have been metal sheets. When they slid open, the revealed passengers looked like prisoners unaccustomed to daylight.

There was no point in looking for a seat. The aisles were mobbed. I was lucky to find a free hanger and a space for my coat. I hung it up and, retreating to the small space between the rack and the partition and putting my briefcase on the floor between my knees, leaned against the Plexiglas and closed my eyes.

"You made it," I heard a voice say but didn't open my eyes till I felt a hand on my shoulder. "You made it," Bud repeated. He was standing beside me, before the window with the fire extinguisher behind it.

A man on the other side of the partition kept flicking his Zippo. The flint was obviously gone, but he wouldn't stop. I was about to lean across and give him a light when someone beat me to it.

We were quiet for a while. The car was overheated and stuffy, dampness coming off coats and umbrellas and galoshes, the fluorescent light pooling at our waists. One man breathed down my neck; the brim of another's hat grazed my ear. Peering through the corner of a window at slate roofs and slate-colored clouds, I wondered how many other passengers I myself was irritating. None showed it, but none would. Among peasants or soldiers there'd have been jokes or songs. We kept to ourselves, more like lobsters in a tank. Where lobsters would have brandished their rubberbanded claws, we raised our elbows and flourished our newspapers.

We pulled into Flushing, where the train sat at the station for a minute or two, fresh air pouring through the open doorway. I glanced across the platform at the billboards beside the opposite track. They were the same as at every other station on the line—"Double Diamond Works Wonders," "Beanz Meanz Heinz," "I'm Margie. Fly me," "Should a Gentleman Offer a Tiparillo to a Lady?"—but when the wind came up and made the snow swirl around them, they reminded me of figures inside snow globes. And again that morning, things seemed insubstantial and dreamlike. I closed my eyes, drew in air sweet with exhaust, ran a fingertip over my lips, and sealed them. I fell into a measured trance. The light penetrated my eyelids in shadowy waves and bars that allowed me to believe as they hovered that I had only blinked. I didn't sleep. Or if I did, I dreamed that I was in a crowded train on a snowy morning.

I opened my eyes, and the gold thread peeking from the knot on Bud's tie pierced the gray of my reverie. "See this guy?" Bud thrust his copy of *Fortune* at me. "I used to know him."

I knew of the man myself, and what I knew didn't make me want to know more.

We left the billboards behind for bramble-choked chain-link fences, warehouses with broken windows, rusting trestles and disused bridges, ailanthus branches bending under the weight of crows, the backs of brick houses and weedy half-paved lots.

Bud poured over the article about his old acquaintance. "He's got himself thirty rooms on Lake Geneva, fountains, pools, stables, hot-and-cold running girls . . ."

"I happen to have it on good authority that he's hustling."

I noticed the throbbing in his temple and looked past it, at the blue and orange corrugated tiles of the new baseball stadium, like a dormitory for a race of giants.

"Really!" he exclaimed, and went back to his *Fortune*.

The scenery raced past too quickly to provide distraction: locust trees shuddered in our blast, signs for Serval zippers and Bohack's and Singer sewing machines passed by faster than any fly could be zipped or any stitch sewn.

"A hustler, is he? I guess I'm not surprised." Bud creased the magazine and put it in his inside pocket. "Still . . ."

There were general signs of restlessness. The man who'd been flicking his lighter went back to it. A passenger fought his way past us to the rack though it was too soon for putting on coats. An overhead fan switched on. A belt snapped and continually slapped the pulley. As we approached the tunnel and the car dimmed, the slapping grew unseemly. The lights flickered, and the rustling of newspapers grew more furious.

"I mean, just think of it," he continued, his hand in the air, and tried two or three times to complete his sentence. The hand was slow to drop.

The sound of the train racing through the tunnel became deafening without being especially loud. We were under water, and its pressurized clatter echoed across all registers. I leaned toward Bud. "Where are you from?"

He brushed back his curl, smoothed down his collar, fussed with the crease in his pants. "Why do you ask? I mean, the fact that you ask, it's a surprise."

The train went dark. The naked bulbs hanging on the tunnel walls cast a dim light but we could barely see farther than the ends of our own noses.

"I come from there." He pointed—westward, I think.

"From the bottom of the East River?"

He chuckled, and the jigsaw edges of his teeth faintly glowed. "I grew up in . . ." I lost him. The pressure inside the train had dropped. It became noisier, though not really louder. Somewhere between his lips and my ears a vacuum was sucking up the syllables.

"I can't hear you!" I shouted.

"Oh, well." He shrugged, then leaned toward me and spoke directly into my ear. I couldn't miss a word now. "It was one place after the next."

The lights came on, the overhead fan switched off, the belt stopped flapping; the car grew quiet. The train slowed and lurched to a stop. Steam puffed from the valves as the doors opened and we were swept onto the platform and up the stairs. I'd never have found a cab in this weather, so I headed for the IRT. Bud was taking the same line in the other direction, and we stayed together.

The crush in the subway was even worse than it had been in the train. Service had been out earlier in the morning. An hour's quota of commuters marched through the tunnels as if to the siege of Broadway. It was impossible to advance against so many. We found ourselves standing with our backs to the wall, like gunfighters making ourselves slim.

"Maybe we'll have better luck upstairs," I said, finding myself speaking softly. The tunnel was oddly quiet given the density of the crowd. Above the footfall, one heard only a repetitive murmur, a dull chant echoing from the tiles.

"It can't go on like this," Bud replied. "It's just a wave."

We got our chance, though not because there was any letup. There were more commuters, and more, till they were packed so tightly that they slowed themselves down. Loss of momentum made them less imposing.

Bud and I waded in. We turned sideways, lowered our shoulders, raised our briefcases, and marched, all the while mumbling excuses and having them mumbled to us in turn. It was only amid the crowd that I understood that this repetition of the phrase "excuse me" was the murmuring I had heard from the side. It sounded devotional. The rapt expressions on the faces of those I crossed, their remote gazes and shuddering lips, bespoke pilgrimage.

The crowd thinned, and the air in the wider passage seemed alpine. We hurried through an intersection lined with newspaper kiosks, flower stands, and shoeshine men and descended to the 1 train, trailed by the odors of ink and shoe polish. "It was good of you to offer me that ride this morning," I said on the platform.

"Spare me the bushwa, Neil."

"No, really. I'm grateful to you."

"Could have fooled me."

"Well, don't be fooled."

Our trains came at the same time. I got into mine and watched through smudged windows as he got into his and found a place between a woman in an Ultrasuede raincoat and a man who had stuffed half a kaiser roll into his mouth. The doors to both cars remained open.

A wino lay sleeping on the platform with a bottle beside him. A man rushed down the steps and into my train and clipped the bottle as he did. It tumbled and the booze began to spill from it, but the wino didn't wake up. Bud hopped out of the car, righted the bottle, and got back in before the doors shut.

A few feet from Bud, a young man hanging onto a strap caught my notice. He was familiar to me, but no matter how I studied him I couldn't say why. As his train started to pull away, he faced me full on and his eyes mesmerized me. They were my son Peter's eyes, the grown-up's eyes that Peter would have had.

chapter four

In the subway we had fought our way through a mob together. For a moment we were more than neighbors, we were comrades. Then he went downtown and I went up.

When I next saw him our common cause had faded and we were back where we'd been, with him looking for something from me that I could easily grant but still begrudged him. Things might have been simpler if I hadn't had anything that he wanted.

But what would there have been between us without it? Bud wanted things. So did everyone else in the neighborhood. Ambitions were defining characteristics, as public as physical features, without the shame attached to deep desires. They were traded on, placed at the forefront of personality. Pure friendships among the new arrivals were rare. They did business with their friends and befriended their colleagues, and if I was a stranger to them it was probably because they couldn't tell what I wanted. But then, sometimes neither could I.

It was easier for me to tell what I didn't want. On an evening the following week, what I especially didn't want was to be where I had agreed to go, to a boat club on a local bay where

Mickey docked the yawl he liked to sail from Westchester. But he hadn't sailed it this time. It was January and the day, almost evening now, was too cold and the water too rough.

The club was out of Mickey's way, not on Bud's or mine either, and figured to be gloomy. But Mickey insisted that we meet there. He preferred to do business where he didn't have to worry about being overheard; his voice tended to boom after he'd had a couple of drinks. "And you know what, Neil?" he asked with false pluck. "If we meet there, it'll make me feel that I'd gotten to sail." He should have said it would make him feel that he'd gotten lucky. He could never get over the fact that during Prohibition the clubhouse had been a brothel, which thrilled him as though it were one still. He'd act especially highhanded, treating the hostess—who'd been there since the bad old days—like a madam and the waitresses like whores.

"One would think you hadn't been out all year," I'd said. He'd gone to Puerto de Habòno for the holidays and was just back. He'd have spent plenty of time on the water.

"Well, it would seem that way. The Caribbean weather let me down this time."

"But you told me you'd gotten only one day of rain." He had never come home uncooked.

"One full day, I meant. It was spotty the rest of the time."

I arrived right before Bud was due. Mickey had asked me to come well beforehand to confer with him, but I was too late for that. I'd spent the day in meetings and had had to force myself to turn up at all. I wanted to spend time with Vicky. Her Christmas break was winding down. She'd gone on vacation with Joyce for the first part and used her stay with me to catch up with her friends: one in particular, a weak-chinned guitar-strumming gawk in denim and desert boots with whom she'd sit around singing inane songs about all the flowers having gone da da da, dee dee dee and who had little more to say to me than "peace"—not a bad choice if one was going to limit oneself to a single word, I had to admit.

Mickey's back was to the bay; only a milky light reached it through the thick clouds, but the olive-drab wavelets skipped and jigged. I took the seat across from his before he had a chance to declare his annoyance by not getting up. "I've been here for nearly half an hour," he hissed. "Nearly half an hour." He leaned forward in his wing chair, grabbed his crossed leg at the shank, and squeezed. "Only you, Neil. You're the only person in the world who keeps me waiting. Know what I'd do if Jeanette made me wait like this?" I didn't dislike Jeanette enough to consider the question. He looked at his watch like someone who already knows the time and said, "We might as well just wait for him. There's no point in trying to figure anything out now."

He was dressed in winter-weight summer clothes—captain's dark blazer and light-colored trousers of a heavy weave. They were what he wore after returning from the Caribbean. He'd had them for years. They were tight on him now, starchily pressed, fatly creased, the lining mildewed. The outfit still served its purpose, however, which was to show off his sunburn, the one he had said he hadn't gotten this time. His hair was longer than usual and bleached by the sun to unmixed patches of gray and dirty blond. Bay Rum wafted from his dewlap.

I offered no excuses but only lit a cigarette for him, then one for myself, the snapping shut of my lighter punctuating my first drag. How often in my life had this sound and this taste corresponded in this way, I wondered. I caught myself wondering and recognized my dread of the upcoming performance, which would really be no performance at all but a genuine episode that had been repeated often enough to ring false. Mickey would lay on the charm with a trowel, become part preacher and part clown, and if the business we'd come to discuss was mentioned at all, it would be as an excuse for a budding friendship.

I don't know whether this was a tactic of his. He might have had some idea of small talk as a blunt weapon for wearing down the other man's resistance. It had never worked, at least not while I was present. My resistance always broke before the other man's. Maybe Mickey counted on my impatience to get them down to brass tacks. But maybe not. It always looked as if he'd go on jabbering all night. He was possibly lonely enough to hold court with whoever was in a position to have to endure it. I can't say. What I can say is that although the scene played to the same end, it was always spontaneous. There was no calculation in my attitude, and there might have been none in Mickey's. We were businessmen, not conspirators. Some had done well in their partnerships with us. Others hadn't.

Mickey pinched a pair of reading glasses on the flange of his nose and looked over some figures in a memo pad he'd taken from the inside pocket of his jacket. I moved an ashtray from the coffee table to my armrest and inspected the clipper-ship insignia on the base.

The clubhouse lounge was meant to recall a ship's cabin. By day the decor worked well enough with the light reflecting off the bay and pouring through the French windows, but at night it was sepulchral. The bar, wall panels, floors, roof beams, tables, and chairs might all have been hewn from the same primeval forest and stained for gloom. The mock oil lanterns were too heavily shaded to reveal the color of the upholstery. Coals in a fireplace between us and the waiters' station gave off no more light than the ends of our cigarettes, which we could make out in a mirror above the mantle. At the far end of the bar, beneath Christmas trimmings, two men hunched over their stools at liar's dice.

"White Russian?" Mickey asked. He directed his question to the waitress rather than to me. He had pushed his glasses farther down his noise and stared up at her with ardor. I looked away.

It embarrassed her too—she looked from him to me. But it was a moment before I understood that his question had been for me.

"Neil, do you or do you not want a White Russian?"

"A Pinch over, please," I said to her. She was young, in her twenties, with frizzed brown hair, hoop earrings, frosted lipstick, a gauzy décolleté blouse, and an inscribed pendant in the opening.

"They make a good White Russian," Mickey said to me, then looked back at the waitress. "Tell the barman to be sure it's well chilled but not watered down. He shouldn't load the shaker up with ice. What's your necklace say?"

"It says 'Robin.'"

"Robin," said Mickey, "Robin—"

The men at the bar slammed their dice cups. "Not again!" one cried.

"Robin, forget what my brother here told you and bring him a White Russian too."

"A Pinch over." I fixed my eyes on hers. She bit her lip.

"Such a mule," Mickey said. "Better do as he says. Will you bring us some nuts with those cocktails?" He pushed up his eyeglasses and returned to his figures.

She hesitated. "Is Pinch the red stuff?"

"It's a whisky," I said. "The bartender will know it."

"The bartender's new here."

Mickey looked up from his figures. "For the love of Mike," he cried. "Where's Jimmy? I didn't see him when I came in. He must be off tonight. Just our luck."

"He died," she said with just the right amount of feeling for a stranger's demise. I liked her, it occurred to me.

"Died?" Mickey asked. "When?"

"A month ago. A little more, maybe."

"That so," he mumbled and glanced down at his memo pad.

She headed with our order to the bar, the cash register like an altarpiece at the back.

"The place is falling off," said Mickey, his eyes still on his pad. I couldn't tell whether he was ciphering or doodling. "So, what do you have in mind for B.Y.?"

"B.Y.?"

"You know, your man next door."

"What do I have in mind? You said there wasn't time to discuss it now." I looked past him toward the water. I couldn't see the current, only the rocking of masts in the slips. The beam of a dock light caught a gull landing clumsily beside it. He was too big for his own good.

"Well, he's not here yet, so—"

"I have precisely nothing in mind."

"Am I not going to get anything out of you even now? I've been after you about this for weeks."

I stubbed out my cigarette. A middle-aged couple had crossed the lounge and begun to play backgammon.

Our drinks arrived along with a bowl of nuts. "You don't have any that are still in their shells?" Mickey asked.

Robin cocked an eyebrow. "These are what we've got," she told him and walked off.

Mickey sipped his White Russian. "Well, this is all right, at least," he said. "It pays to tell them what you want."

My whisky tasted soapy. The glass hadn't been properly rinsed.

Mickey went to work on the nuts. "In Porto . . ." he said while chomping on a mouthful. By *Porto* he meant Puerto de Habòno. Everyone else said *Puerto*.

"Yes?"

He swallowed, then studied the surface of a pecan. "Amazing things, the lines, the texture. . ."

"What are you mumbling about?"

Throwing the pecan into his mouth, he said, "I happened to run into our friend at HABEX." He meant the export bank in Puerto.

He looked past me. I turned and saw one man peering into a trophy case while another checked a coat. "I assume you're not going to offer him anything now," I said. "That would be imprudent."

"Imprudent," Mickey repeated, with his eyes still on Bud, who looked almost too well-turned out for the occasion. His handkerchief was poised to leap from his jacket pocket, his trousers to walk off on their own. Except for a slender bandage on a shaving cut above the chin, he was flawless.

He had seen us at our table and, with the other man in tow, hurried toward us as if pushed from behind. There wasn't a hint of reluctance in that walk, of resistance to that push. The other man raced to keep up. The glass in an old breakfront sideboard rattled as they passed.

Mickey stood up and I followed suit.

"Did he say he was bringing someone?" Mickey whispered as they approached.

"No."

The man looked familiar. "We've met," he said. "At Bud's, wasn't it?"

"I remember."

"Mickey Fox, Garson Eigenart," Bud said, and they shook hands. I recalled that the last time I'd seen him his car was in a ditch, but nothing in his expression showed that he too recalled it. He was too busy being a character—the propriety of his checked suit and oxbloods was offset by his long sideburns, rainbow-colored paisley tie, and pinky ring; his quips by an ingratiating grin; his jumpiness by a mannered calm—to keep track of the other characters he met.

Mickey waved for the waitress, but she had disappeared. "I hope this place will be all right for you. Neil and I were talking about how it's fallen off. We wouldn't have chosen it if we'd known."

As he settled into the couch across from our chairs, Garson accidentally kicked the low coffee table between us. The nuts scattered.

"Sorry, gentlemen. I'm a little cramped here," Garson explained.

Bud and I slid the table away from the couch, and Mickey said, "This is just the kind of thing I'm talking about. There's no one here anymore to see to the placement of the furniture. The place has gone to the dogs." He gestured at the shore. "They've still got themselves a helluva spot, though—they can't ruin a view like that." A moonbeam died in the cloudbank like a floodlight in the glow of a city. "Unfortunately, it's too late to see much of anything now."

"No kidding," Bud said. "You could develop photos in here."

The waitress came to take our order. Mickey took every opportunity to hound her, and there was the same fuss about the drinks as the first time around. "Robin," he said as though shielding his guests from an injustice, "Robin, bring them each one of these," and pointed to his glass. They looked at me in silent appeal.

"They've always kept the lights down," Mickey said. His

twitch was acting up. His shoulder knocked against his chin, but he barreled ahead. "You know what kind of establishment this used to be? There was a gin mill down below. This cove is a natural harbor. Hauling cargo was a cinch. And it was protected. Till they built the pier, the trees went right down to the shore. The coastline is full of secret landing places, but this one was especially good."

He paused for effect, but the effect he struck could not have been the one he was after. The struggle with his twitch hindered his control over his voice. He was speaking too loudly. The lounge had otherwise gone quiet.

I lit another cigarette. A wind-up clock ticktocked on the wall behind me. Outside, a length of cable clanged against a spar. Garson crossed his legs. The jiggling of his foot in the dimness made the perforations of his wingtips seem to swirl. He was close to kicking the table again.

"They made hooch down there," Mickey continued. "Naturally, they brought the party upstairs. This used to be a cathouse."

Bud and Garson seemed not to know what to make of this revelation. Their silence didn't seem at first to trouble Mickey, who might have supposed that so startling a fact would need a moment to sink in. But when that moment was up and another had come and gone, he began rubbing at his fingertips as though the sap of awkwardness stuck to them.

"You don't say," Garson murmured, and spritzed his throat with Binaca. The bartender threw a couple of logs on the fire. The silence persisted.

Bud had an inspiration. He did what came naturally to him: he began to laugh—boisterously.

Mickey frowned. He was after wonder, not hilarity. "You miss my point," he said. "To think that right where we're sitting . . ." He leaned forward and knocked on the coffee table to mark the spot, or the brute simplicity of the business that had been conducted on it. "It wasn't so long ago."

"Not so long ago, not so long ago at all." Bud kept his eyes on Mickey as he spoke. "There are places where the past is acutely present. If I've been a little quiet, it's only because I've been distracted. This room is ripe with the intimacies of bygone days. You can still hear the bedsprings creak."

Mickey was as pleased now as he'd been displeased a moment earlier. He turned to me. "Our friend is very shrewd. The point was a subtle one, if I may say so myself. He's grasped it perfectly. To be so well understood is something."

"It certainly is," I said. "We came to talk business, didn't we? I'm going to need to move along."

"There's no hurry. The first thing Neil learned in law school," my brother explained to the others, "was how to sound busy."

Robin brought our drinks and tried to make her escape. But Mickey couldn't let her get away scot-free. "They say, Robin, that on quiet nights like this you feel the spirits pursuing their dark pleasures. What about it, Robin—seen any ghosts, felt any vibrations?"

"Excuse me?" She bent over to put napkins beside our glasses.

"Echoes of passionate cries?"

When she'd made her retreat, Mickey lifted his glass. "The success of a bold endeavor," he said. We clinked glasses and jumbled the words *success* and *endeavor.*

"And your drinks?" he asked the others. "Did I lead you astray?"

They licked their lips and nodded approvingly.

"A nice change of pace," Garson said.

"Not the kind of thing I'd ever have tried," Bud chimed in. "My habits are tyrannical."

"To the war on tyranny," Mickey cried, and again they clinked their glasses. I didn't join in this time. Mickey pointed at me with his chin and said, "Look at the sober sides."

"I support the tyranny of habit."

"Speaking of tyranny," Mickey said, "the one thing I've never understood about this drink is why they don't call it a 'Menshevik.' That's the proper name for a White Russian, isn't it? I mean the real ones. It would be a much catchier name."

It was time to make my exit. I'd known what to expect but was exasperated all the same. No business would be conducted here. My brother was more interested in palavering, and Bud had shown up with an aspiring hippie whose connection to the enterprise was unknown. They might spend hours getting acquainted. Where in the gloom, among the rutting spirits and the silent stirrings of the bay, was the end? I had wasted enough of the day. I was hungry for supper. "I've got to be going," I said and stood up.

"Going?" Mickey replied. "You can't be . . . why, we're just . . . Siddown, Neil. Please. Neil's evidently got other business—"

"Other business?" I said. "This isn't business. The only whiff of business, Mickey, is in your preparing to proposition the waitress. And if we're here to talk business, what is *he* doing here?" I waved a hand Garson's way. "As far as I know, he has nothing to do with the business I thought we'd come to discuss."

"What's the problem?" Bud asked. "Garson's taking a friendly interest, that's all."

"I understood that you hardly know each other," I said.

"And what of it?" Mickey asked. "New ventures make fast friends. That's the beauty of them." Mickey looked hot. His tan was splotching before our eyes like a paper bag holding a leaky container.

"Is he a principal of the company?" I asked. "I don't recall seeing his name in your documents. Because if he's not a principal, I don't see what he's doing here."

Now Garson stood too. "What I'm doing here is, I'm a friend of Bud's and I'm interested," he said.

"Interested?" I asked. "What's interested? Confidentiality was a concern of yours, Bud. If we're going to become involved with you, then it also has to be one of our concerns."

"Look, I didn't come to horn in. I'm already in more businesses than I can handle," Garson said, arms tightly crossed and voice quivering with outraged dignity.

"Ready for another? I certainly am," Mickey said. He jiggled the ice in his glass and shouted for another round—there was no bantering with Robin now. He turned back. "You'll have to excuse Neil. No one thinks you're horning in. I'm sure you wouldn't have come through the door if you hadn't done the paperwork. You know lawyers, always worrying about risk."

"I don't care how *interested* he may be," I said. "At this stage, any relationship he has to the business is through Bud. I can't see that his presence is called for." I heard a particular exhilaration in my voice, the measured aggression that enters it when I've got a point, the delight in an easy target. A shame that the scenes that excite us most are seldom worth the candle.

Garson fingered the corners of his mustache. "You have a reputation, you know," he said.

"Of course we do," Mickey replied. "And we've earned it. . . . Now please sit down. We've got drinks on the way."

"A reputation for what?" I asked.

"For coming out ahead," Garson said.

The fire had sprung to life, the flame from a lower log licking the one above it, which hissed and popped.

"You know, Bud," Mickey said, staring into the glow, "it may be lucky for us that you brought Garson along, despite what certain people here may think. He may have saved us a lot of trouble. He's right, of course. We do want to win. We want to win and win and win. Would you prefer to have losers for partners? I don't think you would. But . . . " he hesitated, his voice as if faltering. In the regret he projected through them, his eyes seemed a degree shy of liquefaction, the corners of their lids papery as moth's wings. The clock ticktocked.

"But, there's this question of trust. No getting around that, is there? Well, I suppose that if we were going to have this problem, it's better that it happened sooner. A pity, though. I believe we'd have been a real help to you, Bud. And I don't mean just with money, which is an abundant commodity after all. I mean with the intangibles, with contacts and plans and so forth. We'd have opened doors for you. But this is why I say it's better we hit the wall sooner. The arrangements we were prepared to make are exactly the kind that depend on trust. Now, when I say trust, I'm not talking about blind faith. We'd have anticipated your getting outside advice once we'd gone down the road a ways. In fact, we'd have expected it. You'd have had some of your own skin in the game after all. At the same time, Neil and I have found that the key to almost every successful agreement is flexibility, maximum flexibility. Isn't that right, Neil? I'm sure that your own experience bears this out. We may be the four smartest cats in the alley, but there's still no way we're going to foresee every contingency and provide for it. There's just no way. Hence flexibility, hence trust. You end up making too many goddamn false moves without it. The handicap is crippling, crippling. . . ."

I doubt that any of us listened too closely, or that we were meant to. The words were familiar without being especially insincere, and this was their virtue. They weren't exactly empty, and yet the burden of winning agreement wasn't on them. They were like a eulogy delivered by a clergyman who doesn't pretend to have known the departed and who finds sanctuary in a few general truths and the dignity of the occasion. They traded on a mood.

Our round arrived. Mickey sat up in his chair like a rallying convalescent. "You see, Neil," he continued, "we had a business meeting after all. True, it's the end of the venture instead of the beginning, but so it goes." He picked up his glass and waited for us to do the same.

"I'll be on my way," Garson said and, when no one protested, gave his hand coldly to me and to Mickey. As he shook it, Mickey looked at himself in the mirror, at the firelight reflecting against him, the flame's shadow washing over his captain's outfit as if his ship was burning and he was going down with it. "Thanks for the drink," Garson continued. "Fucking thing tastes like rose water if you want to know the truth." Garson took a few steps toward the door and said to Bud in an audible undertone, "Are you gonna hang around with these stickpins?"

They went out together, checking their voices now—the word *neighbor* was about the only one I heard distinctly.

"He comes to us for seed money, and he thinks *he* needs to be protected from *us?*"

I headed for the men's room.

Bud's confabulation with Garson was brief. When I got out, he was on his way back to Mickey, though his step lacked its earlier spring.

I went to the bar for a towel because there were none by the bathroom sink, telephoned Vicky to tell her to go ahead and have dinner without me but got no answer, bought a pack of cigarettes from the machine to get rid of the change rattling in my pockets. I'd said I wanted Mickey and Bud to get down to business, but now that they were ready I found that I had no appetite for it. I went past them to the window overlooking the water and lit a fresh cigarette. It was easy standing there to feel that you'd gained a special prospect. You might imagine that you stood at the head of a continent, or the tail; that you were in the vanguard of a young civilization or bearing the torch for an old one; or that this island was its own world, with its own infinities. In the darkness, through the overlay in the window of my reflection—the face that I watched like a clock—I could see the rocks below, and that was all. But these at least were real. We lived on rocks and stones.

I went back and sat on the couch. Bud had moved to my chair. He looked worn down by the effort of containing himself while the subject he had come to discuss loomed in the background. His curl was dangling, the bandage on his jaw was peeling away, the end of his belt had wiggled out of its loop. "But you said earlier it's just as well he was here," he was telling Mickey.

"Yes, by being here when he shouldn't have been, he showed us that we shouldn't be here either. Better that the partnership fall apart sooner than later."

"Assuming that it has to fall apart."

"If you're wary of us, then it's better it doesn't happen." We'd reached the phony postmortem stage.

"Garson got excited when he heard about the business, so I said to him why don't you come along? I told him more and it turned out he'd heard of you. He's in a small firm himself. Triangle Partners is the name. I doubt they have your kind of capital—"

"Hyperion to a satyr," said Mickey.

"Garson was the suspicious one, not me. He doesn't know Neil the way I do." He shot me a confidential look. "Besides, if you were looking to take me, would you be willing to walk away from this thing on principle?" He brushed back his curl and brought his cigarette to rest at his temple, which throbbed between his fingers. "Not likely. Partners need to stick by each other, I know that."

"It's good you do," said Mickey. "But we're not walking away. You're implying that there was a prior commitment." He was looking better and better. His tan had evened, his clothes had stretched out; there was even a certain grace in the llama-like retraction of his chin as he puffed his cigarette.

"I didn't mean walk away," Bud said. "I meant back off."

"Back off—that's better. Shall we get going?" said Mickey, stirring just enough in his chair to show that it was possible for him to rise from it.

"I suppose," replied Bud. "I mean, unless, that is, there's still something to talk about." Such hesitancy! It surprised me. It was so unlike the man who, from the day he had turned up to borrow my car and driven it like a bandit, had taken one famil-iarity with me after another. Suddenly he was timid. His ap-petite for this venture seemed to override the spontaneity that was ordinarily his foremost quality. I wished I hadn't noticed; to see him at the mercy of his desires wasn't pretty. But there was no mistaking the worry in his eyes and in the creased cor-ners of his mouth. I had seen it overtake him before, evenings in his garden as he looked toward my house or beyond it. I had wondered what he was after. Now I had an answer.

"Still something to talk about," Mickey repeated, appearing genuinely surprised. "Well, after all this, it would be quite a reversal. But it's not impossible, I suppose. . . . No harm in air-ing an idea we had."

"An idea? Lay it on me."

I watched Mickey lean forward and grab Bud's wrist, then

check himself and return again to his regular fat-cat position.
I watched him and knew what was coming, not because we
had discussed any ideas, but when it came to such ideas Mickey
only ever had one. He sat back, pulling at the hairs spilling
from his collar, and said, "What would you think, Bud, about
setting up shop offshore?"

Offshore. In itself the word seemed ordinary enough. There
was no special ring to it, no chime to the syllables either apart
or together. But the mere thought of it had made Mickey start
forward, and now Bud half leapt at the sound. He caught himself and sat back down—quickly, though not quickly enough
to dodge the spell—for now he didn't know how to sit. His
regular straight-backed posture was wrong. He aimed at something more relaxed and in shifting for it imitated Mickey. For a
moment, until Bud caught himself, there were two contented
leopards across from me instead of one.

Offshore, Mickey cried, as if unrolling a magic carpet, ush-
ering Bud on and taking off in one sweep. They flew due south,
down the seaboard, over the Florida panhandle and the Keys—
where, between hacks and expectorations, frame sagging like
an old house, I am writing these words—over the Exumas and
the Mayaguanas, the Sierra Maestra, the Cayo Abaco, and the
Ensenada de la Santanilla; veered eastward—across the middle Antillesian Strait and the Canal de la Cunha—before the
final quick turn back to the north, beyond the southern
Hispanolian coast and the tongue of the Windward Passage,
into the capital of the mountainous kingdom of Aggregente, in
whose capital we kept the vacation house from which he had
just returned. When he said offshore, Mickey was thinking of
Puerto. He proposed that Bud establish his operation there.

The arguments were overwhelming. Labor was a fraction
of its cost at home, taxes practically voluntary, tariff and duty

schedules favored the import of raw material and the export of finished products. The American policy was to use the regime as a bulwark against the bearded foe to Aggregente's north, and manufacturing received every incentive. This, combined with the intrinsic advantages of his own concept, would allow Bud to undersell his competition. It was hard to see how he could miss—as long as the people who mattered received the proper tribute. You needed the right connections. And he would have them: the minister of commerce was a friend, and so were the mayor, the *chef des douaniers,* an executive at the national shipping lines, board members of the trade association, the president of the development bank, even the mistress of the American legislator who oversaw foreign aid to the country— these were all friends. Forging the proper alliances was more than half the battle of doing business there, and it had already been done for him. He was on his way.

Mickey believed he'd carried his point. His interest in drinks, nuts, and ashtrays, in fireplaces, waitresses, and ghosts was all gone. He spoke almost softly, as though he himself had no stake in the matter. He didn't even let his mutterings trespass on the pauses he'd left to give Bud a chance to agree.

And Bud did agree. His nods and smirks and ill-timed chuckles seemed to say as much. He had recovered his spirit; the joyous undertone, the ember of the last laugh and the intimation of the next, was back in his voice. It wouldn't have surprised me if, rough as Mickey's proposal then was—there had been no conditions or figures set—Bud had reached across to shake hands on it. The romance that the word *international* took on when it was attached to *businessman* wouldn't have been lost on him.

It was just what I thought he'd come that evening to find. How else to see the headlong stride with which he'd entered the clubhouse? But Bud was full of small mysteries, and when Mickey was done, Bud took the last, watered-down swallow from his drink, waited for a frown to resolve itself in a puff from a corner of his mouth, and said, "I don't know."

He let the phrase stand at that. It sounded like a refusal. And when he shook his head, it looked like one too.

Mickey's head twitched. Where had Bud's excitement gone? He hadn't raised a single objection.

"We'll talk again when you're ready," Mickey said with strained civility. "Our interest won't last indefinitely, but once you see the sense it makes, you may come around."

Bud and I looked at each other. I lowered my eyes to the coffee table. A patchwork of rings from our glasses looked like a chart of the phases of the moon; cigarette butts spilling from an ashtray were worms from an overflowing bait can. Bud's eyes were still on me. He was waiting for me to say something so that Mickey would stop glowering at him.

"The ashtray," I said as though just learning to put names to things.

Mickey stared at it. "Will you take a look at that?" Mickey said. "Jesus Christ." He half stood, his chair scraping the floor, and looked toward the bar.

"Don't worry about it," I said. "We're all smoked out anyway."

"Bartender!" he shouted. "Some service here, pronto. Where's the girl, where's Robin?" He lowered himself back into his chair and dragged it forward. "Isn't that a pisser?" he said more calmly, then looked back at Bud and added, "The required capital outlay would be anywhere from a third to a half as much offshore as on, while the potential return on offshore operations is higher to at least the same degree. A risk-reward ratio like that is, is . . . how should I put it, Ne-il?"

This wasn't a question at all, but a cue. By pronouncing my

name as he had—breaking the *e* from the *i* and hardening the *l*—he was exercising on me some inscrutable childhood blood claim. He'd said my name in just this way before his big teeth were in. He was expecting more from me than a phrase. I was to help him sell Bud on his proposal. That was one of the last things I wanted. Getting involved with Bud would have been on this list of last things too. So would coming to this meeting. And so would being cued to respond like an organ grinder's monkey. I had no interest in helping my brother.

"How should I put it, Ne-il?" Mickey repeated.

Chalk it up to reflexive obedience, ingrained loyalty, the relative thickness of blood to water, to hunger, irritability, the fatiguing effort of keeping quiet, to being able to hold out for only so long, to the devil. Chalk it up to whom or what you will. I took the cue, joining Bud and Mickey on that magic carpet and going along for the ride. Before I knew it I had embarked on a scattered, tipsy paean to Puerto and its history. Guidebook boilerplate and chamber-of-commerce cliché vied with anecdote and gossip as the people's yearning for civil liberty was said to vie with their love of pleasure, the struggle for democracy and the rule of law with autocracy and debauchery.

I was coming around to scenes of mulatto demimondaines dancing in hillside nightclubs when Bud cut me off. "Count me in!" he cried. "If Neil's on board, I'm on board."

Mickey came to life. "Didn't I say he'd see reason?" His face beamed like that of a minister who has just had the honor of joining a worthy couple in the sacrament of marriage. There had been no seduction as far as he was concerned.

What had come over me? Was it that, unable to be rid of him entirely, I'd seized on the next best chance to get him out of the neighborhood? It didn't seem impossible. But then it also seemed no more probable than another possibility: that I too had worked my way around to the idea that he might be on to something. Encouragement was overdue, if encouragement was what I happened to intend.

It was past ten by the time Mickey had signed the check and thrown a bill from his pigskin wallet on the table for Robin and we had made our phone calls and plans for dinner and gotten our coats and were shaking hands in the parking lot. I thought that I might still be served at a restaurant on the harbor in Dunsinane where I was a regular. Mickey wasn't coming along. He claimed to need to get home before it got to be too late. I wondered what for. Being his partner on certain projects gave me a sense of his business affairs but not of what he did with himself all day, about which he could be oddly secretive. Bud winked and said he'd catch up with me there. "You'd better be quick if you're interested in dinner," I told him. Mickey walked him to his car.

I reached into my breast pocket for a cigarette, punched the lighter on the dash, and when it wouldn't make contact, punched it again, to no avail. That lighter had always been hit-or-miss. The glove compartment had the matches I needed. It also had a Baggie with a couple of hand-rolled cigarettes inside. A sniff revealed that they were reefers. Vicky had had the roadster out the day before. It was her carelessness that struck me. Maybe she thought I wouldn't care, and maybe I didn't. But it bothered me to have to decide. I threw them away and gave myself a light.

Lanes led to roads and roads to the boulevard, where a chain of traffic lights blinked their late-night warning. On an open road and an empty stomach, the blinking lights were incitements to speed up and steal a few moments.

I flew along—past squat prefabs, vacant lots, ramps, bridges, cables, posts, pillars, guardrails, curbs, signs, walls, fences, tracks, trestles, shelters, booths, benches, vending machines, hydrants on over-mown grass sidewalks: everything huddled and desolate in the darkness, the antenna bending like a twig in a gale. I switched on the radio. The dial was where Vicky had left it, which was just as well—the noise and speed would have drowned out music from the stations I knew. A female singer chanted a pop bolero with a studied aloofness. I broke the plane of one traffic light after another. Air concussed. The wheels' hum changed pitch.

The road rose, and, hanging apart from the rest, the last light on the two-lane commercial strip came into view. It seemed to recede as I rushed toward it, and for an instant, I didn't know whether I was coming or going or standing still. Just an instant—then the light got bigger, greener. The song was building to a climax. "Speed ahead," the singer cried, no longer aloof. "Speed ahead," she repeated, and as she did I realized that the blinking was in sync with my racing heart, that the pulse was inside and out. "Speed ahead!" she cried once more. A bright light hit my rearview mirror. I hit the brakes and a car blasted by on the left and crashed through the plane of the last light as if into the next dimension.

The green light turned red. Just past the traffic light, a policeman lay in wait. He took off after the car that had passed me, and when it started to pull over, I saw that the driver was Bud.

By the time Bud arrived at the restaurant, the kitchen was closed. Appetizers from the bar were on offer, nothing more. I was for moving on; the maître d' was eager to close up for the night. And it was time—the rubbery odor of garlic sautéed earlier in the evening drifted out from the kitchen. But Bud wanted to stay. He had invited someone to meet us. "A friend of yours," he said.

Did we have any friends in common? "You stay and I'll go," I said. "You'll have company."

"But you won't."

"I don't mind." I didn't have Bud's endless verve. He was still twitchy and snapped his fingers at his sides, waiting for the next moment, the next line, the next episode—next, next, next.

"You should," he said, retracting a corner of his mouth to allow a low suggestive whistle to escape from it.

Maybe there was something in that smile that won me over. Besides, I was hungry. It had begun to rain and the sound of the rain on the pavement made me hungrier. Feeding him something was the least I could do after he'd been the one to get the speeding ticket. I may have had some idea about explaining the impromptu travelogue I'd delivered at the boat club, if after a little sustenance it became clear to me.

It didn't come to that. We were tucking into a couple of appetizer plates when I felt a small hand on my shoulder, turned, and very nearly knocked heads with Bud, on whose shoulder another such hand had been placed, causing him to turn his head also. The hands belonged to the woman I'd danced with at Bud's party—what was her name? She covered her mouth and cried out at the near collision.

"She's trying to knock us out and steal our plates," Bud said.

She wore the same foblike earrings she'd had on at the party and a belted vinyl coat with a white ruffled blouse and a crucifix pendant underneath. Her hair was shorter and maybe a little wavier from the dampness outside, but she was as long and graceful as I remembered. When she took her hand away from her mouth, it stayed open for a moment and I saw that her teeth had a county-line jaggedness. This I didn't remember.

"Still looking for Lee?" I asked her. How was it that his name had stuck with me but not hers? I was pleased to see her and not only because I'd have a chance to make a better impression than I had before. Though there was certainly that—she'd seen me at my worst and gave no sign of holding it against me, and I was grateful to her for it. But there was something else too, a strange familiarity, strange considering how little I knew her. I didn't think it was particular to us. She seemed to be as comfortable with Bud. Of course she knew him better.

"Lee's busy," she said.

"He's an elusive fellow."

"You've been wondering when we would dance again. I can see it in your hips."

To come up with a suitably hot-blooded response at the same time that I was trying like hell to remember her name was beyond me. I looked down at my hips, which as far as I could tell were minding their own business, and at Bud, who had his hand on her shoulder. Where had he found her and what were they to each other? I didn't care. "Didn't you say that you'd be going back to South America?"

"Maybe she came back again," Bud said.

"And maybe she didn't. Maybe this is another Marta." That was it—I'd remembered.

"Cecilia Marta," Bud corrected me.

"And how did you like Valley Forge?" I asked her.

She licked a fingertip she had dipped in Bud's cocktail sauce and shrugged.

It was raining hard by the time we caravanned back to my house for a nightcap—Cecilia's Beetle bouncing over the

village road like a beach ball between Bud's car and mine—
raining hard and it seemed once we were inside, harder still:
a downpour that drummed on the roof tiles, spilled over the
eaves, cascaded from the gutter spouts, sheeted down the
panes, rippled in ditches, gushed down drains, overflowed
sumps, and raced into estuaries. We were happy, after the blur
of lights and spray on the road, just to be out of it, into the stillness of cabinets, glassware, pans in the dish rack.

"Vicky's gone back to school?" Bud asked when we'd let
ourselves into the dark house. "Neil's daughter's a great kid,"
he told Cecilia. "A tennis champ."

"Hardly a champ," I said. "She's home, but she's out running around most nights." The fact was less disappointing tonight than in general. Though I didn't like to imagine Vicky
driving through this storm, the thought of her wondering what
Cecilia and I were to each other made me uneasy in its own
right. Besides, what were we?

"I guess it's to be expected at her age. What is she, eighteen?"

"Not quite."

Frances didn't hear us come in right away because of the
downpour, and when she rushed in, Bud already had Cecilia's
coat in his hands. He flourished it and yelled "Toro!" Frances's
bark got stuck in her throat and she ran behind the couch
in terror.

While Bud showed Cecilia around the ground floor, I fixed
the drinks and thought that I felt okay. January was half gone,
and it was good to have gotten through the holidays and to be
out of the rain and to be spontaneously awake late at night in
the middle of the week with my good-time Charlie of a neighbor and an alluring woman who for all I knew was anything
from his mistress to a mother superior. I'd seen the taper of
her long shinbones and the quarter-moon of her calves in the

outline of her sheer stockings and didn't care what she was. She'd asked me to make her one of those tiki-bar cocktails that may be as enjoyable to prepare as to drink and that are certainly more enjoyable to prepare than to wake up from, and though I didn't have all the ingredients I had most, including the end of a bottle of Bols that might have been left over from my wedding. If a bottle of liquor has been in your house for twenty-five years, it'll probably be there till you die. Straining to unscrew the top and emptying the curaçao into the shaker, I thought, "Another victory."

I took Cecilia's drink out to her in the living room, poured two straightforward concoctions for Bud and me from the trolley, and started to build a fire. The two of them were crouched over one of the record shelves. "No, you don't want this," he said to her. "This is just one man playing the piano," or, "No, not that. That's just two men playing the violin." I started to say something about manpower as a criterion for music, but I was fooling with the flue, and my words echoed in the chimney. I pulled my head out and referred them to a lower shelf.

Among the souvenirs I'd sent home from Italy at the end of the war were some of the records we used to play there, not the American swing that was played at officers' clubs but an older, less frenetic type of music from South America. This music was tricky to dance to. I hadn't come across anyone who really knew how.

I hadn't gotten around to playing these records at home. When Cecilia put one of them on, I stood up from lighting the kindling I'd shoved under the grate. The music was rich in associations and exquisite even beyond them.

She and Bud began to dance, which took courage, and not only because the music was difficult. The living room was a minefield. The furniture was imposing and eccentrically arranged. There were bibelots and knickknacks wherever you looked. Bud stepped on a lamp stand, upended a bouquetier on a side table, and stumbled over the end of a runner and made the record skip.

He went to the turntable, cued up the record again, and joined me by the fire, where I basked in the heat on my back. "You know, Neil, when you didn't like my prospects before, the fact that you didn't *pretend* to like them, I mean, and have come around, it speaks well—well of *you*, that is. Not to presume . . ." His cheeks flushed. I caught myself putting my hands behind my back for fear that he'd grab one. "I had a feeling you would come around. It reinforces my own conviction. Not that I was in doubt, but a boost is a boost. I know you don't play games."

He didn't mean to presume! He didn't have to mean it, it was second nature to him. I let him, in any case. I had other concerns—Cecilia had kept apart from us, moving in place to the music. Now she beckoned. "She needs a new partner," Bud said, pressing on the small of my back to urge me toward her. I went and let him presume and thought I'd set him straight later.

I hadn't fully appreciated Cecilia's skill when I danced with her at Bud's party, the swanlike arch of her back and swanlike glide. She hadn't had this music to dance to then. It inspired her, and though I was supposedly leading, struggling to remember steps I'd learned more than twenty years back, it was really she who led. She was so quick that she knew what I was going to do before I did, responded in advance, led by following, without a single look or hint of compulsion; it seemed to me that I was in control. Our circuit shortened, the globe our path traced contracted, the points we described grew denser, our torsos pressed closer.

"I think I'll be on my way," Bud said. Cecilia started in my

arms. We were in our own world and hadn't heard him coming. "Sorry to interrupt, but I thought I should say good night
before you got into it any deeper." He gave us a wink. "Didn't
want you thinking I was still hanging around."

Cecilia and I had stopped dancing but kept our arms around
each other and swayed to the music till we could start up again.
"Delighted, Neil, with our understanding." He leaned forward
and gave Cecilia a kiss on the cheek. "G'night, baby," he said.
"You two look fantastic. Neil, if we work together as well as the
pair of you dance together, we'll be in clover. We'll have to get
you a pair of those pointy shoes one of these days. Maybe in
Porto." We shook hands, but this leave-taking put me on edge.
If he wanted to go before Cecilia and I got into it any deeper,
why did he have to say so? And what understanding had we
come to?

"I'll see you out," I said.

"No, go cut it up," Bud said. He lingered a moment—
departure seemed to give him trouble, at least from my house—
and dimmed the lights on his way out of the room.

"So, you and Bud are working together," Cecilia said as he
left. We were still arm in arm, swaying but not dancing again.

"I may put some money into a business he's starting." I
heard myself saying the words and was dismayed that things
had come so far. But of course they have, I thought.

Cecilia studied me, then reached out and ran a fingertip
over a small scar that runs up from the inside corner of my left
eyebrow. "And what does this business do?" she asked.

"I can't really talk about it. Proprietary secret."

She pulled back from me and stood still. The specter of insult lurked in a corner of her smile. "And I'm going to give the
secret away?"

We squared up, embraced, turned our heads, counted, and

set off on our tour, footprint on footprint, breast on breast. The dance came more easily to me now. The boundaries were tighter, our course both freer and more restricted, the trance thicker. I closed my eyes and saw down a boulevard lined with hooded lampposts; on the sea it led to moonlight floated in a motion like our own. When I opened my eyes I thought I saw reflected car lights run along a crossbeam. I listened through the music and rainfall for Vicky's entry but didn't hear it.

Our lines tightened, turns sharpened, and my knee—my bum knee—buckled. One misstep. I faltered and she caught me and for the first time we met below the waist. And accident though it was, this move too was a signal: my right hand, which had lain between her shoulder blades, migrated to her side, where she laid her hand on mine. Together we traced her length: her supple ribs with finger-width hollows between, butter-knife flank, flinty hip, thigh: facts lost with the lifting of the hand.

We danced all the while, or pretended to, to contain our deeds. From her belly—our hands had drifted to the fore—she guided me below. And then it was she who was like a marionette, the wires that held her tightening, constraining her, making her quake, obliging her to exert pressure in order to receive it, urging her to urge me. Only her head moved freely. In contrast to this tension in her limbs, it swung like a baby's, slowly, guyed to no wire but circling as if recapitulating our dance. Our eyes did not meet, but as she rocked against me, I saw that hers were open in unseeing transport. A corner of her mouth worked as if she were in a deep sleep. Two or three times she murmured something that sounded like *crispé*.

I didn't ask her upstairs, much as I'd have liked to. Maybe, if it hadn't been that room, and that bed. It didn't have to be, I suppose. We might have gone elsewhere. But the possibility didn't occur to me. I simply walked her out to her car in the driveway, noted that the temperature had dropped and that Vicky had indeed come home, and sent Cecilia on her way. I am a reflective type, I believe. But when it comes to sex I have always been a little incurious about my motives.

And as I lay in the glow of the clock radio at my bedside, the seconds buzzing and minutes clicking with the shuffling of the numbered tiles, the only motives I looked into were those in my conduct with Bud. They'd become irrelevant, I decided. I'd been trying to protect myself from him and him from Mickey and me. But he'd grown on me; I didn't need to protect myself from him anymore. He'd been given an idea of the kind of partner we were and was undeterred. He didn't want to be protected. What he wanted was his chance. Why shouldn't he have it?

I was glad to settle that in my mind. But another night I hoped to spend with Vicky had gone by without my having so much as clapped eyes on her. She'd be going back in a few days, would no doubt spend the next summer far from home, and leave for college. The snows of yesteryear had hardly melted and already I was longing for them. She was four doors down the hallway but I missed her as though she was far away. I wondered what she'd done tonight, how she'd looked. I thought of her and every picture I called to mind was from long before. Now I'd slip quietly into her room, give her a good-night kiss, and take in the sight of her.

I reached down to stroke her hair and switched on the bedside lamp. The kid, the weak-chinned guitar-strummer, sprang up, without his denim and his desert boots. He sprang up and I sprang back, back and through the body of his guitar, which splintered underfoot.

Served him right for asking where have all the flowers gone. He'd known perfectly well all along.

part two

chapter five

The name Casa Encantada, which the builder had given the house above Puerto de Habòno on Cyclops Hill, itself named for the bare rocky patch that protruded like the giant's single eye from its summit, hadn't stuck. Joyce and I called it the Casa. The simplification was a sign of indifference, not affection. The Casa—a split-level resting on concrete pilings driven into a hillside that, although covered with eucalyptus and pine and a single monkey puzzle, still bore the marks of its clearing—had never felt like ours. Maybe because it was Mickey's too and neither of us nor our wives had done much to put a stamp on it. A few gestures had been made: family photos, seashells, terraria, local craft works carved in driftwood, sisal rugs and tapestries. But with the exception of the faces in the photos, you might have switched the stuff around without any of us being the wiser, at least not at first. Further into our vacation, perhaps, if it rained and they were stuck indoors, one of the children might have noticed the change. *Our vacation, the children,* I write. Recalling our time in Aggregente awakens old habits. It was a family house, and the family had dispersed.

Joyce hadn't been able to get over the fact that we shared it with Mickey and Jeanette. Not that we'd go at the same time. Now and then our visits overlapped by a couple of days, no more. But the very knowledge of their former or future presence didn't sit well with her. Houses, as far as she was concerned, weren't to be shared. She couldn't stand the idea that other bodies had just been in the same space. The creases they'd left in the upholstery, the angles at which they'd lain pencils down on notepads by the phone, the way they'd closed the curtains were intolerable to her. It was almost like having them there, she said, if not worse, because they were around without your being able to find them, hiding in every room.

I could see what she meant, but I wasn't bothered. In fact, I was relieved that Mickey and Jeanette were there as much as they were. The prospect of squatters worried me, not their traces but their flesh-and-blood presence. They hadn't come yet, but with the heat in the barrios below, I figured they were bound to find their way up. We tried not to let the house stay empty for long, lending it to friends and clients and even friends of clients.

So much coming and going turned Jonah, our caretaker, against us—further against us. He hadn't seemed to like us to begin with. It wasn't hard to see malice in the smile with which he'd report misfortune—damage to the roof, for example, or the theft of tools from the workshop. He had no reason to hide it. On the contrary, it served to warn us of what he might do if we were to let him go.

We had our own wiles, Mickey and I. By keeping our associates streaming through the house, we kept Jonah from using it or renting it out himself. We also made work for him; the new visitors tended to inundate him with questions and requests, particularly at night when the shops had shut and they were looking for liquor. Jonah would sell it to them too.

This didn't keep him from grumbling about the disturbance, however. All of which is to say that Joyce had a point. With so many guests passing through and leaving more than traces behind, the Casa could take on the atmosphere of a flophouse. We'd find rum bottles, suntan lotion, magazines, and worse. The cleaning service couldn't tell what to throw away. For all the fine times we'd had in Puerto, Joyce had felt as transient as the others who'd come and gone. And now that she had left and Vicky was more or less grown up, it seemed that there was nothing there for me. Yet it was at the Casa that I found myself, with as much company as I might want.

In that year, Bud had been away from home a good deal. It was a rare weekend when I noticed him working in his garden, a rare evening when the LeSabre with its whitewalls and gleaming chrome pulled up the driveway. His Giulietta I saw even less.

Despite his absence, my efforts to steer clear of the deal I had finally consented to were not entirely successful. My brother saw to that.

Soon after our handshake the anniversary of Aggregente's independence came around. It was the twelfth, I believe. We Americans had been the last masters. The English had preceded us, the French had preceded them and, in the longest and laxest tenure, the Spanish had come first. All the regular players had had their role except the Dutch. But even if the Dutch had come, who would have known the difference?

I attended the Aggregentian delegation's receptions at the U.N. in earlier years, but when I skipped the last one, Mickey raised Cain. My absence, he said, was sabotage: was I trying to cut our connections, didn't I understand that our ability to get anything done down there depended on them, had I forgotten that the ambassador was the brother-in-law of our friend the minister of finance? There were answers to these questions, but instead of explaining, it was easier just to turn up.

On black leather chairs and couches or on barstools before an East River overlook, reporters, public-relations types, spooks and hangers-on hung on or hung out. "You drew a good crowd," I told the ambassador. We crossed from the terrazzo floor over an indigo rug and landed back on hard ground by the bar.

"Yes, the party's still going strong." Glass baton lighting fixtures were suspended at odd angles, like the planes of an enormous crystal, from the ceiling. "But where is your brother? He tells me your associate has plans for a factory in Puerto. We were supposed to discuss it." A giant of a man—toy flags hanging from a rack at the far end of the bar grazed his toque— waved to the ambassador, who excused himself.

I lit a cigarette and wallowed in the crowd's polyglot murmur. Laughter pealed and glasses clinked. The river's darkness merged with the evening's. The current eddied past a weedy islet poking out halfway across, a metal buoy rocking in its swell. A small boat crept like a glowworm toward the Queensborough Bridge. On the far shore, a big red neon sign told us to drink Pepsi-Cola.

A clap on the shoulder made me jump.

"Didn't mean to startle you, Neil." It was Bud.

We traded greetings. It had been a while since we'd seen each other. He wore a checked sport coat with a silk handkerchief in the breast pocket. His skin was tanned and the whites of his eyes and his teeth stood out against it.

"You got my message?" he asked. He had called to thank me for use of the Casa.

"I did. You're very welcome. I hope you found everything all right. No problems?"

"None to speak of. The power went down a couple of times."

"That's common. When it lasts, you can start to miss the air conditioning."

"It was cool most of the time." He looked restless. At least, his glance was restless.

"And it wasn't too noisy with the roofer there?"

Bud's back was nearly to me at this point. "What'd you say?"

"The roofer. I hope the noise didn't disturb you."

The ambassador came into view across the room and appeared to be headed our way when he ran into a stout man in a burnoose.

"The roofer. Sure, he came around. He said to tell you that he was waiting for some money from you. Didn't I tell you? Must be Mickey I told."

"Do you mean he's stopped working on the roof?"

"That's right. It was Mickey. Have you seen him?" Bud unbuttoned his sport coat and turned back toward me. "I thought he'd be here. I was supposed to meet him beforehand, and we were going to come over together. But I was a few minutes late, and after I sat there for a while, I figured he must have gotten tired of waiting for me and gone on ahead. He was going to introduce me to the ambassador."

"I'll introduce you as soon as he comes back. He's expecting you anyway. Mickey already told him about you."

"Well, that's good to know. The muckamucks in Puerto always ask whether I've met the ambassador."

"He greases the wheels."

"I've been able to grease a few on my own but it wouldn't hurt to have his help with the others."

I had turned toward the bar for a second, and when I turned back, the ambassador stood next to us. He gave no sign of having heard the last thing I'd said—not that it really mattered—but I was disconcerted all the same. In the growing dimness in the lounge, expressions were hard to read. Though it was nearly dark outside, the lights hadn't been turned up and the neon Pepsi sign blinked brighter. His wire-rimmed glasses and shiny pate shone in red flashes.

I introduced him to Bud. "You've come just as we've let our hair down," the ambassador said to him. "It won't stay down for long. The lights are on a timer. They'll come up in a minute."

"And till then we drink Pepsi?"

"They don't even serve it anymore. The U.N. tried to get the sign moved. Know what Pepsi told them? 'We were here before you came and we will be here after you go.' Anyway, I like a bit of darkness. It's racy. Of course, you've got to be careful. One evening last summer I was regaling a young lady from Prague with a perfectly amusing story, but when the lights came up I saw that she was crying. 'My dear,' I said, 'was my story as bad as that?' 'No, no, not at all,' she said. 'Forgive me, I was thinking of Dubček.'"

They had turned toward each other, and now their profiles were displayed in neon flashes, the clenching and relaxing of their jaws, the minting of self-interest in the corners of their eyes.

"Thinking of Dubček, eh? At least you weren't in bed at the time."

"At least? You wouldn't have said that if you'd seen her!"

Bud rested his hand on my shoulder and said, "Watch out, you'll make Neil blush." The overhead lights came up. There was quiet while everyone blinked. "And now he won't be able to hide it."

"You don't know the fellow the way I do. A seasoned operator, this one." It was the ambassador's turn to rest a hand on my other shoulder. "He may have a few gray hairs, but experience has taught him craft."

"I've seen him at work, Ambassador."

I squirmed under the weight of their hands. Bud removed his, but the ambassador's stayed. "Which reminds me, Neil," Bud said, "your, ah, *petite amie*—"

"Neil," the ambassador interrupted, "how is it possible that you let Bud go to Puerto without telling me? At the Ministry of Commerce, they thrust export-license applications at him. And some dead weight at the national development bank kept him waiting for twenty minutes. Bud, my brother-in-law is the director. He's more afraid of my sister, his wife, than of the chief of internal security—and he's right to be. A call from me is like the combination to the safe. So sorry that your time was wasted, Bud. If only I had known. You have to wonder sometimes whether these Foxes are really so sly."

He smiled, tapping my shoulder with the hand that had been resting on it.

"Tell it to Mickey, if you see him," I said, leaving a tip on the bar. "I'll leave you gentlemen to your discussion. Congratulations, Ambassador, on your national anniversary."

A man in a blue serge suit with a boutonniere in one lapel and an unfamiliar symbol on a pin in the other came up behind the ambassador and started talking to him.

"But I was about to say, Neil, that your lady friend is around," Bud said. "You won't stay?"

"I'm not sure I see what you mean."

"Cecilia. She told me she was free tonight."

I shrugged and took a step toward the exit. Through the lounge's brightness, the river was visible only as a shadow in which you could perceive motion but not form.

"She was asking me about you. She says you're too moody for her to read. I told her not to worry. I didn't know what else to say. What should I have told her?"

I might have asked the same question about her. We had continued to see each other now and then. It was always pleasant—or more than pleasant. Yet there was a cloudiness about the romance, if romance it was.

In my living room on that rainy night she and Bud came back with me, the music Cecilia and I danced to reminded me of the liaisons I had had in the army. The similarity didn't stop with the music. There was the same sense of anonymity and chance. I had thought that my association with Cecilia would be similarly temporary, but one way or another she'd stuck around. There was neither a foreseeable end to our romance nor an order in its continuation. Who she was and what she wanted from me were unavoidable questions, and yet I did avoid them. To ask them would have been inappropriate to our occasions.

"She's got nothing to worry about," I told Bud. I saw him steal a glance at the ambassador and got the feeling that Bud didn't want to let him get away. "Your answer was fine."

As I left the reception area and stepped on to the descending escalator, I looked down the well and saw Mickey coming up. His hat was in his hand and the collar of his overcoat was up high. Against that background, I watched a series of expressions cross his face. He might have been taking both parts in a debate. He looked furious, then sorry, then uncertain, like someone waiting to catch the sense of someone else's words.

In my surprise I forgot to turn away to avoid his seeing me, and he'd have had to—we weren't far from each other by now and my escalator was practically empty. He turned, put on his hat, and faced straight ahead. I felt remorse for his embarrassment. But I didn't call up to him. My remorse was not so strong as that.

Bud and I hardly ran across each other for what seemed a long while after that. He was gone, and I was busy.

I certainly looked busy. After my abbreviated night of passion with Cecilia, my knee began to give out, and I consented to have it operated on for the second time. It was a minor procedure, but when the surgeon postponed the operation, my recovery coincided with a hectic period at work. We—Weissmer, Schiff, Marne, that is—had settled with the insurance company to whom we'd sold the shaky debentures. There were negotiations within negotiations. I hobbled into meetings all over, and whether I was dealing with the buy side in Philadelphia or the sell side in Boston, there was always the same crack about how I'd brought the crutches along as a bargaining ploy.

Mickey continued to vie for my attention. The stream of prospectuses was unending. I'd toss them aside, but a day or two later he'd call and badger me to look. Although some—like Buccaneer's Cove, a beachfront development outside Puerto— seemed to be straightforward enough, the bulk of them ran to outlandishness. The anticonventionality of the time put a premium on eccentricity, as if whatever was brilliant also had to be far out. American hucksters and European engineers who'd come over in the brain drain were teaming up on all manner of gizmos and gadgets: lathes that could grind glass so finely that it would be possible to make lenses for palm-sized cameras, microscopic transistors that could be scattered from the sky by the thousands to eavesdrop on our enemies, a meter that counted the number of glasses of beer a bartender dispensed from a tap to prevent him from cheating the owner. I told Mickey that he'd missed his calling, that he should have been a patent officer.

"No percentage in it," he barked.

And I seemed to have to face another private trial every time I turned around: the filing of marital separation papers, Leon's endless tinkering with her will, a change in the zoning code that reduced the minimum size of a building lot in Dunsinane Gardens to allow for further subdivisions, blighted elms, a root canal, another railroad strike, Vicky's dramas.

Her anger at me for barging in on her and her folk-singing boyfriend lasted past the end of her vacation and well into her final term. She had sworn off speaking to me, but in the early spring she finally called from school. "I need you to send me pocket money, Daddy. I can't even go to the movies."

I had tried to apologize, but now, after having been snubbed for so long, I found that there was an edge to my regret. "Who is this, please?" I replied. "I'd think it was my daughter, except she isn't speaking to me."

"I'll get you," she said and hung up.

I called back several times over the next few nights, but she wouldn't come to the phone, not even after I'd sent her a check. The other girls in her dorm had gotten to know my voice.

A high wind came up late on one of those nights, when my desire to keep calling Vicky wasn't quelled by the knowledge that I would have to wait for her to come around. It had been a gusty week; with all its huffing and puffing, winter was going out less like a lion or lamb than a big bad wolf. But the gale that night was something else. I'd stepped out with Frances and watched its blasts sweep clouds in from the bay and rip off their tails. A flash of lightning made Frances run back inside. She nearly upended the sofa trying to crawl underneath.

I returned to my chair, emptied my tumbler, and picked up my book. But it was impossible to read. The wind's howling was like a kind of inverted scream, a vacuum that absorbed every other sound within itself. I knew that the doors and dormers must be rattling, the shutters and gates clattering, the wind whistling down the chimneys and vents and through the cracks between the sashes and sills. It seemed to me that I could feel if not hear them and that the rain spattering against the panes was enveloping me in mist. The lights flickered, then failed. I might have made my way to the pantry for a candle but instead stayed put, letting the darkness settle around me. I remember thinking that I had never felt less like myself, that I might be anyone. I dozed off.

I came to at dawn, my glasses dangling from the arm of my chair. The storm had blown over and the lights come back on, pale yellow in the morning pink. The picture frames seemed crooked, the pictures themselves to have receded, and the outlines of the furniture to have smudged. The room was like a memory, as though I had been gone for a long time and come back to a faded reality. Running my fingertips along the edges of a matchbook I'd picked up from the table, I went to the window and looked across the lawn, which still lay in shadow. I could see the night lights from Bud's. I hadn't noticed them before. I saw them again from the next bay and climbed the stairs.

I awoke at noon. When I went out for the paper, I understood why the view had been so clear. Beyond strewing everything across the lawn that could be strewn—limbs, sticks, stems, branches, early blooming flowers, their petals scattered like plucked plumage, and the tarp from the woodpile the storm had brought down one of my biggest trees, a white ash that had stood on a shallow rise near the hedges along the property line. The gale had not only knocked the tree down but also drowned out the sound of its crash. I felt that I had fallen asleep on my watch and failed to guard a family treasure. My children had swung from this ash, and now it lay toppled, its trunk splintered near the base and again farther along where it had smashed against a boulder, its limbs spread over planting beds, its crown reaching to the driveway. I walked its length, the sky pressing on me as if the tree had been holding it up, inspecting its warts and knobs. An empty bird's nest lay intact in a cleft between branches.

"It's like a beached whale." Irene's voice startled me. I hadn't heard her coming. She was dressed for yard work, in a smock and long skirt and a beaded choker that she must have forgotten to take off. She held her daughter by the hand.

"It must have been loud," I said. "But I didn't hear it. That wind sounded like the end of the world, didn't it?"

"It shook us all up. The children got scared and came to sleep with me. They eventually nodded off."

"And you? I'm sure that with the baby—"

Her daughter leaned back and swung from her mother's arm. "Easy, Lizzy," Irene told her. She turned back to me. "Not a wink," she said.

We stood over the fallen ash, the fluttering of its fringed leaves like the twitching tail of a dying animal. "I should have Charlie come over to count the rings. He's been learning all about it in school."

"I hadn't thought of anything so practical."

"You'll have firewood for years to come."

"I already have a pretty good supply." I nodded in the direction of the woodshed behind her. "I count on you to take some off my hands."

She reached over to me and brushed something away from my chin with her fingertips. I stepped back in surprise.

"Excuse me!" she cried. "I didn't know what I was doing. You had a little something, it looked like a seed from some jam, on your chin. I'm in the habit from the kids. I didn't even think."

"I didn't have any jam this morning. I must have nicked myself shaving."

"That's what it must have been. My mistake. I hope I didn't irritate the cut."

"Not at all."

We fell silent. We could hear an amplified voice from the road, possibly a telephone repairman's. "Is your phone out?" I asked. Her daughter tugged at her sleeve.

"By the way, Neil, there's—"

"I haven't thought to check mine."

"There's something I've wanted to talk to you about." She shifted toward me, and I caught sight of the pulse at the base of her neck.

"Fire away."

She seemed at a loss for a beginning. My invitation hadn't helped. I hadn't meant to sound quite so breezy, and now I couldn't think of how to put her at her ease.

Her daughter, meanwhile, had thrown herself on the ground and was clambering along a horizontal branch, pretending to climb it. "Mommy!" she cried, "look how high I am!"

"Hold on tight," I said. The girl laughed.

"I know that you put up some money for Bud's new business. He's grateful for that. *We're* grateful. I hope you know that. The business is going well. There's lots of interest. And because of all this interest, well, he needs more money. I guess you know that too."

"I'm sure he does, but the extent of our commitment has already been decided. We're not in a position to—"

"I didn't mean to imply, for heaven's sake . . . I wasn't asking *you* for more, Neil."

"I didn't think you were."

"I'm asking whether, with your knowledge of finance, you might be able to suggest another way for him to get what he needs. He's dealing with a bank down there where the plant is. Before this bank'll give him a loan, it wants some kind of security, and he hasn't got any, except . . ."

"Except?"

The answer came to me as soon as the question had crossed my lips. Or maybe I had known it beforehand. I heard myself sigh. Through the void where the ash had stood, the early afternoon light overspread the Youngers' yard, catching a cluster of cherry branches, a brick barbecue and, nearer the front walk, a bicycle leaning on its kickstand.

Though no one besides her daughter could hear us, Irene lowered her voice and moved closer to me. "Except the house," she continued. "He wants to stake the house on the business."

"The house. If you don't mind my asking, haven't you got a mortgage?"

"We do, but we made a good down payment."

"And then there's appreciation."

"So they say." She fingered the beads on her choker.

"And you want to borrow against your equity."

"*I* don't want to. Bud does. But he needs me to sign on. The house is in my name too. I imagine . . . you can imagine how I feel, Neil."

I couldn't imagine it. But I could see that it cost her to speak to me in this way. Her voice seemed about to break. Still there was determination in it, a physical resistance to the words. Her strangeness to money made it an intimate subject.

Her daughter hung slothlike from a branch of the fallen ash, which bent under her weight. I started to think about how big the cleanup job would be, and it took me a moment to summon the called-for response.

"I wouldn't worry too much about it," I said to Irene. "They have to ask for security. It's a formality, practically. No foreign development bank wants to be in the American real-estate business. They'd rather wait for their money if they have to. Foreclosure is their last resort."

"But they'll do it if it comes to that."

"Of course. But the bank director is a friend of my brother's. He's brought in plenty of business over the years. This director would figure to be reluctant to move against Bud."

"Sometimes I think there's something about Bud that tempts people to move against him." A bleak laugh escaped her. She turned away from her daughter to look me in the eye. "Neil, suppose you were to guarantee the loan. We could give you the same security the bank's asking for. Then I know I'd be dealing with someone trustworthy."

Her scent was soft in the April sharpness. Negotiations are carried on from behind desks for a reason—her nearness changed the nature of her appeal. I picked up a few twigs and inspected the shoots.

"I don't know. We're already making a sizable investment in Bud's business. Being guarantors as well would heighten our exposure, and I doubt you'd want it that way. Unless of course it'd allow Bud to cut a better deal." I was snapping the twigs, one by one. "On the other hand, rates are already artificially low. It could make us jumpier without helping him in the long run. You may be better off with the bank."

"But I don't know the bank director. I know you."

"I'm not sure there's much to know. I'm a businessman. So's he."

"You asked whether I'd slept through the storm last night. The truth is that with this loan hanging over us, I haven't been able to sleep even on calm nights."

"Listen, Irene, I'm hardly involved. You may want to speak to my brother. It's really his project."

"Your brother? I haven't even met him. I couldn't possibly."

"Mommy, look!" The girl dangled upside down a foot or two off the ground near the end of the branch. She held on with one hand and waved at us with the other.

As Irene looked back, the branch gave out, and the back of the girl's head hit the ground. She was quiet for an instant while she grasped what had happened. Then, having measured her distress, she screamed bloody murder. Irene ran to her.

"It's nothing," I tried to stop myself from saying. I'd meant to reassure the mother, not make light of her daughter's wailing.

Irene was bent over her. "She was frightened," she said, in explanation or rebuke.

"Of course she was."

A phone-company repair van pulled up the driveway. The crookedness of one of its hubcaps made the wheel appear to wobble. The driver looked gray behind a dirty window but when he hopped out, he showed himself to be young and golden haired.

The girl's sobs subsided. "Think about it," Irene said as I walked off to deal with the repairman, "won't you, Neil?" The vulnerability in her voice was tempered by a domestic strain, as if we were a couple and she asking me for an everyday courtesy, to let her sleep, perhaps. We had been through an intimate experience after all. After intimacy, sleep. It seemed to follow. To be allowed to sleep, what humbler request could there be?

"Of course," I said, innocuously enough. But who was I kidding? If there'd been any chance of my turning Irene down, it

would have come then. By agreeing to think about her proposition, I was more than halfway to accepting it. And within
a couple of weeks I had accepted it, personally floating the
Youngers a loan—I had the cash on hand and no compelling
investment anyway—secured by the equity in their house.
They were oddly casual about the deed of title, slipping it like
a tradesman's bill inside my front storm door, and this odd-
ness seemed to infect my sense of the deed itself. Finding it on
my way in from work and absentmindedly bringing it upstairs,
where I went to change out of my suit, I slid it beneath the lamp
on a clothes dresser in my bedroom, meaning to put it in a safe
deposit box on my next stop at the bank or to file it in my office. But weeks passed without my doing either. One morning I
found myself shoving it to the back of my sock drawer.

　I see now that by agreeing to consider Irene's request, I
had practically granted it. Irene was too vulnerable, too much
alone, to let down. Busy as I was, I couldn't help noticing how
often Bud was gone. It'd be Irene and the boys with the blower
and shovel after a snowfall, on a ladder pulling vines from the
coping, touching up the paint on the shutters, nailing down a
plank on the front steps, hauling out the trash cans, bundling
the newspapers, weeding, mowing, raking, mulching. The
customarily masculine share of the home-maintenance burden had fallen to her, and she set herself to it like a drafted
soldier's wife. Except that her husband hadn't been drafted. He
had gone willingly. He might have counted being apart from
his children a hardship. And he might have been pleased with
Irene. From where I stood, he ought to be.

　But I might not have been in a position to make that judg-
ment. Others I'd made about Bud had come to seem partial. I'd
been quick enough to guess that he wanted what I had, but it
had taken longer to recognize that the envy went both ways,

that I might want what he had: a decade in hand and a family that was together and in need of him. To see that I might want those things was to have to consider my wanting them so badly that I'd try to deprive him of them. Was there less reluctance in my concessions to my brother and to Bud himself than I had supposed? I didn't like to think so, though an exchange with Irene on her lawn one evening that spring made me wonder. She was late taking down her storm windows—vinca budding around the flagstones, a lantern at the end of their walk throwing shadows from a moth trapped in its panes—and I'd gone across to ask her whether she'd like me to send over a handyman who was tending to a few things for me. "I'm all right," she replied, and then, when I asked again to be sure she wasn't refusing from politeness, she put down the frame she was carrying, glared at me, and coldly said, "Really, I'm fine." The offer seemed to insult her. I started back across, last year's leaves soggy underfoot.

"No one made him go," I turned to say. But she had already headed in another direction and gave no sign of having heard me. I was glad she hadn't.

The more politic reply would have been something along the lines of "I'm sorry you're alone." There'd have been something to it. It wasn't that I missed Bud. But as I made the circuit of my days, I might find myself thinking of him, wondering how he was faring in Puerto. From my familiarity with the country and the reports he sent Mickey, I could imagine him scouting factory sites, meeting customs officials, shipping agents and bankers, losing his way by day in the import-export maze, making friends by night who would promise to get him out. The life he'd be leading down there was more accessible to me than the one he led next door. I knew what he'd need to do and could surmise that at a certain moment he might be doing it. He had been an overbearing presence as my neighbor, but now that he was off in a place I knew, I'd developed a sense of concurrency with him. He'd become one of the people I was habitually aware of, a spoke in the wheel of my consciousness.

Telexes from him would come in to my office. "What's keeping you, fella?" they'd say, or "Come on down!" He might have walked in; I could almost hear his voice. And I'd remember what he couldn't have known: how well distance became him. I might have put down my credit-risk report, pulled my glasses off my nose, leaned back in my chair, and dictated a reply. But I wouldn't have gone in any case. Travel fifteen hundred miles to see a man who breathed down my neck from next door? There'd have been more sense in walking a mile for a Camel and ramming it through the eye of a needle. I might visit Puerto again, but not on his account.

When Vicky had said before hanging up on me "I'll get you," I didn't take the threat seriously. I'd heard it from her before, and she'd never stayed angry for long. But as the weeks, then months went by without a word from her, I found out that this time she'd meant it.

I'd given up calling her. A guidance counselor kept me current on the status of her college applications—I wouldn't give Joyce the satisfaction—but I'd have traded this news and more besides for a word from Vicky herself. I'd stare at her signature on the back of the check I had sent after our last call or comb the mail for a letter. Short of driving up to New England for a confrontation that would likely go wrong or taking a perverse consolation in the strengthening of her will, I could see nothing for it but to wait her out.

Our feud, I often thought, was prolonged by her being away. If we'd been living together, she'd have had a way of getting even. But from school she had no way, or none that she could be sure I'd see, and could only let her threat stand. Or maybe, prep school sharpening her instinct for punishment, she understood that it wasn't her threat that worked on me but her silence. And it did work on me. Her favor was a right, a need. She had said she'd get me, but by freezing me out, she already was.

At last she called. Our talk was no different from one we might have had had we been in touch all along. She made no mention of her silence and I was too cautious to bring it up. I didn't let on that I already knew her news. I congratulated her on her admission to some fine schools, made myself available for her graduation, and gave her what I hoped were the expected responses on every other subject. I didn't tell her how I had missed her. It wasn't that kind of conversation. I didn't want her to know how she'd subdued me. The feud was over.

I stepped out into the spring evening, lit a cigarette, and could hardly stop smiling long enough to draw on it. A crocus patch had sprung up near the trunk of the ash. The ground was almost blue. Birds twittered. A whiff of lighter fluid hung in the air. I had my daughter back.

Things with her went back to what they had been, to weekly phone calls given over to dues, duties, arrangements, negotiations not so different from those I carried on at work. I was relieved, and grateful simply to hear her voice. But this gratitude lasted only so long, and then it was hard to keep myself from thinking that my worry when she'd stopped talking to me was out of proportion to the pleasure I got when she started again. I hoped for more from our conversations and had to hide my disappointment at not getting it.

I was finishing dinner when one of these calls came through. The phone on the wall in the hallway between the kitchen and the dining room rang so loudly that you'd snatch the receiver from the hook to make it stop. But I was happy to hear from Vicky, at least until she worked her way around to saying that she'd been thinking that it'd be hard for Joyce and me to attend her graduation together.

"I wasn't expecting to go together," I said.

"It'd be uncomfortable for you two to be in the same place, is what I meant." I had drifted out of the hallway, through a swinging door back into the dining room, and was facing a series of built-in shelves in a corner on which decorative plates, an antique dinner gong, and an erasable alabaster writing tablet with the word *menu* gilded at the top were displayed.

"We're not talking about a dinner party, honey. Hundreds of people will be there. I'm sure we can handle it."

"Well, Mom said she'd be uncomfortable. . . ."

"Then she doesn't have to go."

"But it's a big deal for her. She's been talking about it for months. She's already bought a special hat and everything. And you know yourself, you can't stand ceremonies."

"I've been looking forward to this one."

"God, I thought you'd be glad to be excused! And so did Mom."

"She's just worried she'll feel self-conscious if I see her in some desperately foolish hat. Better tell her to leave it behind. You don't need the embarrassment." I leaned against the swinging door, which started to give way, causing me to lose my balance. The mouthpiece knocked against the door frame.

"Daddy?"

"Right here." I returned to the dining room. "You know, I can picture that hat already. It'll block the view from the row behind. What's the matter with that woman? She *looks* for occasions to make herself absurd. Don't listen to her, Vick. Her opinions have absolutely no bearing on anything but her own—"

"She still knows you. She was married to you for a long time." My eyes ran over the alabaster tablet. A fancy dinner menu from years earlier was still printed on it. The ink had faded, but the writing was legible. Years back, Joyce had plunged into French cuisine and started to prepare elaborate meals, most of which hadn't come off. Vicky would sometimes keep her company in the kitchen and, with Joyce's help, write the names of the dishes on the tablet. *Cuisse de canard confite en pot-au feu et ses légumes,* I read in a child's loopy hand. "But listen," she continued, "if it means a lot to you to go . . ."

"That's all right. I understand. Let her wear her silly hat in peace." My back was to the swinging door again, but this time I caught myself before I leaned against it. "Only, you might have—we might have discussed it."

"Discuss it? We are discussing it."

"We used to discuss . . . that is, have discussions, talks." A kind of shakiness had come into my voice. I could feel her discomfort on the other end of the line.

"When I was little, you mean? Those weren't discussions."

"Of course things change with age. I understand that."

"Someone's been waiting to use the phone. I've got to go. We've been on for a while."

"You know, I've been thinking, why don't we take a trip? How would that be?"

"Great. I really should get off the phone."

"Naturally I can't set a date right now, but when some time opens up."

"Sure, Dad. This girl who's waiting for the phone looks fit to strangle me."

"Well, don't let her do that. It'd spoil our trip."

It had been a difficult conversation, to conduct and to escape. Vicky had had to make her excuses and I mine. It had seemed obvious that there was no girl waiting for the phone and no trip to Aggregente in the offing. But then winter came around and we were making plans for it.

chapter six

I didn't have to hold Vicky to taking the trip. The push for it came from her.

At Thanksgiving she had come home from her first semester at college with a sore throat and a fever, nursed it over the short holiday, and gone back to finish the term. But the symptoms had mushroomed into a case of mononucleosis, and she'd had to come home again. Christmas found her rallying but still bedridden, giving me an excuse for not spending it with Leon and Mickey and Jeanette. By New Year's she was coming around. She was well enough a week later, but a term's worth of final essays and exams overwhelmed her. Her powers of concentration weren't the strongest, and the quantity of work expected of her was itself a distraction. Taking up any single task felt like an avoidance of the whole. After so much rest she was stir crazy, she told me, and needed a change of scene.

I remembered our phone conversation in the spring. A trip together had seemed a farfetched, stopgap hope. But now the occasion presented itself. I too had some writing to do. A merchant-banking firm was making overtures to buy Weissmer in our weakened condition and it had fallen to me to assess the offer. And thinking that there was still the Casa's roof to be dealt with, I welcomed the idea of some time in the sun, especially in Vicky's company. I imagined us working, taking quiet meals and walks on the beach together. I hoped we might be at the end of our tiresome parent-child conflicts and at the start of something like a friendship.

I booked seats on a flight at the end of the week. When I showed Vicky her ticket that evening, she told me she had set plans for the day after we were to leave. A *happening,* she called it.

We were having dinner. The familiar tension crept into our voices. She picked up her knife and fork as if taking arms.

"People are gathering to talk about social change." She wore a deerskin jacket and a needlepoint choker in imitation of an Indian squaw.

"Then what you're going to is a colloquium."

"Jesus, it's not a colloquium. There's music."

"That's called a concert, last I knew. Even when the music happens to be earsplitting."

All that can be said for the ensuing quarrel was that it was short. I raised standard objections, she countered them all, and in the end I agreed to her flying down to meet me a couple of days later.

The only direct flight to Puerto was at night, always on an older plane and always half full.

The engines droned. The cabin lights were dim. The stewardesses plied us with spirits from miniature bottles and disappeared behind orange mesh curtains that, clashing with the red upholstery on the seats, went to our heads even more directly than the liquor.

Between Philadelphia and Baltimore a calm came over me,

in spite of, or because of, the fact that I was inside a machine hurtling high above the Earth. I'd drift off, come to, and drift off again, till the sound of the engines was indistinguishable from the workings of consciousness. Was I flying or dreaming that I was flying? I hovered between a sleep in which I'd dream of being just where I was and a waking in which I suspected I might be asleep, until, as dawn crept under the crack at the bottom of the window shade, I raised it to behold the Caribbean looking so blue that at first I doubted it was the sea I was seeing and not a lower section of the atmosphere. The conch pink rays that dissolved the darkness were themselves dissolved in a whiter light. The sun cleared the horizon and the tiny scratches on the double-glazing of the plane's windows were like scratches on my eyes. The stewardess came around with hot towels. I put mine over my face and heard myself sigh. When I next looked out the window, the spine of one of the islands humped out of the water—a clump of trees, the belly of a quarry, the glare of a corrugated iron roof, a muddy river dividing rust-colored banks.

My cab from the airport moved into traffic on the avenida: trucks with bouncing cargo bearing cryptic stencil marks, buses and brightly painted vans packed with passengers, mud-splattered cyclists and, on the sidewalk thoroughfares, peasants hauling their wares to market on their heads or backs. Tow-headed missionaries handed out pamphlets beneath a peepal tree that dwarfed the market gate; as the tallest of the group extended a pamphlet to a passerby, he slipped on the blossoms. My driver saw it too and couldn't stop howling. In the rearview mirror, his teeth looked like broken tablets. Government cars raced by stalls and kiosks. We followed in their wake and found a route leading out of the valley, past villas behind limestone walls and mahogany phalanxes. Along the last stretch of road

I saw Jonah on foot, a machete tethered to a sack on his shoulder. He spat as the cab approached, but when I stuck my head out the window and greeted him he was friendly. He had aged since I last saw him. Dark streaks marbled his eyes.

I let myself into the house. The anticipated eeriness of returning alone to empty rooms and half-forgotten objects, the confrontation with absence and auras, had made me uneasy. But I prowled around and at the sight of dust and cobwebs and dead flies, faded upholstery, bubbling Plexiglas, exposed rafters in the wing where the roofer had left off working—at every sign of deterioration—felt only that I wasn't there yet, that the rooms might have been empty. My mind was still up north.

I unpacked my bag and threw open my bedroom window, but seeing that the screen was torn lowered it to within an inch of the sill. I lay down on the bed with my hands behind my head, a twisted mosquito net dangling above me. Drawing deep breaths of musty air and looking past the blades of the ceiling fan at a crack in the stucco ceiling, I said to myself that it was not so strange after all to be here without Joyce, who had never stopped complaining about the house anyway and who, if she had been here, would be complaining now. Drowsiness began to overtake me. I felt the corners of my mouth slacken. A cock crowed down the hillside, too far away to bother me, I thought, anticipating a nap.

It was not to be. I came to with a start, in no more than a moment or two, not long enough to dignify with the name of sleep. In the closeness of the air in the room my throat and chest had tightened and a familiar panic stirred. This panic had in it more than the fear of suffocation. I don't remember my dreams, but it seems to me that my son, Peter, is sometimes in them. I awake with a sense of him, a feeling that he has been nearby. It wasn't that I had that sense now. I hadn't dreamed, but this tightness in my chest brought him to mind nonetheless. He had died of an asthma attack.

It happened in summer, at the end of his second week at a sleepaway camp. He hadn't wanted to leave home, but we figured that he ought to be ready to. He cried when, after he'd been gone for a few days, we called him. He was the only new boy in his cabin, he said. The other boys had been there before, knew one another, and wouldn't accept him. But by the time Joyce, Vicky—who was too young for camp—and I left for Puerto the following week, he seemed to be getting used to the place. Or so we told ourselves.

A couple of days into the trip, we got the call, or I did. It was from my secretary, who thought I'd already heard the news. Peter had died the night before, but the camp had been unable to get through to me in the Casa and called my office after hours. The answering service passed the message on to my secretary without telling her that I hadn't gotten it. When she called me to find out what return flight we'd be on, I had no idea why we'd be returning sooner than we had planned.

I was grief-stricken but calm. My composure might have looked like reserve. It wasn't. Nor was it that I had foreseen Peter's death. I was as surprised as anyone else. The asthma attack was his first. There had been no indication that he even *had* asthma. The counselor who slept in Peter's cabin mistook the boy's gasps for sobs. He thought Peter was crying himself to sleep. By the time he understood that Peter was wheezing, he was too far gone.

I started a family late, after I had made partner. My standing at the firm allowed me to spend extra time at home with Peter. I'd steal an hour in the morning and sometimes two in the evening. Being able to come and go from the office as I liked didn't diminish my responsibilities, but I was too charmed to mind letting my work suffer. Peter was either on my knee or in my arms. I spoke and sang to him, hummed and prattled, talked sense and nonsense, buzzed my lips.

I'd stand watch over his crib while he slept, often restlessly. His legs kicked and his arms waved as though he was learning to swim. His face was restless too. His world seemed to be full of angels and devils, none of whom stuck around for more than a moment. His expression was so various—the longer I'd watch him, the less familiar he seemed. But maybe faces are like this. Take them in once or twice and you recognize them, study them and they look stranger and stranger.

This privilege of Peter's company had its cost, however. His charm was more than I could bear. I grew deeply attached, and this attachment had a morbid side. He might smile, coo, clutch my finger in his fist while his eyes glowed in a rush of joy. Or he might turn serious or sad, his lower lip protruding in a way that would make Joyce marvel at our resemblance. Whatever his mood, he delighted me. But then, in the midst of this delight, it would come to me that I had waited too long to have him. And thinking of how old I would be when he reached a certain age, how old he would be when I died, I'd wish I was younger. "Leave it to you," Joyce said, "to develop a biological clock *after* the child is born."

So I might always have been preparing myself to lose him. But if I had been, the loss that occurred was not the one I'd been preparing for. Panic, or the possibility of panic, had stayed with me. It took only the close air of a shut-in room to bring it on.

I got up, opened the window all the way, turned up the ceiling fan, untangled the mosquito net, and crawled under.

I awoke in the late afternoon, stepped onto the deck beside the swimming pool, and looked downhill at the light quivering on the bay, at the coral-darkened shallows and the brighter depths dotted by a pair of islands. A couple of fishermen were out, no one else. The lively surf and white sand beaches and hulking hotels were on the other side.

A few lengths in the pool made me hungry. In the kitchen, I found a bottle of Tia Maria alongside a note from the last person to use the place, an associate of Mickey's with a spelling problem. The man's difficulties made me hope that he'd left some food behind, as though his not being much of a writer meant that he had to be a chef. But the fridge was a bleak landscape of punctured tins, the condition of their contents not worth the risk of discovery: anchovy relish, smoked oysters in oil, condensed milk, its label drip-obscured. The pantry was no better: a box of salt, a packet of coffee, a carton of biscuits, and a box of mosquito coils. The biscuits were too stale to break.

I threw on some clothes, fired up the Mercury wagon we kept there, and started down Cyclops Hill. Big new houses peeked from behind bougainvillea. The needle on the fuel gauge didn't move off the red line. I cursed Mickey for leaving it empty, then his associate with the spelling problem, whoever had been the last driver. I had intended to grab a bite at a café near the house but for fuel I'd have to go farther. A needle hovering around the empty line on the downhill would sink below it going back up.

The filling station lay on the outskirts of town. At the junction midway down the hill, I headed toward it, the Mercury's motor knocking like an outboard. The jungle green yielded to scrubbier ground—mango and papaya trees to thorn bush and prickly pear; houses of brick, glass, and tile to those of cinderblock and tin. The road narrowed as it wound, ditches deepened, vines crept through overhanging branches. Through thinner undergrowth, I saw a rusted-out car chassis at the bottom of a gully. When the road dipped, my eyes would shoot back to the fuel gauge, where the needle had also dipped below empty. I put the transmission in neutral and coasted when I could.

Around a steep bend, I entered a dust cloud. A gamey odor quickened my nostrils. The cloud cleared to reveal an open truckload of goats. I had to hit the brakes hard to avoid rear-ending the truck, which bounced along, the mudguards behind its rear wheels flapping over every rut in the unpaved road. The goats themselves stood steady. Their coats were thin, which made them look like tall, shorn sheep. A few of them stuck their heads over the rail and fixed their stares on me. I backed off, away from their stench, and took another peek at the gas gauge.

A car approached from the other direction. It too had to slow down, and as it edged past the truck, I saw that Bud was the driver. His mind must have been elsewhere. He looked at me blankly and it was well after we'd crossed that he shouted back. I stuck my hand out the window and waved.

If I hadn't seen him then, Bud would have turned up soon enough. At half the stops I made that afternoon, collecting the local mail, laying in supplies, reserving a table for the night of Vicky's arrival, Bud was known too.

"Nice to see you, Mr. Fox," the pro at the local tennis club said when I stuck my nose in the door. He was standing at a racquet-stringing machine that looked like a sextant, his long blond hair curled under itself, the skin peeling on his upturned nose, seashells strung on a leather lace hanging from his neck.

"And you, Dennis," I answered. "Anyone looking for a game?" I stepped inside.

"Today? But, it's late."

"No. Tomorrow or Sunday."

"There was that lefty—"

"He's gone. Transferred somewhere cold."

"Doesn't sound good for his game."

A brunette wearing a capless brim and a short skirt stuck her head in a door on the other side of the pro shop and said her good-byes.

"There's Jean-Luc."

"He cheats."

"Miguel?" Dennis pulled on the racquet string with one hand and worked a clamp with the other.

"Talks too much."

"I don't think I have anyone else for you." He stepped over to the counter and reached behind it for a clipboard. "What about your friend?"

"My friend?"

"Monsieur Younger."

"Monsieur Younger," I repeated.

"He's a nice player." He pushed the phone and clipboard toward me.

"I don't think so," I told Dennis and took down some other numbers from the clipboard.

Wherever I showed my face it was the same. They'd all met my friend. I might have sent him ahead to prepare for my arrival. And now, as I drove back to the Casa, with dusk settling on the banana fronds and jacaranda blossoms ringing the city's reservoir—from which an egret took off—only now did the misgivings I'd expected hit me. A delayed reaction. I couldn't have said where they came from or what they were, but being impossible to name they were impossible to dismiss. I knew only that Bud had brought them on. He'd been everywhere before me. His use of the Casa in the fall suddenly seemed as intrusive to me as it might have to Joyce. At home it had been comfortable to imagine him going about his business here, but now that I was in Puerto myself such imaginings were a straitjacket.

At the crossroads I turned away from Cyclops Hill and took the long way home, up and down cobbled streets, past open ditches of running water, sidewalks and steps and bright ramshackle houses. Barefoot men and women carried calabashes or charcoal, children chased one another, vendors' braziers glowed from alcoves. Atop the old quarter outside the gates of the Justice Ministry, a Moorish fortress that had been turned into a prison, an outdoor market was in full swing. In the courtyard overlooking the water, a café had opened, a terrace strung with colored lights. I pulled over and ate a bag of grilled peanuts against a stone parapet overlooking the palisades and currents of the northern coast, the view striking me as flat and postcardlike after so many humbler scenes. On a terrace steps away stood a coin-operated telescope with a smashed lens.

A group of beggar children began working on me. I forked over my change and moved farther down the wall. They followed. Before driving off I tossed the remaining peanuts to a dog whose itchiness made his begging seem more benign than the children's—he couldn't beg for more than a few moments without stopping to scratch himself.

It was a squalid scene, but at least it was a scene. On the street in Dunsinane there were only cars.

Minutes before Vicky's plane was due, a single storm cloud like a plane itself rolled in without warning—no thunderheads, lowering skies, or pressure drops. I waited at the airport terminal—a hangar with one side open to the tarmac—skimming a local paper. A gust fluttered the pages; the groundswell of dust and grit made me cover my face. When I opened my eyes, the rain was pounding the terminal's metal roof so hard that it would have been impossible to tell it was falling in drops if not for the sight of them smashing like asteroids against the concrete apron. I could have screamed without hearing myself. Workmen rushed from the tarred runway to adjacent hangars. Behind the cloud the sky was clear, and, even while the rain continued to pour down, a rainbow arced over the hills. Then the cloud rolled past as if on wires and took the rain with it. The plane followed—it seemed to be driving the cloud onward—landing under a bright sky. The baggage and signal crews hustled back to meet it. By the time they'd wheeled out the gangway and the stewardess had thrown open the hatch, the puddles on the runway were evaporating.

As the passengers clomped down the metal steps, I felt a hand on the small of my back. I knew whose it was before I turned to look. "Don't tell me we've come for the same bird," Bud said.

I glanced back at the plane. A pair of swallows was harrying the flight. One of the baggage porters was taking cover under a wing of the plane and the others were laughing at him. Vicky stepped onto the landing. Even from that distance she looked tired. She was slouching and pulled at her ponytail. I turned to Bud. His time down here had added to his swarthiness. Against this background, his lips showed redder than they had, his eyes more liquid. There was a chalk mark on his lapel that his tailor must have forgotten to rub out. "I would think I had the privilege of greeting my daughter myself."

He returned my look, and I had half a mind to knock the twinkle out of his eye. "I can't think of anyone who'd deny you that privilege." Vicky was still a short distance away. He moved off and cried, "Salut!" to Cecilia, who was coming down the gangway and who, from the expansiveness of her wave, might have been greeting the whole island. I wondered what to make of that wave. It was easier than wondering what to make of her being there in the first place.

Bud granted me the privilege I'd claimed, and he kept to it. Over Vicky's shoulder at the baggage claim, I saw Cecilia start toward me and him call her back. I was sorry that he did, and sorrier still for the way I'd spoken to him. I'd have liked to say so then.

The nearest chance I got was by the curb as we were leaving. His car was five or six back from mine. I waved at Cecilia and shouted "I'll call you" to him. I meant it this time.

Vicky had looked tired from a distance, but it was when she reached me that I saw the depth of her fatigue. She was wobbly and sallow.

"It'll be nice to lie down," she said when we were in the car.

"Why do I have to keep after you to take care of yourself?" I asked.

"Jesus, all I said is I feel like taking a nap. It was a long trip."

"You didn't need to say anything. Don't try to tell me that the trip by itself is responsible for how run-down you look. I shouldn't have let you stay behind on your own."

"You shouldn't have let me? What should you have done, Dad, lock me up?"

"All I'm saying, honey, is that for a smart girl . . ."

"For a smart girl? For a smart girl, what? Spare me the sermon, will you? I'll be fine after a nap. All I did was have a blast. When's the last time you did that? Have you *ever*?"

We lapsed into silence, passing a man on a mule-drawn cart bearing sacks of charcoal and the crumbling wall, rusted gate, and orange-blossomed immortelles of an old cocoa plantation. When I next looked at Vicky, she had dozed off.

What was her idea of a blast anyway? I knew how to enjoy

myself when it was called for. And if I didn't, then what could I do about it? For someone who took herself for an idealist, Vicky was awfully concerned about pleasure. But then, her friends were all like that.

I slowed as we approached a roadside crab shack—a conch shack, really. Conch fritters and conch chowder were on offer, not crabs. In her girlhood, Vicky had been crazy about the fritters. "Hungry?" I said to her, softly enough not to wake her if she was really sleeping.

"No," she answered without opening her eyes. "Who was that woman?"

I took my hand off the gearshift, pulled a cigarette from my breast pocket, and gave the car lighter a push. "Which woman?" I asked, but she had dozed off again.

I had wondered before about the nature of Cecilia's connection to Bud, but as long as he and Irene were my neighbors and my own connection to her—to Cecilia—had remained casual, I had preferred not to wonder long. It had been possible till that afternoon to treat our encounters as coincidences. But one didn't turn up in Puerto as a matter of course. Her appearance here had to mean something. And even if that something was respectable—as the lack of embarrassment in her and Bud's manner suggested—I thought I should find out what it was.

But another part of me rebelled against doing the finding out. I had come to relax, if not quite to retreat. I intended to write my report, spend time with my daughter, enjoy the sunlight and sea. Anything that might get in the way came in for resistance.

I hadn't let myself worry about the possibility of other things coming up. I knew that Bud might be around and that if he was I could expect to run into him. It'd be fine with me if he was and I did, fine too if he wasn't and I didn't. To spend an hour with him wouldn't have been an undue intrusion. I was prepared for it. But I wasn't prepared for Cecilia's appearance or for the greater commitment that it might entail. At the same time, I couldn't convince myself that her presence was unwelcome to me; I couldn't even try very hard. But before I gave up the effort, I thought I'd better figure out whose girl she was.

"So now you're feeling friendly," Bud exclaimed when I called that evening. "I can't imagine what's come over you," and figuring I'd earned his sarcasm, I agreed to stop by his place the next afternoon. I wondered whether he was planning to talk business and hoped not. I wondered whether his visitor would be there and hoped so.

We stood on Bud's deck with identical drinks in our hands, Bloody Marys, in nearly identical dress—tortoiseshell sunglasses, polo shirts, Bermudas, and water buffaloes. There was no sign of Cecilia, and I didn't let on that I was looking for any.

I looked down on the sleepy harbor. A breeze was just stiff enough to swish in my ear. "It isn't a bad spot," I said.

"You mean for sitting back and watching the world go by?"

"Something like that."

"If only! I've been chasing around like a March hare."

I nodded. We were leaning against the house. I turned from it and caught sight over Bud's shoulder of a cat slinking along the deck railing. Bud looked back and saw it too.

"But things are falling into place for us. I've found a site in the new industrial zone, near the airport."

Again I nodded.

"We've got power and water lines and a backup generator. There's an experienced overseer who may come to work for us. His name's—"

"The name won't mean anything to me. I don't know any-one like that here."

"He gave me the inside track on some machinery. I don't know how much you know about making edges."

The cat was stalking something in the lavender below the railing. "Not a thing."

"Most of the stamps and dies we need are right here. I thought we were going to have to import them."

I had finished my drink and was running my ice around the edge of my glass, practically rattling it, but Bud stayed on the subject. Something in him, or in us, made him keep going, a fixed quotient of energy, or of sociability. His insistence on my hearing about his business increased in proportion to my resistance to it.

I heard a car below working its way up the road.

"They were used to make gas masks," Bud continued. "Some firm down here had a commission to make gas masks for Uncle Sam. The canisters happen to be the very shape we're after."

The car I'd heard below was nearer now. Bud was listening for it too. He walked to the railing and lit a cigarette. I lit one for myself. Green hills were at his back, blue sea before him. "You see, we're on our way."

"Glad to hear it," I said without pretending to mean it. Yet he seemed sincerely pleased that I'd said it.

The car's wheels crunched against the gravel driveway. "A visitor," Bud said unwonderingly. He slid open the glass doors and went in.

The deck was too exposed; the hillside's trees offered no cover. I approached a grillwork table in a corner, reeled open the central umbrella and, seating myself in its shade, stubbed out my cigarette.

Even before I heard Bud come back through the house and Cecilia's voice behind him—that soft lilt giving everything she said an air of invitation—even before this, I felt myself quicken.

She squinted as she came onto the deck but didn't look my way and started fiddling with the sliding screen door. "This screen won't close," she called in to Bud. "It's off the track."

"Don't worry about it," he answered. He came through the door and handed Cecilia a glass. "You've got to knock the wheel up there." He jammed the flat of his palm against the top of the frame and slid the door shut.

Cecilia turned to take in the view. She took taking in herself, dark and slender beneath a gauzy frock.

"Oh, *there's* Neil!" she cried. "You said he'd come out of the woodwork."

"Where'd you pick up that expression?" I asked and started toward them.

"He looks so different when he smiles," she said to Bud. "Like another man."

"I taught her that expression," Bud declared. "But I also told her that you hear it only at parties."

"Isn't this a party?" she said.

She went over to a chaise beside the pool, and Bud and I followed. Bud sat down on the edge and dangled his legs in the water. I remained standing.

"It's hot," Cecilia said. "I'm going in." She stood up, wiggled out of her sundress, snapped a strap on her bikini top and tightened a bow on the bottom, flounced to the edge where Bud sat, leaned on his shoulder, dipped in a toe, and dived in. She covered the length of the pool under water, her hair a pulsing blur as she stroked, rested, and stroked again.

Bud cocked his head and said, "I'll bet you're not sorry to have run into her." He spoke in an undertone, but it was a theatrical undertone, louder than it needed to be, loud enough for Cecilia if she was listening to gather that we were talking about her. But then, I suppose she might have assumed as much, whatever she could hear.

"Yes," I said more quietly, "it's quite a coincidence."

"I see you have your doubts," he replied.

"I often have my doubts. They're not especially significant in themselves." Speaking quietly was making me sound confidential. "But the fact is, she has a way of turning up where you do."

"Where I do? I'm surprised to hear that. Though I can see how you might think so."

Cecilia kept swimming, her head above water, seeming to take no notice of us.

"Well, yes, I do think so. You wouldn't expect me to believe that the only times you're spending with her are the ones when I happen to come along."

"You don't make it sound very likely."

"It isn't likely."

"How likely is it that if I was with her I'd have encouraged you two the way I have?"

"I've wondered about that myself."

"And?"

The cost of satisfying my curiosity was too high. The subject was private, after all, and delving into it could only bring us closer. "And I don't know that I want to pry any further into your business. It's good of you to entertain my questions as far as you have. But maybe we should leave it at that."

"We passed the knife-and-fork stage a long time ago, Neil. You don't have to mind your manners around me. What is it?" He nodded at Cecilia. She was floating on her back, the islands of her breasts, hips, and toes peeking from the water. "Do you think I get some extra charge from passing my mistress around?"

"She's right over there," I objected.

"With her head under water." To prove his point, he spoke up. "See?" he said to me when she showed no sign of having heard him.

"I don't like the thought, but it has crossed my mind," I said at length. "It wouldn't be unheard of."

"I know, I know. It takes all kinds." A band of clouds had slid in over us and fractured the daylight. We held up our hands against the sharper rays. "But I'm not one of them," he continued. "There's no dark secret. I don't believe in secrets. What's doing between her and me is nothing. I won't tell you I've never thought of it. She's too attractive for me not to have. But I will say that what we've got, Neil, is basically—basically it's a business relationship. Now I wouldn't expect Irene to understand that, but I know you can. She's working for me, and there's an end on it. Have I mentioned that she's got experience in shipping? She worked for a container company down in South America. That's one way she can help us. And can't you see her working the booth at conventions? She's an absolute natural for drawing a crowd. And that's as far as it goes for us. It so happens that you're here and she's here. I just want to get out of the way."

"I don't know that there's a call for that. I don't know that I'd want you to. Or that she would."

He leaned back and looked straight at me. "Oh, I think she would."

I'd begun to feel uncomfortable. The deck was an inhospitable spot, despite the view. The heat and the breeze made for a kind of static in the air, a buzz below the atmospheric hush. "Maybe so, but for now I'll be the one to get out of the way. I should be moving along."

"I should have known better than to level with you. You're so easily scared off. Do you know that Mickey calls you 'Neil of the Hasty Departures'?"

"There's nothing hasty about it." I glanced at my watch. "Vicky's been running herself ragged. I want to keep an eye on her while we're here."

"Have her come over."

"Another day."

"Cecilia," Bud said across the pool. "Excuse me for a moment. If it wasn't urgent I wouldn't interrupt. Neil is threatening to break up the party."

"Leaving?" Cecilia said. "But it's impossible."

They tried to talk me out of it. Cecilia claimed that I really wanted to stay, that the smile I couldn't quite keep off my lips gave me away. "What smile?" I asked. "I'm not smiling."

Cecilia crossed to our end of the pool, hoisted herself out, and came over to me. "This smile," she said, lifting the corners of my mouth with her fingertips. It was a pleasant sensation—better, in fact: her touch was familiar though her hands were wet; so was her scent beneath a chlorine draft. Now I really did feel myself smile. "See?" Cecilia said. "That one."

What exactly was I smiling at? I didn't wonder at the time. But as I drove back—I was heading home over their objections and with the promise to meet them that night or the next—I had to admire her timing, the way her gesture had capped Bud's explanation, as though she'd heard or guessed at our conversation. Whether it had been the prescience of her approach or the simple pleasure of her touch that had made me smile, I didn't bother to decide. It was enough to have smiled at all, and as I thought of it, I looked in the rearview mirror and saw that I was smiling again.

Bud had been trying to get me to lower my guard. He might not have succeeded in getting me to lower it on his own account; there was more between us than could be cleared away in a few gestures. But on me, on my own general outlook, he did seem to be having an effect. I felt different from the way I had when I had arrived. The late afternoon light was soft, the breeze a whisper. I would take Cecilia as she came, I thought, and imagined myself diving into Bud's pool, swimming to her as she floated on her back and grabbing her around the waist. I had half a mind to turn the car around, but I was already on my way up Cyclops Hill. Another peek at myself in the rearview showed a face no longer smiling, but purposeful. I'd catch up to her later.

I found Vicky over her books at the high Formica bar between the kitchen and the dining room—the extent to which she was *over* them was the question. The room was dim for study. I had overlooked it when I'd first come in, gone to look for her in her room and on the balcony with the red poinciana flowers drooping on the sloped roof. Back in the dining room, the slatted blinds were angled against the sunlight, which crept across the table to her. From the tilt of her head in her hand, I thought she might have nodded off. Her eyes were open, but her pen rested against the page. I started to speak, then thought better of it, and drew close enough to see her heavy lids and deep pout. "Hello, Daddy," she said, lazily.

"Hellooo, Daaaddy," I answered. I circled the table and kissed her on the cheek. "Sorry to be away so long."

"Were you? I didn't notice. I was working." She put down her pen and began to play with the ends of her hair. Her foot began to twitch on the base bar of her stool. Her tranquility was gone.

"It'd still have been good to be here with you."

"I'm sure you had more fun doing whatever you did."

I pointed to a writing pad in front of her on the bar. "Is that what you were brooding over when I came in?"

"No brooding. I figured out what I'm supposed to say and I said it. See?" She leafed through the pages. She'd covered quite a few. "I'm nearly done with it."

"That's good news. But why are you sitting in the shadows? I thought you were asleep."

"I wasn't asleep."

I turned toward her, the stool creaking as it swiveled, and studied her profile: soft yet obdurate, the slope of the jaw descending from the earlobe peeking through the chestnut waves. Though she must have felt me looking at her, she didn't flinch. She had never minded being looked at. She had other ways of keeping her distance. "I'd like to know what goes through your mind these days."

"Nothing very interesting, believe me."

"What, for example?"

"Oh, things like Gregory."

Gregory, Gregory. I searched my mind for a face to match the name. None surfaced. I played for time. "Isn't he interesting?"

"I guess it depends. Funny he should come up, though. That's what I was thinking about, him."

"That *is* funny."

"You never did say much about him."

"You didn't ask me."

"That's true. I was so angry after you barged into my room, I don't think I'd have cared."

That was Gregory. I thought it odd that a creature like

that should even have a name. He had to, though. Generation follows generation and all must have a name. "Is he still in the picture?"

"I didn't know you were interested in the picture."

"Sure I am."

"I hardly know myself. He's over in Rhode Island, you know. We've tried to keep it going, but we just end up having a lot of difficult phone calls. Then when we see each other, there are so many misunderstandings to straighten out."

"Sounds tough."

"He's such a boy. He has no idea what's really going on with me. I've got to explain everything to him. He's awfully cute, and his fumbling was entertaining for a while. . . ."

"I see," I tried to say but had to clear my throat. She was right. I didn't really want to hear about her boyfriends. Not so much from a lack of interest. It was more a question of relevance. I didn't see that the subject was worth our time. "I see," I said again.

"Oh, no you don't. You don't really care."

"Sure I do. It's a matter of maturity. You're more grown up than he is."

"It kind of seems that way, doesn't it?"

"It does to me." I was happy to have slid through.

"He'll catch up. I guess I'll have to wait."

"I don't know. I wouldn't say that necessarily," I said. "I mean, that's not the inescapable conclusion."

We were managing, Vicky and I. An hour passed without contention, an afternoon, a day, and another. In light of the way things had been going, it felt like half a miracle. Being on vacation made getting along easier and so did the taste she'd developed for wine. It took her edge off, diminished her inclination to put the worst construction on my words. I was too pleased with the change to mind how it came about.

On one of these afternoons—we'd had lunch on the patio while a storm came up, then moved inside, made inroads into a second bottle, and watched it pass through—I was well into a siesta when a knocking on the front door woke me. This knocking must have gone on for a while—it had to penetrate to the depths of my slumber. By the time I'd come to, it might have knocked down a fortress. In clambering up from my sleep, I'd had to knock one down too. I staggered to the screen door in a bathrobe.

"We've got a court in a half hour," Bud said. With the sun in my eyes, and the mosquito-proof mesh between us, I could hardly make him out. It was like trying to peer into a confessional. "We got lucky. There was a cancellation."

"A half hour? What are you talking about?" My robe was open. I felt along the sides for the belt.

"I heard you were looking for a game."

"I might have been, with a little notice."

He pressed his head against the screen. "Cranky, are we? Sorry to wake you, but I couldn't call. Your number's not on file at the club, and I left my address book at home. There wasn't time for me to go there and back."

The belt was nowhere to be found. I held the robe closed. "Why can't you leave a man in peace? What's the matter with you?"

"What's the matter with me? Jesus, Neil. I heard that you wanted to play, and when a court opened up, I had no other way to reach you. I went out of my way to come here. That's what's the matter with me." He turned and walked back toward his car.

"For Chrissake," I called after him, "come on in. I'll be with you in a minute."

"That's more like it."

I went back to my room, threw on some clothes, and rejoined him in the entryway. He held a pair of racquets—the newfangled round-headed steel kind that serious players generally regarded as uncouth and unplayable—under his arm like schoolbooks. An extra shot of Vitalis he'd put in his hair to keep it out of his eyes made him look like a Latin bandleader. "Now grab your gear and we'll see whether all those trophies you've got up in Dunsinane are for real."

"They're from the dark past. See this knee?" I shook my leg like a stick. "I don't fool with singles anymore. Go pick on someone your own age."

"Don't wag that thing at me. You forget that I've seen you on the dance floor." He whacked my leg gently with his racquet and tried again to slip by me into the house. I stood my ground. "You've never been picked on in your life."

I tapped the spot on my wrist where my watch would have been if I'd put it on. "I'd offer you a cup of coffee, but if you're going to pick up a game you'd better be on your way."

"You mean if *we* didn't need to be on *our* way. Come on, fella. It's clearing." I stepped outside. The sun had started to burn through clouds that were the gray of old coins. "We'll knock it around. Sweat out yesterday's punch to make room for today's."

"I've already had today's," I protested.

He wore me down. I was up and around anyway and could use the workout. "We'll just hit," I said. "We won't play a match."

"Won't Vicky play?"

"She must still be napping. Besides, she's been down with a cold."

I went to the kitchen to leave her a note and found one she'd left for me. She'd gone to the beach with some friends and would be back for dinner. I started to wonder which friends these could be but decided it wasn't worth the bother.

I had never seen so many players milling around the courts— mostly guests at a new hotel with which the club had come to an arrangement, I gathered.

We wouldn't have waited. The cool the rain had brought was already dissipating, the breeze dying down, the warblers in the ornamental lemon trees piping up, the fitful clicking of the fronds of the coconut palms above the court like the applause of apathetic spectators. Vapor trails formed overhead; the club gardeners might, if they could, have floated up with their shears and clipped through them. Drops of moisture clinging to the bougainvillea dangling over the walls behind us portended our sweaty brows.

The heat felt good at first. We were spontaneously limber and drove the ball from the start. I had forgotten how mechanically Bud played, how neatly, like someone intent on following instructions. He hit the ball the same way every time: hard, straight, flat, low over the net and not too deep—it would land in the middle of the court, behind the service line but well in front of the baseline. His shots incited you to hit the same ones back. Repetition begat repetition. We were more or less stationary. When a ball went too far to the side of us, we let it go, apologized for the error, and hit another. You wouldn't have thought from watching us that hitting it past your opponent was the object of the game. It was more like playing catch.

The grandstand framing three sides of the court next to ours had been built when the club hosted a pan-Caribbean amateur tournament. That this court stood empty was puzzling, given the demand for it. It had been newly swept after the rain, and everyone who passed it must have gone back to the desk to point out its availability.

A few spectators entered the grandstand: a pair of military officers, one whose head was shaped like an anvil; an unshaved young swinger with sunglasses on top of his head and hair spilling from his open shirt; and three women, two blondes and a doe-eyed wavy-haired brunette. Security-agency types took up positions in the stands and assumed sanctioned looks of boredom. Others brought out a canopy to shelter the seats along the sideline. Another pro, not Dennis but a whiskery Latin who kept the arms of a tennis sweater tied across his chest, came onto the court and flashed his smile at the spectators. Whoever they were waiting for was taking his time about it. In the meantime, they watched Bud and me hopping on our toes at the baseline.

"Who's winning?" one of the military officers shouted over to us during a water break.

The man they were waiting for was escorted by the director of the club onto the court through a portal at the base of the stands. He was young, overfed, and even from the distance between courts gave off a whiff of cologne. His shirt was tight, his shorts tighter. His sunglasses were too big and kept sliding down his nose. His mouth was set between a smirk and a sneer, though this might have been the face he made when he was out of breath, which he seemed to be instantly.

"Who's that?" Bud asked the next time we stopped to pick up balls at the net.

"It's Ramses Alonso, the former president's son, the national playboy. He plays polo and flies fighter jets. But mostly what he does is chase tail. I've seen him scoping out prospects at the Tropicana. The aristocrats all worry that he'll jump their daughters' bones."

"A swordsman, eh? He's certainly not much of a tennis player." In fact he wielded his racquet like a sword, thrusting and parrying at the ball more than stroking it, leaping like a swash-buckler, exulting whenever he chanced to hit it inside the lines, swearing when he failed. Or so it appeared—my Spanish is slim.

His followers in the grandstand laughed, whistled, cheered, whooped. The convention by which the game is played in silence was evidently unknown to them. When we paused, Bud would try to stare Ramses down. But Ramses was too caught up to notice.

"I've half a mind to tell him to put a lid on it," Bud told me across the net.

"Better not," I said. "We're lucky they let us on at all. When his father played, they kept the court next to his empty. I'd have thought it was the same with him. He must have given permission for us to stay."

"Imagine his needing two courts," Bud replied in a some-what louder voice than the one in which I had spoken. "One is too much for him."

I sidled farther from the other court and turned my back to it. "Pipe down," I whispered. "You don't want to get that kid's back up. He's an army general, you know. His father had him commissioned when he was thirteen."

Bud faced the grandstand court now, not disguising the fact that he was talking about Ramses, who stomped around, hold-ing his ill-fitting sunglasses in front of him, throwing them on the ground and crushing them underfoot, then commandeered an officer's Ray Bans. "You think we should humor a punk like him?" Bud asked me.

"How do you think he got to be that way? He can do whatever he wants."

Ramses retreated to his canopy for a breather. His camp followers grew louder and more animated now that he'd stopped playing. The officer whose glasses Ramses had taken climbed down from the grandstand and tried to take them back. Ramses gave him a hat instead. The pro began to clown with the glasses Ramses had cracked. An officer tossed one of the women's shoes over the rail. She retaliated by tearing a medal off his uniform and tossing it after her shoe. The officer shouted at the woman. Ramses picked up the medal and pinned it to his shorts.

In the rumpus I took my eye off a ball and shanked it. It rolled toward Ramses; by the time he retrieved it, Bud and I had already started hitting another. We kept it in play for a while, and Ramses waited for us to miss to throw the ball back. He was impressed and made his followers quiet down. At the end of our next rally, they applauded. Their talk grew quieter.

Ramses came over to our court. "Excuse me, gentlemen," he said in deliberate, courtly English, removing the sunglasses. "As you see, I cannot play this game. But you, you can play. Please, come over here and play for us."

This display of humility was startling. He had a gift for regal condescension, for making you feel honored to be spoken to. "Thank you, but we're nearly done, General."

"Finished? But it isn't possible. I am asking you to play for us." He opened his palm in a gesture of supplication. You could see from the flintiness of his eye that he was unaccustomed to refusal. "These courts are mine," he continued. "Please, I invite you."

If he wanted an exhibition, I said, he had one pro right there and could surely dig up another.

There was nothing more for him to say. He gave me a menacing look, put the sunglasses on, and sauntered back to his court.

Bud came up to the net to find out what the matter was. "Nothing much," I told him. "He wants us to play for them on his court. He couldn't believe we'd forego the honor."

Bud followed me to the far sideline, where I toweled off. "It doesn't matter to me where we play," he said. "I don't mind moving over a court, especially if it'll keep them quiet."

I took a cup of water from the cooler. It tasted metallic and I had to resist the urge to spit it out. "A minute ago you didn't seem to have much patience for him."

"That was before you advised me to stay on his good side."

I agreed to move over for a few minutes before we quit. We had already hit a lot of balls and I was nearly out of gas.

Almost as soon as we set foot on the grandstand court, Ramses came out from under his canopy and said, "Please, please, you play a game for us. A competition. A winner, a loser."

I protested. So did Bud. But Ramses wouldn't hear of our refusing. The dispute grew embarrassing, then tedious.

As I was about to give up and walk off, Bud waved me up to the net. "We'll keep doing what we've been doing," he said. "We'll hit it back and forth to each other like before. Only we'll start the points with a serve and keep score to satisfy them." He gave a quick glance at the grandstand. "What do we care who comes out ahead? It's all in fun."

"It's all in fun." When you hear that, you know that none of it is likely to be. How could it not have occurred to me that an urge to settle the score might grow up in Bud? And if it had, wasn't he entitled to it? A friendly tennis match—there were surely more spiteful methods of revenge he might have tried to exact. I was getting off easy, if this was even what he was doing.

He certainly seemed to be taking something out on me. He had said we'd bat it back and forth but the plan hadn't stuck. We had agreed to try to hit the ball straight, but we hadn't said anything about how hard we would hit it. And the harder we hit it, the more difficult it became to control. Sooner or later, one of us would make the other scramble, and all bets were off.

Bud could scramble better than I. My bum knee prevented me from covering the court as well as I'd have needed to keep up with him—my knee and the heat of the afternoon. Though past its meridian ferocity, the sun had come back strong. The clouds were in tatters; the last of the rainwater rose in a mist from the grandstand's metal seats.

In all our dealings, in our every negotiation and exchange, the ten or dozen years I had on Bud had never mattered in so brute a fashion. Being faster and stronger was no use to him at the dinner table or on the phone, but it certainly was here. And what about experience, what could it have done for me? Mightn't it have permitted me to opt out, put me past caring whether he beat me, let me let him have his revenge and the in-nocent satisfaction it might bring him? If I needed reassurance, I might have reminded myself that I had a handicap, an injury, and that I was easily the more skilled player. I mightn't have minded about the outcome of our match. But I did mind. The competitive fires kicked in on their own.

I lost the first game. In the middle of the second, the swinger and one of the women got up and left. I expected the rest of the group to follow, but they didn't. Something about our match held them. They watched closely, applauding and making clipped, teeth-gnashing remarks under their breath between points. I found it hard to take their interest seriously. I thought they were mocking us.

I lost that game too and was trailing in the third. It's odd that so frivolous a thing as a tennis match can feel like a prison sentence, but it can: you are bound by strict rules in a circumscribed space until you win, which sometimes seems impossible, or lose, which is often unacceptable.

The woman who had gotten up came back. I thought I heard her ask the score—3–0 for Bud, by then—and sigh when she heard the answer. It was a down-but-not-out sigh with a combative edge to it. I felt that she was counting on me.

One of the officers suddenly leapt over the grandstand rail and came toward us, the butt of his revolver undulating in his holster. He veered toward Bud and stood over him like a boxing trainer. I couldn't hear him, but his anvil-shaped head looked ready to crack Bud's skull open if he was disobedient.

Ramses came down to give me a pep talk too. His breath hung in the heavy air as he barked at me. His face looked more dissolute up close.

But there was something in this fight-corner reveille. I might at least have been putting up more resistance to Bud, though not by trying to out-hit him. I couldn't cover enough of the court. I'd have to finesse him, feed him dinks, floaters, lobs, slices—junk—to throw off his rhythm, sabotage the game, lower the level of play in the hope that he'd sink further than I. But I was reluctant. This was an older man's strategy, an older man's game. It might have been only fitting. Still, I didn't like the idea.

But to lose to him would also have been a sign of age, an even clearer one. And now Ramses and his followers had adopted me. I had fans to play for. As holiday dilemmas go, it was a thorny one. Or would have been—Bud looked defeated

from the moment we walked back onto the court. His step had
lost its bounce. His shoulders hunched. His eyes gazed into the
distance. His curl had detached itself from the mass of his hair
and dangled in his eyes.

Bud served—his usual serve, flat and without much of a hop
to it, but no lollypop either. I bunted the return back short. He
ran to get it and netted the reply. I hit another short one after
that. He chased my shot down and hit it back to me. I chipped
it to the other side of the court. He didn't even bother chasing
it. "Nice shot," he said without enthusiasm.

Our next points followed the pattern. He'd hit the soft,
spinny balls of mine that he had chased down right back to me
or miss trying. I won them either way.

He might have started to play the same game I was, hitting bunts and dinks to exploit my immobility. Lame as I was,
he wouldn't have had to do it well. But he was evidently too
gentlemanly to play this way, if it even occurred to him. He'd
either knock the ball right back to me or let it go, and soon I
took the lead without so much as a look from him that said,
why are you spoiling the fun?

The fun wasn't ours, though, but some of our spectators'.
They were gleeful at the turn the match had taken. Ramses
clapped everyone on the back, even the women, and strummed
his racquet like a guitar. One of the blondes twirled her harem
jacket in a mock striptease. The brunette, her doe eyes suddenly heavy-lidded, threw me amorous looks. The hairy-
chested swinger and the pro were as depressed as the others
were jubilant. They'd gone for Bud, and though he'd occasionally fire a ball past me, more often than not I had the answers.

Bud looked resigned. The heat had taken the stuffing out
of him. Or maybe the way I was playing was so irritating to
him that he couldn't be bothered to extend himself. The fewer

points he won, the less he seemed to care. He was in a hurry to get it over with. This suited me, though near the end I couldn't suppress a certain shame at the tactics I'd resorted to, at having wanted to win enough to do whatever it took.

I glanced at the grandstand on my way off the court. It looked like a tableau from the Rialto in Venice's heyday. The officers, the swinger, the brunette, and the blondes: everyone was exchanging cash. Some paid, others pocketed, and Ramses, grinning, collected from them all.

I'd wondered why they'd stuck around to watch us, why they hadn't gone off to the next lark. Now I knew why. We were the next lark.

"You taught me a lesson," Bud said in the car, our progress reflected in the spill of light and shadow across the hood and dash and along his profile.

"And you let an old man have his day."

"Not at all. I was thrown, I admit, when that hatchet-faced thug came down and ranted at me."

"What did he want?" I asked distractedly. We had picked up more speed than I'd have liked, but I tried to hold my tongue.

"Nothing to do with the match. I'm not exactly sure what he wanted. To rattle me, I guess. He said it was his duty to remind me to show the authorities their due respect. I thought he was going to try to coach me. I got a civics lesson instead."

He was driving like a local cabbie, bouncing down the middle of the road, passing around blind curves, doing fifty where the rusty signs from colonial days set the limit at thirty, gesticulating, sometimes with both hands, and turning to look at me. "I can see why you lost your concentration," I said to remind him of the concept.

"Evidently that joker was taking bets on us. Like we were fighting cocks."

"I know." Acacia blossoms had blown in through the windows and were flurrying around us. "There's no driving test here, you know. Licenses are for sale. You've really got to watch out."

"While you were hitting me all those fancy shots, I kept wondering what kind of place you'd brought me to."

"Say, Bud, would you mind slowing down a little? I'm in no hurry, and the way they drive—"

"Don't worry," he replied, training his gaze on me.

"Keep your eyes on the road, will you?" I leaned forward in my seat and pulled at my shirt where it was sticking to my back, till a bump in the road had me pressing my hands against the dash.

We got stuck in a row of cars behind a bus. Bud kept waving his hand at the line of traffic ahead of us. The driver of a crowded taxi-van tooted his horn. The acacia petals that had been swirling in the wind settled over us.

The bus turned off. Bud checked his watch, kicked the accelerator, and raced up the national road—the harbor, a leaden sliver with an oil derrick bobbing like a hen pecking for worms, coming into sight below—and down.

"You missed your turn," I said.

He didn't hear me or chose not to. I was about to say it again but decided that a detour was preferable to a palaver over directions.

We drove through an open chain-link gate into an industrial park: old trucks and a rusty forklift, crates, a dumpster surrounded by weeds, and a cavernous metal shed with a wooden sign that read "Revtex Ltd." above the double doorway. A desk chair propped open one of the doors.

Bud stopped a good distance from the shed. He left the motor and air conditioning running.

"Your site?"

"I'd invite you in to look around if there was anything to see," he said. "We're still getting things off the ground. I'll be back in a minute."

Five minutes later I was still there, with nothing to look at but used nails, wood shavings, and empty cigarette cartons on the ground beside the car. I got out to see what was keeping him.

He was on his way out of an office in the far corner when I went in. "You got it," I heard him say. The interior had no other partitions. The close air smacked of sheet metal and coffee. Bands of dusty light splashed through high louvered windows in which fans turned, striking ductwork or spilling across the concrete floor. An array of heavy machinery ran along the back wall. Pipes, lighting fixtures, and rolls of fiberglass were stacked at the sides. At the head of a row of workbenches, a fantailed pigeon stared at me with vacant impudence.

"You've got plenty of room," I said as Bud hustled me out. Not that I needed the encouragement—the air in the parking lot was cool by comparison.

"The machines needed a bit of retrofitting. It'll be done in a matter of days. There's no use air-conditioning a space that size in the meantime. Your investment's got to take me a long way. I'm running a tight ship."

I had to admire his thrift. "Good for you."

"For us, you mean." The road followed a ridge along the coast and was reinforced on one side by new concrete piling. "We're meeting the engineer for a drink. You can hear all about our process, though you may get distracted."

"I don't know. When's that?"

"Not when, who. Your friend Cecilia will be joining us. You know, she looked crestfallen when you left us the other afternoon. How many more days have you got down here—just a few, right? You don't want to waste her sweetness on the desert air."

"When did you have in mind?"

"Why, now! It's as good as on your way home."

It wasn't a place I'd have gone on my own, but he drove there reasonably, and that was enough for me. We parked on one side of a lagoon and took a ferry to the other. Frangipani lined a steep upward path that ended in a fountain. Inside the bar, sea fans, conch shells, coral, and stuffed blowfish collected dust. Outside again, on one end of a panoramic terrace, where begonias spilled from terra cotta pots in front of an iron balcony, the mainland opened behind the lagoon—white sand and sea grapes, hills dotted by tile-roofed villas shielding the town below, with the saw-toothed cordillera in the background. At the other end, a crowd was gathering to watch the sun set over the water.

Cecilia hadn't turned up yet, but the engineer had, a long lean jumpy type who twisted his metal watchband with the fingers of his free hand while he talked. He had a lot to say. I wasn't listening. Every now and then, one or the other would make an inclusive gesture, but I wasn't that curious. Newcomers squeezed past our table and jostled our drinks. "She'll be here any minute," Bud called to me over the crowd. The shadows that had been creeping along the stonework lengthened.

I stood up. "I've got to make a call," I told Bud.

He laid a hand on the table, which canted under his weight. "I can't imagine what's keeping her. I'll follow you in and see if I can reach her."

"Don't worry about it."

I went in to have the maître d' call me a cab, shouting to make myself heard over cocktail mixers being shaken like

maracas. Batlike birds soared and swooped over the lagoon behind them.

"It's going," someone whispered as I came back outside,
and I stopped to take in the pinking of the west, the gilt-edged
clouds and etched horizon, the descent of the orb into the sea,
the waves' sudden quiet, the gulls' keening, the rocking of fishing boats in twilight.

A waitress set a candle in the center of the table, the flame
casting over us the shadow of the nylon webbing encasing its
glass chimney.

A steel drum kit was wheeled out from behind the bar.
Flambeaux were lit beside it. Musicians in straw hats and cut-
away flour sacks began to play "Sugar Boom." The limbo stick
was sure to follow. I took my leave of Bud and the engineer.

"Cecilia will be sorry she missed you," he said.

She didn't miss me. As I was getting on the ferry, she was getting off. "I got lost," she said, taking my hand.

I was happy to see her. I'd underestimated my expectancy
up on the terrace.

I stroked her wrist with my thumb. "Will you stay?" she
asked me.

"Not tonight," I told her. I'd been keeping my distance
from her, though it wasn't my inclination, or my habit—I'd
been married for too long not to take regular intimacy as an
expression of a deeper feeling. Resisting this assumption and
seeing our intimacies as an end in themselves had required vigi-
lance. But how long could I go on this way without confirmation that the effort of restraint was worthwhile? I'd waited for
evidence against her to come to light, and waited some more.
But none had. I found that I was tired of keeping my guard up.
"Tomorrow. Can I see you in the afternoon?"

I'd meant to spend the whole week with Vicky, but now that we were getting along again, the plan seemed excessive. She didn't expect it anyway. We were back on the right foot, which was the important thing. And maybe her taunting me on the way back from the airport about not knowing how to have a good time had given me something to prove.

I crossed the lagoon beneath a quarter-moon lying on its back. It had risen while reclining. I too rose, in homage to this feat of levitation.

chapter seven

Cecilia showed up a half-hour late at the Casa the next afternoon.

"How about showing me around?" she said with a tilt of her head. Her dark muslin dress wasn't quite see-through, but it invited an attempt.

Her directness took me aback and pleased me too. Vicky had gone off with a friend after lunch.

"There isn't much to the place," I said. I wandered into the living room, expecting her to follow.

"Around the island, I meant," she said from the doorway.

I went back to her.

"You don't want to?" she asked me.

"Sure I do." She had slipped out of one of her sandals and was tapping her heel against the stone floor.

"Well, then, why are you looking at me like that?" she asked, moving closer to me.

"Like what?" She leaned into me and ran her fingers down my back. A hibiscus bush stood outside the diamond-shaped window near the top of the front door. A hummingbird flew up to one of the flowers and hovered, its wings fluttering in a blur. I grazed the tip of Cecilia's ear, she jumped, and the hummingbird darted into the light.

"I thought you wanted to show me around."

"I do. But the fact is, I can't be much of a guide. I hardly know this place. I never go anywhere when I'm here."

"Good," she said. "You won't be bored."

Wherever Cecilia and I went on our jaunt around Puerto that afternoon, we were taken for man and wife. Merchants, beggars, hawkers, policemen, missionaries, nuns—everyone seemed to think we were married. Some showed it in their address, others in their looks.

We didn't just tolerate their error, we indulged it. Whatever they asked me to buy for her, I bought, in payment for the compliment of thinking her my wife. And she let me buy, happy at the presumption: jewelry and handicrafts and tourists' trinkets, all going straight up to the attic, if they even made it home. The urge to buy and to be bought for came with our roles. Beside the endless flagpoles of the field of Mars, down a pastel-colored row of foreign embassies with a bird sanctuary in the middle of the plaza, to the spiked gates of the legislature, through the city within a city built a decade earlier to host an international fair, wherever I took her, Cecilia played the part of the adoring wife so well that I could forget that she was acting.

This would look beautiful on your wife, *Señor.* This would please your wife. *Tu esposa,* they said, and made it sound natural.

We picked up some beer and headed out of town. Our route led to a switchback road up a hillside that gave us shifting views of the places we were leaving behind. Cecilia put up the armrest and slid close to me on the bench seat; we were like kids on a cruising date. She tilted her head and twisted one way and another to take in the changing scene, and the veins and sinews of her neck and shoulders beneath the straps of her dress were a topography of their own. A last set of curves wound us out of sight of the town, to the island's lusher leeward side. I saw the hand-lettered sign I was looking for and veered onto an unpaved road.

We hit a rut that bounced Cecilia against me and the top of my head against the roof. "The way down's a little rough," I said and readjusted my glasses.

"And the way back up?" she asked. She pulled the top off a can of beer, took a swig, handed it to me and, while I took a drink, caressed the back of my neck.

"We'll be all right, and once we're there you won't care about coming back."

"I don't know about that. I'm a very practical girl."

There were plenty of other beaches we might have gone to. But the one I was taking us to was a hidden gem, provided that it remained hidden. I had always meant to find out whether whoever owned it might be interested in selling. I'd never gotten around to it and on every return was relieved to find that it had been left alone.

We jolted onward, past tangles of tall grass, scaly ferns, bamboo thickets, lilies whose sickly perfume engulfed us. In the crooks of trees, termite nests swelled several feet across. Midges swarmed in sunbeams. Bird calls and cries sounded between the creaking of our shocks. The decline got steeper and even our brakes' screeching seemed wild.

The climate turned more arid. The ground, which had been muddy in patches, became flintier and redder. Thorn bushes and succulents with bright flowers appeared. A dry wind came up and gave us the taste of the dust the car was kicking up. I tried rolling up the windows but immediately got too hot. As I was rolling them down again, a stone thudded against the front axle and the Mercury shuddered. We had come to the end of the dirt road. A half-mile walking trail led down to the surf. I grabbed the beer and an old plaid quilt from the backseat. Cecilia kicked off her sandals and took my arm.

"Keep those on," I said. "The path is as rough as the road."

"I'll be all right," she said.

"Take them along. I'll carry them. It'll be easier than carrying you."

I was wrong. She didn't need them, though the path wasn't any smoother than I remembered. It was if anything more overgrown. But Cecilia's soles were like thick leather. Even with my sandals on, I trod gingerly through stretches where she marched. No stone was too jagged, no root too knobby for her.

"How do you do it?" I asked when she stopped for a minute to let me catch up at the edge of a pine grove.

"I didn't wear shoes till I was eight or nine. I still have my calluses." She rubbed the bottom of one foot.

"You didn't wear shoes because you were wild or because you were poor?"

"Both," she said after a moment.

"But I thought your father was an officer?"

"He is now."

A millipede wiggled over the ground at our feet. It was at least half a foot long, bright red, with crooked horns at the front and what looked like a stinger behind—the kind of bug that, were it to turn up in your bathroom at home, would make you consider calling the fire department. "Don't step on him," I said, "no matter how thick your calluses are."

Down the path, where the ground was changing from dirt to sand, I noticed a bit of fluttering cloth, red and about knee high. It looked like a tattered sleeve snared on a low tree branch. Closer inspection revealed it to be a triangle attached to a wire post pitched in the ground and supported by a coconut husk: a surveyor's flag. Ten or fifteen feet farther along, there was another, and another, and so on the rest of the way down the path. Not all were red; some drooped instead of fluttering, some caught the light coming through the palm fronds, some hid in the shade of their trunks, others lay in the sand. But whatever their aspects, they told a single tale: surveyors had been here, and where surveyors went, builders would follow. I stepped onto the strand certain of a coming despoilment.

Cecilia took in the scene and gasped. "Where am I?" she cried. I understood her reaction. It was one of those places that is too lovely to seem real. You looked at the fleshy pink of the sand, at the mirror images of sea and sky, at the clouds' late-afternoon radiance—you looked and were disconcerted. You were intruding on a dream.

We couldn't decide where to spread our blanket and throw ourselves down. This spot was too near the water—we'd have to move when the tide came in. But maybe the tide already had come in. When was high tide? I didn't know. That spot, nearer the coconut grove on the rim, was too far from the water—you needed to hear the beating of the waves. Another spot was too much in the middle of the beach—who wants to sit smack in the middle of anything? Farther on we went so far as to throw down the quilt before realizing that the angle was wrong.

We trudged onward, Cecilia approaching the red cliffs near the end of the stretch that had been visible from the foot of the path. And there, at the base of the cliffs, near a couple of boulders, a placard came into view, a printed sign. It was narrow, but standing tall on a metal post it looked more official than the surveyor's flags. "How about here?" I suggested.

"And that?" She pointed at the sign.

"I don't want to read it. It won't say anything we'd care to know."

We put down the quilt, setting stones on the corners. I turned my back while Cecilia slipped out of her sundress, and looked out at the water. The tide was indeed coming in, but slowly, its lapping alternating with the rattle of shells and pebbles in its retreats. I took my cigarettes and lighter from the pocket of my shorts and tried to light up but couldn't keep the flame out of the breeze. I gave up and turned back.

Cecilia had already lain down. Her lingerie was bikini-like, dark, narrowly cut, and not lacy. Sitting down beside her, I gave my lighter a few more flicks but still couldn't get my cigarette to catch. "Here," she said, pulling my head down and toward her so that her body shielded me from the breeze. Even after I'd lit the cigarette, she kept hold of my head just long enough to make the action suggestive. She released me and I leaned back, drew on the cigarette again, and brought it to her lips for a puff. When she'd blown out the smoke, she laid her head on my shoulder and put her hand on my chest. Again it struck me that we were acting like kids on a date, desire giving spontaneous actions a studied air. I ran the fingers of my other hand through the sand. It was coarse, heavy, soft.

"Shall we go in?" I asked after the cigarette was done.

"Not yet. I'll wait till I'm hot."

I went ahead on my own. I was plenty warm, despite the breeze and the beer, which was no longer cold anyway. But the sea itself was a bath, barely cooler than the air. After wading in I had to turn around when I realized I was still wearing my sunglasses.

Without the glasses and their prescription lenses, the surface of the water was a broad shimmer. It was like opening my eyes after a long sleep, over and over again. The tide had come in farther than I'd thought. The shallows seemed to go on and on; only their color deepened. I went from one band of blue to the next, each slightly darker than the last but always transparent. Meanwhile, parallel to the shore, the grooves in which the sand on the bottom had settled were endless, their ranks broken only by an occasional starfish. The admixture of sun, beer, and myopia gave me a sense of heroism, a sense that the march through those bands of blue and across the miniature mountains in the sand was a march across a continent or a geologic era.

I reached a sand bar. A gull scattered as I stepped onto it. Though I hadn't gone more than fifty yards, I'd have planted a flag there. I looked back to shore and waved at Cecilia; my vision was too blurry for me to tell whether she saw me or was waving back. Much nearer, a pelican flew past, dived, pulled up short, regained its height, hovered, and dived again. I couldn't tell whether he had come up with a fish in his bill, but something in the way he flew off made me think that he had. His success—the assumption of his success—fueled my exaltation. I plunged off the other side of the sandbar and started swimming—powerfully, it seemed to me. I imagined the breadth of the expanse traversed with every stroke, the water parting before me. Again I felt that I was covering a great distance. My legs were pistons, my arms the paddles of a millwheel. My muscles strained, and with every turn of my head I breathed harder. With shortness of breath came an awareness of breathing. My thoughts turned to my son, Peter.

I had gone alone to collect his body. Joyce had Vicky to look after, a funeral to prepare for.

I flew to White River Junction in a little plane the whir of whose propellers Peter would have enjoyed. The day was windy and overcast, and I imagined him as a littler boy, sitting on my lap during the flight and looking out the window as the cloud wisps trailed past.

His body was at an undertaker's nearby, in Lebanon. I stopped there to make arrangements and drove on to the summer camp.

The camp director tried to trap me in his office, in a single-story building of wooden shingle with an outsized front deck. The office itself teemed with plaques and certificates from summer camp associations and photos of camp scenes. An old air conditioner blasted away, and the director roared over it. He was forty, bright-eyed and double-chinned, with the camp insignia monogrammed on his polo shirt. The straight-in-the-eye look he fixed on me, meant presumably to convey his sincerity, was oppressive. I had come to find out what had happened to Peter, not to meet the camp director.

His talk moved from sympathy to regret to reproof. Had there really been no hint of Peter's being asthmatic, none whatsoever? If only the camp had been made aware of even the possibility of the condition, the necessary medication would have been at the ready, the counselors and nurses prepared.

I saw what he was after. "I don't intend to give you any trouble," I told him. "Have your insurance company send me a release."

He pretended not to catch my meaning, and then, having dropped the pretense, to be embarrassed by it. But soon enough he showed me out of the office and up a hill, to Peter's cabin.

I was hoping to look it over alone, but lunch had just ended and it was rest hour—Peter's cabinmates were in. I heard their shouts and laughter as we approached. It had been three days since Peter's attack, three days and four nights; the boys' mourning period was over. The director heard them too and rushed ahead to prepare them for my arrival. I paused at the foot of the steps and waited for him to call me in. A bird twittered in the pines, which swished in the wind.

The five boys had composed themselves in solemn attitudes, the two bunkmates standing side by side with bowed heads at the foot of their beds and Peter's lone bunkmate assuming the same posture alone. Peter's bed, a lower bunk, had been stripped. A red bandana was tied to the top rail.

"The boys have a few memories they'd like to share with you," the director said to me.

One by one they introduced themselves, shook my hand, and recited their lines. A mop-topped boy said that in their last soccer game, Peter had scored an acrobatic goal on a header. A boy with a mouthful of braces said that in his first archery competition, Peter had tied for high score. An overweight boy in a tight sleeveless T-shirt said that Peter wasn't afraid of spiders and even let them crawl up his arm. Peter's bunkmate, who wore a thin leather strap around his wrist, said that he was generous about lending out his stuff—his flashlight, for example, which he hadn't had a chance to give back.

He tried to hand me the flashlight. "Keep it," I told him.

They were a perfectly fine group of boys, I supposed, and I'd have liked to be well disposed to them. But remembering their laughter as I approached the cabin, I couldn't refrain from asking myself, was any the boy that Peter had been? If one of these boys had needed a friend as Peter had needed one, would Peter have spurned him as Peter had himself been spurned?

The counselor drew me aside and told me what I already knew. "I thought he was crying," he said. "He'd cried himself to sleep other nights. Some boys do that in the beginning." He shrugged and lowered his eyes.

A bell pealed, signaling the end of rest hour. The camp

director sent the boys on their way. The counselor started to follow but paused at the door. "If I knew he had asthma things might have turned out different," he said.

I asked the camp director for a few minutes alone in the cabin. I paced the uneven floorboards but heard no echo of his footfall in mine. I looked at the toilet kits, cans of insect repellent, plastic hand-held battery-powered fans, boxes of envelopes, shoe bags, baseball gloves and caps that he would have looked at but couldn't see through them to him. I lay down on his bed but got no sense of his form. The screen door rattled in the wind.

My eyes drifted up to the rafters, on which old campers had carved their initials and dates. On a shelf beside the bunk, a Swiss Army knife lay in view. I picked it up. It was one of the bigger models, with many knives and tools. I began to inspect them, wondering which would be best for carving.

The door swung open and slammed to again. I thought nothing of it and continued running a blade over my fingertip. Then there were quick footsteps. I turned to look but the top of the bunk obstructed my view of the boy's face. "Oh. Sorry," I heard him say. The sound of his voice surprised me. He wasn't one of the boys I had met. Before I could sit up, he was gone.

I came back to myself. I'd gotten caught up in my own momentum and swum farther out than I should, I supposed. I stopped and looked back and, blurry vision and all, saw that I'd hardly gotten anywhere. I was nearer the sand bar than was the sand bar itself to the shore. I'd been swimming against the tide, running in place. Well, I thought, it's all the same, and drifted back toward the bar. The gull I'd chased away had returned. He flew off again at my approach, and as I lumbered up the bar I saw Cecilia wading toward me. It wasn't until she was close that I could tell that she was speaking to me. The shoreward breeze swept her voice away. "I can't hear you," I said.

"Why did you swim so far out? You frightened me." I had never heard her sound like this. Her exuberant singsong was gone.

"I had no idea. But I didn't go far at all, you know. Maybe it looked that way, but—"

"Didn't you see me waving?"

"I didn't. I mean, I thought you might have been. I couldn't tell without my glasses." I didn't need them right then. She was directly in front of me, on the rim of the sand bar. Now that it was wet, her lingerie functioned less well as a bikini than it had, insofar as a bikini is intended to function as clothing. I drew closer to her, in part to shield her from my own eyes.

"I had a friend who drowned at the beach." The anger was gone from her voice.

"I'll bet he didn't drown in water like this, did he? It'd be work to drown in this." She didn't answer. "Anyway," I continued, "you're here now to protect me."

I jumped back into the water and pulled her in after me. We romped around, chased and splashed each other, swam side by side, floated on our backs, and while I lay back holding her hand with the orb of the sun and the shadows of clouds behind my closed eyelids she sang a song that nearly put me to sleep.

"Look," Cecilia exclaimed as we were coming out of the water. "How cute!"

On the beach a dog awaited us, one of those short-haired, big-eared Anubises you see in the tropics. He was nosing around our quilt. Cecilia picked up the quilt, gave it a shake, and wrapped herself in it. "He doesn't look so cute to me," I replied. From his lowly bearing I took him for a stray, but when I'd put my sunglasses back on I saw that he wasn't lean enough, and when Cecilia reached her hand out to him I saw that he wasn't skittish enough either. He wasn't entirely trusting, but he'd let her get within a couple of feet of him before springing back.

"Better leave him alone," I said.

She ignored me and again advanced toward him, more slowly than the last time. He let her get closer, but before she touched him retreated. "He could be rabid," I said, following along.

"This dog? He isn't rabid," she replied. "He reminds me of Frances."

"Of Frances? He's nothing like Frances."

"It's the color. They're the same color."

She kept trying to pet the dog, which kept retreating. She was determined to win his trust. The dog did seem to want to let Cecilia touch him. He'd whine whenever she started to give up and walk away from him and look longingly when she reached out to pet him. Even when he recoiled he looked reluctant, as though it was his job to lead us somewhere. We almost had to follow.

At last, at the head of the beach, they gave up on each other. He headed for the coconut palms and she didn't follow. "It's just as well," I said. "A dog like that might have bitten you sooner than let you pet him."

The dog stopped in front of the sign, lifted its leg on the post, and disappeared into the grove.

The sign was angled away from us. Cecilia went up to it and read it. "We're on private property," she said, turning to me with her hands on her hips.

I surveyed the beach, and sighed. "Well, it's ours for the afternoon."

I moved closer to Cecilia and brushed some sand from her

shoulder. Then I went over to her and read the sign for myself. Below NO TRESPASSING, it said PROPERTY OF BUCCANEER'S COVE.

Buccaneer's Cove—the name rang a bell.

"How about that?" I said, thinking aloud. "He bought it." It was a development project I had reviewed for Mickey.

"What?"

"This beach." I recollected myself. "It belongs to my brother. To him and me, that is. I mean, it seems to be ours."

"It's yours? How come you didn't know?"

"My brother buys things and puts my name on them. I try not to pay attention. But I just realized that this is one of them."

She moved beside me and gave me a friendly bump with her hip. "Poor Neil. You own so much you don't know what you've got."

"Not exactly. Anyway, the point is we're all right here."

We went back to where we'd been lying. Cecilia unwrapped the quilt and spread it over the sand. We lay down, side by side on our backs. Evening was still a long way off, but the moon hung in the sky.

I sat up and popped open the last beer. I passed her the can and she took a drink.

"It makes me hungry," she said.

"I know. It gives me a craving for something salty."

I turned to look at her as I spoke, and as I did, saw a salt mark on the top of her drying shoulder. I rolled onto my side and kissed it. Then I licked the salt off my lips. "Tasty," I said, and, leaning down, did it again, nearer the strap of her brassiere.

She sat up on an elbow and, raising her sunglasses to the top of her forehead, looked straight at me. "Have some more," she said. It wasn't the seductiveness of the invitation that struck me. There was something new in the way she looked at me. The restless, goading hardness in her eyes—a look that transmitted a stronger sense of her own predispositions to what was in front of her than of engagement with it, the look that had made me wonder how much she really let in—that look was gone. The eyes with which she now took me in were steady and appraising, and the hand she placed on the back of my neck as I kissed her collarbone was slow and heavy.

"I never noticed that before," I said, running my finger over a small mole near the base of her neck.

"Oh that." She touched it and took her hand away. "It's ugly, I know."

"Not in the least."

To stop me touching it she took my hand in hers. I kissed the back of it, and tasted my lips.

"You're less salty there. There's no hollow." I looked at her hand. The nail on her little finger was bitten down to the cuticle. She saw me looking, and took her hand away.

I kissed the salt from her stomach and found a small scar. I kissed the salt from her hip and found a bruise. I kissed the salt from her thigh and felt scratches she had gotten coming down the path. I lingered over them all. Each time she caught me lingering, she'd pull me away, thinking I was finding fault. She was wrong, though. The marks I studied weren't blemishes. They were perfections. They made her seem knowable as she hadn't seemed before. I looked at her and she looked back, and even in her eye I saw something new: a flaw in the membrane of an iris, a crack through which a trace of its brown pigment marbled the white, like a trace of blood in a fertile egg. And if it's ever possible to identify the moment when our feelings for another change decisively, I'd say it happened right then.

This was hardly the end of our skirmish. It wasn't likely that it would be in those surroundings. Of course, they took up less of our attention the more we devoted to each other. They inspired us and then receded. The clouds, moon, and sea were reflections in Cecilia's eyes, tracings in a glaze of pleasure.

At the edge of my vision, beyond her dark hair against the plaid of the quilt, lay her sunglasses, my wallet, a pack of cigarettes, and a beer can. I lifted my head and the wind blew sand in my eyes. I opened them and saw that it wasn't the wind. The dog that had come along earlier was back. He was bounding, yapping, pawing the sand.

I shouted at him to go away, stamped my hand, menaced him as best I could without getting up. But my shouts and threats only encouraged him. He was irrepressible. He continued to bark and wag his tail.

"He's jealous," Cecilia said. "He doesn't want to be left out of the fun."

I lay back and waited for him to go away, the sun's brightness pouring through my closed eyes. In the floodlit theater of my mind I saw her as she had just been, as if what had happened a moment ago was of another time. "My sunglasses," she said.

I handed them to her but couldn't find my own and wrapped the quilt around us. She resumed her attentions to me.

"If only he'd stop that yapping," I said. I was as tense as I had been taut.

"Relax, Neil. The dog doesn't know what he sees. He's not about to take our photo for the newspaper, is he?"

The dog quieted down. Still it was no good with him standing over us. Picking up where we'd left off was beyond me.

My shyness, if that's what it was, seemed to surprise her. She expected me to be more rough-and-ready. I might have expected her to be less.

"It's getting stuffy under here," she said and tried to uncover us, but I held the cover down. "Do you realize that you're spending your afternoon in heaven hiding from a dog?"

When she put it that way, it did sound ridiculous. "I'm not hiding from him." To make my point I threw the quilt off us and turned away from her, toward the dog. "Hiding has nothing to do with it."

I looked the dog's way. There in the sand beside him was a pair of lace-up, leather-uppered, rubber-soled army boots. These boots were attached to a pair of legs in khaki trousers, which led in turn to a beefy torso, and then the pudgy pink face of a grinning man in sunglasses. I pulled the quilt over us again. Cecilia giggled.

Our visitor marshaled his features in a soberer array and ceremoniously cleared his throat. "You are trespassing," he said in a Spanish accent.

"No," I said. "You are trespassing."

This seemed to throw him off. Appearing to consider the matter, he reverted to the script. "*You* are trespassing," he repeated, changing his emphasis and bowing slightly, which dislodged his sunglasses from their perch on the high bridge of his nose, so high that it gave him the look of a totemic carving. He pushed the glasses back over the hump.

"Would you please?" I hissed at Cecilia, who had taken to stroking my thigh under the quilt while I carried on the argument.

I turned back to the guard. "But you are *committing* a trespass," I replied, and instantly regretted it. The comeback wasn't so sly as I'd thought. And even if it had been, this slyness would have been misplaced. A single phrase was enough to tell you that the man hardly spoke English. But then, I was at a disadvantage myself. I'd have liked to put on my shorts and discuss the matter standing up. "Will you excuse me?" I asked.

This request also baffled him. It wasn't in the script. "You are trespassing," he said yet again. Only this time he left out the bow and raised his voice. He leaned back, sticking his thumbs in his thick, low-slung leather belt, which I now saw had an outdated walkie-talkie clipped to it. "I must ask you to leave."

"Would I please what?" Cecilia whispered. She continued making trouble under the quilt.

I grabbed her hand and looked back at the guard. "You don't understand. I own Buccaneer's Cove." I heard myself speaking like a jingo, slowly and loudly. "This is mine." I made a sweeping motion with my arm and tapped my hand on the ground. I might still have been trying to scare off the dog.

The guard tapped his hand on the ground in turn, causing the dog, which thought his master was inviting him to play, to run in circles. "Property of the Buccaneer Development Corporation," he said.

"You've got it—the Buccaneer Development Corporation." I patted my chest to identify myself with that entity.

"McNeil Brothers, Limited," he added, leading me up the chain of ownership. *Brothers* he pronounced lovingly. *Limited* was strictly an afterthought.

"Exactly! McNeil Brothers, that's me." If I could have reached it, I might have shaken his hand.

"You are Señor McNeil?"

"So to speak," I mumbled. "I mean, to all intents and purposes."

His look turned cautious. "You have identification?"

"Well, sure."

I picked up my wallet from the sand and looked through it for what I doubted would be there: a business card for Mickey's and my partnership. I'd had no use for those cards for a long time. It wasn't likely I'd have one. When I'd confirmed my suspicion, I took out my driver's license to show him. I still couldn't get up to hand it to him. He had to bend down.

He stood back up and studied it.

"No McNeil," the guard said.

"Not 'McNeil,' just 'Neil,' you see? The 'Mc' is for my brother. We're partners. Business partners. The 'Mc' is for him and the 'Neil' is for me. It says 'Neil,' see? That's me." I took other cards out of my wallet to show him. "'Neil,' 'Neil,' 'Neil,' they all tell you I'm Neil."

"No McNeil," he shrugged. "No good."

I took a look over my shoulder at the water, at a fishing dory that had sailed into the bay. I turned back to him. "Now, come on. Use your head, put two and two together. My brother's Mickey, I'm Neil, it's called McNeil Brothers. It makes perfect sense." I looked at Cecilia for confirmation. She didn't look amused anymore, just bored. "Explain it to him in Spanish," I told her.

"He gets it, Neil. He doesn't believe you."

He bent down and handed me my cards. "You must go." He sounded reluctant but resolute. His brow arched with sincerity. "Please. It is my job."

Cecilia started to get up and, unless we were going to play tug-of-war with the quilt, I had to follow. The time had come anyway. The punkies were coming out, and though the dory was drifting far from shore, we were no longer alone, or so alone as we thought we had been.

Cecilia made one last attempt to pet the dog but he still wouldn't let her. We collected our things and marched toward the path, the quilt enfolding us.

"I'll make it up to you later," I told her.

"Yes you will," she replied. "Many times."

part three

chapter eight

"There's another," Mickey said from the passenger side of my station wagon. If I had gotten my way, we'd have been in separate cars. But I hadn't and we weren't. "Whose is it?"

"Whose? How should I know?" I asked. We had gone upstate together over Labor Day to see Leon, who had broken her hip in a fall. Her doctor had been gloomy on the phone. Only after we'd gotten there did I understand that his gloom wasn't at the prognosis but at the likelihood of treating her for years to come. She seemed to be no nearer her end than either of her sons and might by the time we left her have been further from it. Age had brought her a talent for taking back in drops and drams the life she'd given us practically all at once.

I had called Mickey after getting off the phone with her doctor. "I can't drop everything whenever she sneezes," he said.

"Everything? So you're busy now, are you?"

"I have got quite a few balls in the air, as it happens."

I'd have been happier paying the visit alone. But Jeanette had prevailed on him to go along by predicting his regret if he stayed home and it turned out that Leon's number was really up.

It's possible that Jeanette was right, that neglecting the old lady at the end might have become a lasting regret, except that regret wasn't one of Mickey's capacities. It required more reflection than he cared to engage in. Jeanette must have been loath to miss the chance to spend a few days without him.

In any case, Mickey's reward for being dutiful was to sprain an ankle on the way down the steps of Leon's house, on the very afternoon that we'd turned up, unannounced.

"Both of you," she cried in mock delight, leaning on the kitchen table as she rose to greet us. "Come for the deathbed scene, have you?" She wore one of the cotton blouses she'd brought back from Mexico; reading glasses dangled from a string above its embroidered yoke. I squinted in the late-summer, late-afternoon light, at once brittle and hazy, sifting in through the drawn curtains. Mickey lowered the bill of his fishing cap. "I must be a terrible sight. You won't even pretend to look at me."

Behind her, on the open shelves of a sideboard, family memorabilia collected dust: scrolled diplomas, medals, ribbons, photos. In the most prominent photo, Mickey and I stood in starched linens beneath the elm canopy of an Ivy League courtyard with our father, whom through age and girth Mickey had come to resemble.

Leon continued to rail at us. "Shall we act out Old Mother Hubbard passes on?" she asked. "Is that what you came for? I'll put on a bonnet and gown and lay knitting needles by the bedside that I might have put down when the pain got too bad."

Seeing what we'd let ourselves in for, Mickey and I exchanged sympathetic glances. Little else had the power to bring us together.

That afternoon we were on our way out for a swim when

Mickey sprained his ankle. The house was warm, and he had suggested to Leon switching on the air conditioner. "Air conditioning?" she replied. "If you're going to try to get me to poison myself, you'd better be subtler about it." He was looking over his shoulder, trying to see which direction the next volley from the maternal fusillade might come from, when he missed a step.

This wasn't his story, though. Once he'd left off howling, he insisted that he had tripped over a stone that had come loose from the mortar.

"You were running away from her," I said. "Fleeing."

"Those stairs are crumbling. You've said so yourself."

"You'd rather be a klutz than a coward?"

The thought of having to wait around till he was fit to ride back had sapped my powers of commiseration. He adjusted his wince to reflect not only the pain of his injury but also the disbelief at such a lack of compassion in the face of it. Or so I surmised. I could see him only in profile. We were back in the car, on our way to the emergency room. I saw more of his ankle, though, much more. It had ballooned.

But I needn't have worried about being held up. The swelling quickly went down. Mickey's joints could be as full of hot air as his manner. We were able to leave the next day. For all her venom, Leon made it clear that she expected us to stay overnight anyway. As our departure approached, she even invited us to stay longer. She always did this, and I always pretended to consider the invitation.

So we had come and gone, with only Mickey the worse for wear. With the help of painkillers, he dozed through much of the ride back, a blessing adulterated by the talc-overlaid odor of his uninjured foot. Not long into his nap, he had kicked off his boating moc, confronting me with the Hobson's choice of enduring it or waking him and disturbing the peace. I chose peace.

He woke up mumbling about coming home with me. I hoped he was talking in his sleep. But when he repeated himself in his regular deafening tone, this hope was dashed. He had meetings the next morning in the vicinity of Dunsinane that traveling all the way from home in his condition would make hard for him to keep. And by the way, did I think my orthopedist might be able to squeeze him in tomorrow?

"I don't know. Do me a favor and put your shoe back on, will you?"

"I can't put a shoe on that foot. It's swollen."

"It's the other one I mean."

"So you'll call him?"

"Do you really need to see him? You seem to be getting better on your own."

"You never know. Take your case. You let your knee go, and what happened? It destroyed you."

"Destroyed me? What do you mean by that?"

"A manner of speaking. Forget about it." He waved away my question. "I only meant that when a man loses something as fundamental as the full strength in his legs—" He broke off—the waved hand had been left to hover, and on discovering it in front of him he began fingering the hair on his chest below his collar.

"Yes?"

"Oh, nothing. Why take a chance, is all? Especially since I have other obligations close by."

Had this been the first word of these obligations, I'd have suspected him of scheming to be waited on while he was laid up. But he had mentioned them in his balls-in-the-air speech. He was waiting for me to ask about them now.

He waited. It was no more than a few moments, but to him it must have been an eon; the silence couldn't have been heavier. I lowered the windows.

I'd left the state thruway for the greener parkway that ran parallel to it. Plane trees above a brook running through the median took on a blue green cast through the aquamarine tint of the windshield. Something in the change roused Mickey's powers of inanity. "Still," he said, apropos of nothing, "it's good we went."

I didn't reply. But silence was impossible. The stripes on the parkway were like the ticking of his mind.

"You don't think so?"

"Maybe. But only for our own sakes. It didn't seem to make any difference to her."

"I don't know about that. Didn't you notice that her mood improved?" He spoke about as loudly as possible without shouting, loudly enough for the woman driving in the next lane to look our way. The corner of her long collar started flapping against her jaw. When she looked back at the road, it stopped.

"Doesn't it always when she knows she's about to be free of you and feels she's made it through the visit?"

"It seemed to happen sooner this time. Last night, on the patio. She actually laughed. Don't you remember?"

"I must have missed it." It had been a not unpleasant evening, the cicadas and fireflies filling in the gaps. "I don't know how I could have, though. I think I'd have fallen off my chair."

"Oh, that's right," he said. "It was while you were mixing the drinks. You were at it for a while."

I pulled into a gas station and, while the tank was filling, called the house and let Magda know that there'd be another for dinner. She didn't sound pleased—some trouble about her

wayward daughter not looking after her little girl—but agreed
to see what she could scare up.

"And what did she laugh at?" I asked when we were back
on the road.

"What did she laugh at?"

"Yes, that's what I said."

"Well, that's just it."

"What's just it?"

"I can't exactly say. Something about Joyce, I believe, something less than flattering. Because of my loyalty to you, I haven't
got much to say for her these days."

"You never had much to say for her." He laughed, but I
hadn't been joking. "What did you tell her about Joyce?"

"I think I was reminding Leon of how fussy Joyce was at
restaurants. My God, she was fit to be tied when she didn't get
exactly what she wanted."

The sunlight sharpened. I lowered my visor, put a cigarette
in my mouth, tapped the car's lighter, and ran my hand over
the seat's brocade. "Where are you going with this, Mickey?
What did Leon say?"

"About Joyce?" His voice fluttered in phony surprise. "Oh,
nothing much really. She only said, when I was describing
Joyce's expression when she was tasting something new—you
know how she screws up her face—Leon said to watch out, that
whatever her foibles I ought to respect the fact that Joyce was
your wife."

At a dip in the road, the fumes from a power mower mingled with the scent of the grass it was cutting and made me
sneeze. Above a meadow, a flock of swifts dived and climbed,
swooning and waking through the haze. "And then you blurted
to her that we aren't together anymore."

I thought I saw the corner of his mouth crease. But if his

first reaction was to smile, he had composed himself by the time he turned to face me. "Hardly," he said. "How long has it been, Neil? I thought I was reminding her of what she must know by now."

"You didn't think anything first. You just blabbed."

"Blabbed? I don't blab. And I don't see what you're getting testy about. It can't possibly matter now."

"Who said it did?"

"Well, it doesn't. I was telling you, she laughed when she heard. 'Do you mean they're through?' she asked me. And when I confirmed it, she laughed again. 'I've had my suspicions since he came to see me alone last year. Earlier, even. With the likes of her it was only a matter of time.'"

"She probably wonders why I kept it from her."

"She did wonder. I told her I didn't know. Maybe she thinks you're attached to Joyce. 'He'd have to be blind to believe that,' she said, 'but you never know what he'll take it into his head to believe.' And we started to chuckle over that too. Then she asked about your dishes. 'She didn't take the china with her, did she? That china crossed the ocean with us.' I didn't know what to tell her. What do I know about your dishes? 'I wouldn't put it past her,' Leon said. 'That woman isn't just venal. She has a wandering eye, and where the eye wanders . . . I remember a long time ago, when she was pregnant with Vicky. We went shopping together in the city. We'd come out of a shop on Fifth Avenue, and this rather large black fellow walks past and Joyce's eyes follow him up the street. Now there's a real buck, she says. Excuse me? I said. She saw that she was out of line and wouldn't repeat it. But I heard her the first time. Who knows what a woman like that was getting up to in her spare time. And let me tell you, with the hours that Neil puts in, she's had her chances.'"

It was a crude performance, what I saw of it in glances stolen from the road. Mickey's rendition of Leon had all the subtlety of the Big Bad Wolf's impersonation of Little Red Riding Hood's granny, the pursed sourpuss frown, the scrunched cheeks and beady eyes. It didn't come off. But he found another way to bring her across, or it found him. He seemed to go back in time as he talked, back physically that is, to pass through youth and even childhood in the telling. The younger and more boyish he looked, the greater his resemblance to our mother. The fleshy bag hanging from his Adam's apple, the long-lobed ears, the bulbous nose with its wide pores, the broken blood vessels around the cheekbone and the swollen vein at the corner of a papery eyelid—all the weatheredness of his maturity—melted in the spite of his recollection. His features looked finer now, firmer, sharper. It had been a very long time since he'd been able to get to me in this way, and the rediscovery of this child-hood power brought with it something of the manner and even the look of childhood. He drew nearer to his origins in the very parent whose part he happened to be acting out. Children may take their features from both parents, but they can really look like only one at a time. Mickey had grown into his resemblance to our father. Now he grew out of it again, for as long as his mood lasted. Only malice could make him young again.

"I don't like to be the one to say it, Neil, but have you ever had yourself checked out? To make sure you're clean, I mean. Who knows whether there's anything in—"

"You don't like to be the one to say it? Admit it, you're hav-ing a ball! Do you think I believe for a moment that you're tell-ing me this for my own good?"

He shifted in his seat and one of his feet knocked against the underside of the dash. The injured one, I hoped.

"Dammit! You'd think a boat like this would give you more legroom."

I gave him a hard stare. "Answer me. Do you expect me to believe that you're telling me this for my own good?"

"Why shouldn't I? Why shouldn't you, I mean, in the interest of—look out!"

I had kept my eyes off the road for too long and let the car drift from the left lane onto the median. The front tire bumped against the curb, but before the whole front end hurdled, I had time to jerk the wheel back to the right. We lurched into the right lane. It was lucky that the driver of the car beside us had been quick to hit his brakes.

"For Chrissake, will you watch where you're going?"

"All right!"

The near miss shook us up. I drove on in silence; he'd gotten under my skin again. But then I thought, so what? How was this out of the ordinary? It was no more than my brother's usual effect on me. What I felt and what I did in his case had little to do with each other. The tolerance and fitful accommodation that marked my policy with him were all despite myself. Distrust, exasperation, disdain—I'd voice them all, but when did I act on them?

At the approach to the Throgs Neck, with traffic backed up at the toll, he had insisted—though I had already searched my pockets for coins and come up empty—that I move into the shorter line, in the exact-change lane. He had a load of change, he said. It was in his blazer, underneath his crutches in the backseat. His sprained ankle made him even less agile than usual, however, and while he was leaning over the back of the front seat, he lost his balance and grabbed the end of one of the crutches, causing the other end to fly up and clip me on the back of the head. He pretended not to notice. I'd have swatted him back, but his head was in the backseat. That there wasn't any change in his blazer need hardly be added. But he did find a few cigars in there. "We could slip one to the toll collector," I suggested.

"Are you kidding? These are no nickel weeds. They're real Havanas," he said. "Esplendidos. You'd bribe Abe Fortas with these, not a toll collector."

We might have gone through twice in the time it took us to nose our way back into a regular line, finally winning a game of chicken with a monsignor in a newish Lincoln who, when he had no choice but to let us in, gave us the finger.

"Isn't it posted on the boards?" Mickey asked. We had come off the highway a few miles from Dunsinane and sat at a red light at the bottom of the ramp. He wanted to see who was building a subdivision that was set back from the road we were about to turn onto, on a sprinkler-soaked field. Mist rose from depressions in miniature rainbows.

"Those aren't signboards, they're building panels. Can't you tell the difference?" Either he needed to have his eyes checked or this was another case of his seeing what he would, and he seemed to see well enough when appearances corresponded to his wishes.

"Oh, right. So they are." He pulled his sunglasses off his nose and wiped at them with his shirttail. "Will you look at that? They haven't even picked the stakes up yet and it looks like they've already got fifty-percent occupancy. Somebody's making a mint. Unbelievable," Mickey exclaimed with a shake of his head. "Unbelievable."

I didn't find it unbelievable. Hillocks had been leveled, loam churned, weeds and brush cleared, burrowers routed, plots hollowed, foundations set, pipes laid, septic tanks embedded, bricks stacked, walls erected, doors, windows, and chimneys framed, staircases blocked, roofs pitched, ground sodded, saplings planted, roads paved, deeds exchanged and reexchanged. I had no trouble at all believing it. It was right before our eyes.

He put his sunglasses back on, and putting his arm back over the seat, bumped one of his crutches, which flew up and knocked me in the back of the head again.

"Goddammit, Mickey!"

The light changed and we went on our way. "Seriously, Neil. These missed opportunities are a damn shame. The prime's, what, three and a quarter? When will money be this cheap again?"

We stopped at another light. An old man with a cane stepped off the curb. Across the street, along the far corner, a bright yellow hardhat from the local electric company hung from a telephone pole. A tool belt was strapped to the stud below its numbered aluminum plate. "Looks like a man walked off the job," I said, trying to call Mickey's attention to the hat and belt.

"Him?" He pointed at the old man crossing the road. "The old gink can hardly walk."

"Not that man."

"Oh, right." Turning his head toward the window on his side, he stuck his thumb and forefinger in his nose and gave a yank. "So, what do you say, Neil? There's a site in—"

"Go ahead, Mickey. Build. Build! What's stopping you? You don't need me."

"Work without you, here? I wouldn't think of it. In your back yard?"

We rounded the last turn and passed the back edge of my property. Light splashed from the fluttering leaves of a row of viburnums. Mickey hounded me right to the top of the driveway. He'd be gone tomorrow, I reminded myself on the lawn, and the pressure that had accumulated in the car dispersed in the nearsighted black and blue of dusk: lightest in the sky, darkest around the wooden palings bordering the perennials. Cicadas whirred, frogs thrummed, the screen door gasped and creaked. Frances bounded out, tail waving.

He'll be gone tomorrow, I told myself again. There'd be other evenings like this. And as for his blabbing to Leon about Joyce, I had put off telling her for too long. What he had said about her being pleased when she heard the news rang true. After twenty-five years, she'd been proved right. An overdue vindication, that's what it would have meant to her. If I hadn't gotten around to telling her, maybe it was because I wasn't looking forward to seeing her smile when she found out. Now I wouldn't have to. Mickey had done me a favor.

"These goddamn bugs," he said as we were taking our luggage from the back of the wagon. "You could choke on them. Don't you have the place sprayed?"

"Don't get carried away. They're gnats, not roaches." Mickey swatted at them as at a pack of devils.

"Don't they spray for gnats? They should. They're a goddamn menace."

"And how would you propose they do that? Gnats go where the wind blows. What do you want them to do, spray the wind?"

"I don't know. They can't be flying all the time. Hit 'em where they live, like anything else."

The pattern our conversation had followed in the car held through dinner. There were things Mickey wanted to tell me, but he wouldn't come out with them. He'd drop a hint or two to make me curious. I wouldn't take the bait, though, and he'd go quiet, then get impatient and, to break the silence, say anything at all, which would lead us to digress from whatever he'd been scheming to get me to ask him about. Finally showing his hand, he'd tell me whatever it was he'd had to say all along, denying meanwhile that it was of any importance to him.

Only by being as stubborn as Mickey was I able to dictate the rules of the game. Of course it'd have been better had there been no gamesmanship at all, but this wasn't likely in light of his guile. It was to be expected that his motives would be self-interested. What I wouldn't accept was their tortuousness. If he'd wanted me to know that he'd told Leon about my separation, why did I have to draw it out of him? His evasions carried a slippery self-justification: if it appeared that I was forcing him to tell me what he'd told her, it might also appear that she had forced him to let on to her what he had. I wasn't about to let him get away with this kind of thing. Yet on the bigger questions I'd let him have his way without much thought. I drew the wrong lines in the sand.

My immediate concern was to get through dinner—Magda had improvised a scampi that was too garlicky for Mickey; I saw him trying to avoid the bite of the sauce by chewing the shrimp with his front teeth—and I did get through it, with nary a mention of McNeil Brothers' enterprises, current or prospective. What's more, I got through it equably, which was more than you could say for Mickey, who twice bit Magda's head off, first for forgetting to serve his salad before she dressed it—his distaste for salad dressing was nearly a mania—and then for failing to understand that he wanted his coffee *with* his strawberry shortcake, not afterward. She held her tongue and looked to me to defend her, but I was committed to my own equanimity and kept out of it.

I got up from the table intending to take Frances for a stroll.

"Hadn't you better stay on your crutches?" I asked him as he hopped after me, the house shaking under his weight.

"I'm all right."

"I'm sure you are. It's the pictures I'm worried about. I want them to stay on the walls."

"Then fix me a drink." He leaned on a short balustrade above the living room.

The thought of watching him decide what he wanted and sitting with him while he nursed it was itself tiring, and I yawned one of those yawns that begins as a fake but turns real once you've got your mouth open wide.

The dimensions of my fatigue were nothing to Mickey. It would never have occurred to him not to insist. "Well, what are you hiding, some dusty old cognac perchance?"

"I've got cognac."

"No, not on top of Pouilly-Fuissé. I don't think so."

"How about port?"

"In summertime?"

While foraging in the liquor cabinet, I heard him drop heavily into the Eames chair, which rocked back and snapped forward under his weight. Then Frances yelped: in plumping down, Mickey had stepped on her. She jumped to her feet, raised her injured paw, and limped behind the sofa. I pulled my head out of the cabinet and scowled at him. "Why is he always underfoot?" he said. "That's no dog, it's a horse. He's too big to get out of the way."

"It's a she. And now she'll be on crutches too. Do you want a drink or not?"

"A cordial, Neil—anything will do. I'm not feeling particular."

I pulled out several bottles from the back of the cabinet and put them on top. "Kahlua, Pernod, Cinzano, Fernet, Benedictine, Grappa—what's your pleasure?"

As he looked over the selection, his mouth fell into a frown through which he mumbled what I had no doubt was his disapproval.

"What did you say? Out with it."

His nervous tic flared up. His shoulder started to twitch and his head strained toward it with an awkward twist; the twitching shoulder bobbed against his chin; the sinew in his neck bulged through the padding of flesh. This was how he might look on the executioner's block.

He tried to speak through it, but his jaw tightened up on him. "Pwa whee, pwa whee hundory."

"Pwa whee hundory? Haven't heard of that one. Is it Japanese?"

His twitch was bordering on the convulsive. He was helpless to reply.

I looked away, my eyes straying to a new tower of Magda's design on the coffee table. It had the usual foundation of records, books, and magazines; the innovation was all at the top, where a humidor rampart, an urn steeple, and a letter-opener spire teetered heavenward. I took the urn out of harm's way.

But when the tower was dismantled, I saw that it had served as a fortress: the nut bowl on the lacquered tray had been concealed behind it. Magda had refreshed the bowl, depleted in my brother's last visit, and polished the contents. The heaping, lustrous shells were a regular horn of plenty. The last thing I needed was for Mickey to get started cracking nuts. What was cracked would be bitten, fastidiously chewed, and—with a cough and a grimace, for it was apparent that the taste of the nuts it so thrilled him to crack was a disappointment to him— swallowed, giving rise to thirst and thence to more drinking. Over this tedious largo, his talk would trickle through the night. I rushed to rebuild the tower high enough to block his view of the bowl.

"I was saying that a Poire William would be hunky-dory." He had shaken off his fit, but his face was flushed. His eyeballs quivered and his hands trembled.

"Poire William? My, my, we're getting awfully esoteric in our old age, aren't we?"

There was no sign that he'd noticed the nuts. I plunged back into the depths of the cabinet. "Here's Eau de Vie—will that do?"

"It's . . . perfect."

Disregarding his tentativeness, I poured him a few dribbles; I wanted this over quickly. He stuck his nose so far into the snifter that his eyebrows glanced the rim. I wondered whether there'd be anything left for him to drink after he was finished inhaling. "Now I know how an aardvark drinks brandy," I said.

I served myself a soft drink, lit up, and reached for an ashtray across the coffee table. "I'm just trying to find it. There isn't much here."

"It's called a nightcap. You throw it back and go to sleep."

"And what the hell is Wink?" He scowled at the soda bottle beside my glass. "It isn't very hospitable of you to make me drink alone."

"I'm not making you drink."

"I hope those shrimp hadn't gone off. It is a good thing I went easy on them. She may have been hiding something under all that garlic."

"I ate the shrimp and I feel fine."

He shrugged, and—palm upward, stem between his fingers—raised the snifter to his lips. Then he stopped and, recovering his sour expression, lowered it again. Again I pretended not to notice.

Before I'd left for upstate, Magda had put fresh lilies on the piano. Now they were on their last legs. Stamens lay at the base of the vase, and though the petals were still hanging on, they were bent back. The muslin curtain behind the piano was yellowing. I had never liked those curtains. It was possible that I had never liked any curtains.

"So how is Vicky liking Radcliffe?"

"She's not at Radcliffe."

"That's no reason to get snippy." He pushed the ottoman forward and crossed his injured foot over his knee. The Ace bandage had begun to unravel, revealing the inside of his foot at the top of the heel below the ankle, a puckered line of sea green veins where his arch would have begun if he'd had one. Its lack made for an ugly sight. It had also kept him out of the war. "Lucky for her she's not in Boston. That's nowhere to be young. What a cesspool."

I didn't object. He was easiest on general topics.

Once more he raised the snifter to his lips and lowered it without drinking. "Say, Neil, that port you, ah, mentioned earlier—was it ruby or tawny?"

"You've got to be kidding me."

"Because if it's the tawny, then I think I'd, ah, like to take you up on it." He slipped his finger under the gap in his bandage and began to pull at it. "It's really only the ruby that cloys in the heat."

My recollection is dim here. I imagine that I adjusted my eyeglasses, that my eyes narrowed and my lips curled. But my composure was stretched too thin to say for certain. "I see. Ruby cloys in the heat."

"This isn't some sort of eccentricity. In the universe of taste, it's an overwhelming consensus, a fact, to all intents and purposes."

Helpless before such a fact, I exchanged the brandy for a liberal pour of tawny port. "Why, thank you," he said as if to an unasked-for courtesy. He took a sip, smacked his lips, and sat back, giving the swathe of bandage he'd been fingering a last pluck. He'd worked a hole in the wrap now, exposing the dirty hollow below the ankle and the discolored parabola of the bone itself. "Not bad, for nonvintage. Almost calls for a cigar."

He caught my eye and led it to the humidor I had taken off Magda's pile. I reached over to it and, pushing open the top, showed him that it was empty. "I've got those esplendidos in my jacket, but I don't think this is quite the occasion." He lit a cigarette instead, snapping the lighter shut with a man-who-knows-what-he's-about air. "But where were we?" he asked.

I didn't bother to shrug.

"Oh, yes. College—I remember. I was reading in a study on purchasing patterns how when you take a bevy of women and put them together in one place that before long they all start to get their monthlies at the same time. Some kind of sympathetic reaction, evidently. How many are there at some of the larger schools? Multitudes! And at some point in the month they're all on it. Imagine that."

"Imagine what? What exactly do you want me to imagine?"

"For God's sake, don't be disgusting."

"I'm going to bed. I've got to be up early tomorrow."

"But it isn't late. We were settling in here so nicely." His ankle was still crossed over his knee. He leaned forward in the chair to rub it—the betrayal of my retirement to bed was salt to the wound. "Besides, there's news." He waited for me to ask about it. When I didn't, he gave a slow nod, letting his chin come to rest on his chest. "Fresh developments."

I stood up. "Whatever they are, these developments, I leave them to you."

"Don't be this way, Neil. Siddown. It's barely ten o'clock."

"It's ten thirty."

"We're partners. You can't leave things to me. It's a question of"—he sought in the air for an operative principle—"a question of stewardship."

"You had all day to tell me whatever you liked. Why do you wait till now?"

"It didn't come up."

"Didn't come up? Then you should have brought it up. Most things don't come up by themselves. Whatever it is that you have to say, you could have just said it."

"We were caught up in other subjects. Everything in good time."

"Precisely. And so I'm going to bed."

"What's gotten into you?" His voice rose even beyond its usual roar. "You don't invite a man to sit down with you for a drink and abandon him. It isn't . . . it's not . . ." He twitched a few times, then shook it off. "Who do you think you are?" Outrage pushed him forward in his seat. It was in such states that arteries burst. I saw him slumped over the chair, martyred to a sham propriety.

"Fine, I'll stay up with you for a few minutes. But keep it down, will you?" I glanced at the staircase, a vestigial reflex: more than a week remained before Vicky would be going back to school. She was probably gadding about with her latest boyfriend, who groomed himself like one of Jesus' disciples and comported himself like one of Satan's.

"Why should I?" he asked. Swiveling, he too looked at the empty staircase. The chandelier in the hallway lit the balustrade but not the steps. "Don't tell me you've got that chiquita who's been sniffing after you—"

"Sniffing after me?"

It was then, as he swiveled back, that the nut bowl loomed

up before him. The eyes that had first narrowed in pain and shone with fury now widened with enthusiasm. "Hey, hey," he said, pointing at the bowl. "Slide those over this way."

"I don't know that I like the sound of that."

"Of what?"

"What exactly did you mean by 'sniffing after'?"

"Oh, that. Just an expression. Say, those are some meaty-looking nuts you've got there. I think I'd like to try a few, if you don't mind."

"An expression of what?"

"For God's sake, will you let it go? We've got business to discuss. Now, how about sending those nice shiny nuts over to me? Your table tonight was hardly replete."

I didn't so much as look at the nut bowl. I sipped my drink, sat back, and checked my watch. Since I'd last checked, thirteen minutes had passed. I begrudged him each one.

"Are you going deaf?"

"No."

"Then pass me the goddamn nuts."

"You were asking me something. About a chiquita. 'Don't tell me that that chiquita . . .' you started to say. What was it that you didn't want me to tell you?"

His disbelief at my refusal to meet or even acknowledge his simple request was too much for him. He sprang out of the chair and, kneeling on the ottoman, lunged for the nut bowl across the coffee table.

He'd never been quick, and the sprain made him slower still. I seized the bowl ahead of him and jerked it away, but a handful of nuts spilled in the tussle. They bounced around the table, and before I could put down the bowl, Mickey had swept them over to his side, out of my reach. He lunged again, grabbed the nutcracker, dropped back into his seat, and inventoried his capture. It was enough to keep him busy for a while. He brandished the nutcracker and gave me a look that said that the game was up.

I slid the bowl over to him. "Care for a nut?"

"Thanks, I've already got some."

He nestled a walnut in his palm, fingered the grooves, conked the shell against the edge of the table. I might have been awaiting a diagnosis from a medicine man. The smoke from my cigarette end rose in a double stream, each following its own course before converging in a vanishing lasso.

"Linda's threatening to leave us," he finally said. "She's bluffing, of course."

"How do you know?"

He frowned, then puffed his cheeks and snorted. "Because that's what people do."

"*Sauve qui peut,* right?" The phrase was pretty nearly all the nonrestaurant French he had.

"You said it."

I switched on the lamp beside my chair and the nutcracker, which he flexed like a set of brass knuckles, caught the light.

"I don't say it wouldn't be trouble if she followed through. She's got some kind of reverse double-entry system that's as loopy as she is herself. She's scared away the IRS."

"And you're willing to take the chance she'll walk?"

"What chance is that? House rules. We sponsored her visa application. She's got migrant labor status. We let Immigration know that she's no longer working for us and they'll be on her back."

"I'd assumed she was a citizen by now."

With a killer's scowl, he cracked the walnut he'd been all but fondling and set about picking off the shards and tossing them in an ashtray. He worked slowly and silently, in full expectation of my sitting and waiting. The fan in the freezer rattled on its startup; the fridge hummed beneath it.

"Well, you were wrong. You don't keep up," he said over my unstifled yawn. "You're above concerning yourself with such things."

"Someone else might hire her."

"To clean their house maybe, but not to do their books. Without a reference from us, what credentials has she got?"

"If she backs down, she could get angry, even sabotage the books. Quite a mess that'd be."

"Not in her nature."

He went to work on the next nut. I thought I'd put on some music, as a distraction if not an antidote. In none of the three records I chose did the records match the jackets. I sifted through Magda's tower on the coffee table and found the Boccherini, unjacketed beneath a crystal ashtray. As the viola was reiterating the opening theme, the needle skipped. Within a few measures, it had vaulted to the second movement. It was leaping back in the other direction by the time I pried the record off the turntable and snapped it in two.

On the way back to my chair, I came up behind my brother. "Allow me," I said and gently took the nutcracker out of his hand. He was too surprised to resist, and now I took my turn, which was unlike his in that I talked while I worked and didn't stop to eat the nuts I'd cracked but stockpiled them like a squirrel's treasurer.

"What's she want," I asked. "Money?"

"What else?"

"And we're paying her . . . ?"

"Ten." It sounded on his lips like a settled fact, a long sentence or a short life span.

"Ten."

"Plus a bonus."

"How much did you give her?"

"Oh, she didn't make out too badly. I gave her about what we agreed on."

"You took my suggestion? There's news."

"I took it under advisement and halved it, roughly, as we decided."

"I decided that?"

"Your decision was to leave it to me." He picked through the shell fragments he'd thrown in the ashtray.

"And 'roughly'? What does that mean—you gave her even less than half?"

"It might have been a little light. Our cash flow has been choppy. We've got too many deferrals, too much tied up in escrow and foreign accounts. There are write-downs and amortization expenses. *We* didn't get a bonus, did we?"

"Not so called, but our year-end distribution seemed all right to me."

"That's a nondiscretionary item, not a bonus. We're the principals. We assume the risk."

"If we're illiquid, it isn't because of escrow holdings and currency conversions, Mickey. I mean, come on! You know they're footnotes. We're not running Manufacturer's Hanover. Litigation's the real drain. Never mind representation; how much did we post in bonds alone last year?"

"The least of our worries. We'll get it all back with interest," he cried—hollowly, I thought—his features coarsening into a mask of beleaguerment. The words had probably run through his mind so often that he could hardly bear to hear himself say them. Though maybe it was just the moment. To be deprived of his distraction seemed to leave him out of sorts. He slid his empty glass back and forth on the table.

I made no move to fill it. My fingers were busy cracking shells. I'd gone through a good dozen, and my pile of nuts was just the right size to present to my brother. I pushed it across the coffee table. He sat back in his chair.

"It's my offering, the product of my recent labors, the wages of the last five minutes of my life. Dedicated to you."

He still made no move to accept it. "Take it, Mickey. For all you do."

An uncertain smile played on his lips. "They're all yours," he said. "Thanks, though."

"It's a gift. Where's your sense of occasion?"

I gave the pile another push, and a hazelnut bounced over the edge. He sprang back as from a staining liquid. "All right," he said, "all right."

I waited for him to start eating.

"Have an almond."

He put an almond in his mouth—awkwardly, beginning a habitual motion in the middle—and chewed it with a grimace and a light cough and no hint of pleasure.

"Have a walnut."

He didn't oblige.

"How much was the bonus?"

He cleared his throat. "I could do with a glass of water."

I didn't stir.

"Two hundred," he added.

"Two percent. You'd give her a couple of fivers if you could get away with it. Have two walnuts."

His gaze shifted from the sprained ankle, crossed over his

knee with hair peeking out of the gaps in the bandage, to the
nut pile, and returned to the ankle. He didn't eat.

I got up, walked around the table, leaned over him, and
picked up a handful of nuts. He looked at me over his shoulder. With my free hand, I grabbed the hair on the back of his
head, turned him around, and tried to shove the nuts down
his throat.

My brother's strength was less than his bulk, but in certain
situations one serves as well as the other. He might easily have
fought me off. His arms were free, and his fists. Once he'd gotten over the surprise, he might have made me pay for my attack. But maybe it didn't really surprise him, reminiscent as
it was of scenes in our childhood when I had helped to force
him to swallow his medicine. His reaction was the same now
as then: to resist the substance but not the agent, the feeding
but not the feeder. There was submission in it—I might still
have been administering medicine that a part of him believed
he ought to take. For a moment he was still and slack, and a
Brazil nut as big as a quarter moon slipped between his teeth.
That, and maybe something more, got through.

He got up and hobbled away, spluttering and choking. Over
the sound of the kitchen tap, I heard him coughing. I had returned to my seat. Our scuffle had been orderly. Nothing had
toppled, and Frances was making quick work of the nuts on
the floor. One chewed piece had wound up on the arm of my
chair and my shoes were scuffed and that was all. I waited, but
on hearing the front door open and shut, I stepped out the side
door with Frances. The brightness of the moon dimmed the
stars, though Venus shone through. I came back in, went upstairs, and ran my shoes under the electric buffer in my dressing closet.

I was washing up for bed when my brother appeared

in the bathroom doorway. When he'd arrived was another matter—he was leaning against a doorjamb with his arms folded. I'd been longer over the sink than usual, with the hot water running full bore and a nailbrush in hand.

Mickey's posture was all I could reliably see of him. My eyeglasses were off, and the length of the tub that separated us was enough to blur my view. But he was different. His voice was distant. As soon as I looked up at him, he started in. "There's another thing. I'll come straight to it."

"Leave it till tomorrow. I'm wiped out."

"Your friend next door. He's yawing some, I'm afraid. The authorities in Puerto have been giving him a hard time about his export-license renewal. He got hung up at a bad time. There was a changing of the guard at the trade ministry, and he didn't get wind of it. I warned him early on not to take his eye off the revolving door. Apparently he's been lining the wrong pockets for months. The former chief wasn't about to set him straight, of course. I've spoken to the ambassador. Someone should have told Mr. Younger."

"Someone like us." I had done with my hands and was washing my face. My words slopped through soap and water and reverberated in the bowl of the sink.

"Well, no one did, and the mistake caught up with him. They held up his cargo. It was impounded at the harbor, loaded, unloaded, sent back to the factory. Finally the favors were tendered in the proper quarter and the stuff got off. But at a deficit, and the late arrival won't help. It was a big order. He needed it to go off smoothly. He's pretty well extended, and his distributors won't even think of paying him till they have the product in hand."

"Over a barrel," I said. "Already." I pulled a towel off the rack and dried my face.

"The holdup was unfortunate, but there are others who've made the same mistake."

He meant a man named Freddy we'd partnered with a few years back. He'd bought the rights to manufacture tires in North America under a European brand name and set up a plant in a cape town in the Aggregentine north. Freddy hadn't made his mistake all on his own. Our information had gone stale. The partnership had ended in receivership. "We've made it ourselves. We ought to figure it in." I picked up my toothbrush.

"You'll get no argument here, Neil. It's a tricky business. Which is why I'm for indulging him."

There was more to Bud's troubles than the impounding of his shipment, Mickey reported, and not all were matters of dumb luck: the unexpected imposition of a surcharge on electricity, unexpectedly long drying times for resin resulting from poor ventilation and high humidity in the factory, the unexpected rate of worker absenteeism owing to the unreliability of the public transport system.

I took my toothbrush out of my mouth, raised it like a baton, and tried to say, *unexpected*? But the word drowned in a slurry of toothpaste foam. I rinsed my mouth.

"How much," I said.

"How much?" The foam followed the lapis drip line in the sink's enamel and slithered down the drain. "That's for him to decide."

I hadn't known Mickey to deal in blank checks. Our stake in the business was already high. Raising it would effectively make Bud our employee, not our partner. To protect our interest we might have to come in and run the business. I wasn't about to do this. I didn't think that Mickey was either. An hour earlier, he'd been crying poverty. Maybe our scene downstairs really had shaken him up.

"You don't say," I said. I ran my tongue over my teeth. They'd gotten a better scrubbing than usual while Mickey held forth. "I don't mind admitting that you've wrong-footed me this time. I'd have thought you were for tightening the reins, not letting them out. But I guess we knew we might have to raise the float."

"Us? We couldn't possibly. It'd kill his incentive."

"Whose money then?"

"Vogel's."

Vogel was a factor whose services a few of our partners had resorted to, Freddy among them. If they had already incurred a fair amount of debt, Mickey would encourage our partners to deal with Vogel because, unlike the banks, he would accept a borrower's accounts receivable as collateral. It was insecure, and the rates on his loans could be near to usurious. Now, it would appear not to have been in our interest for our partners to carry high-interest loans; our success lay axiomatically in theirs. But Mickey had found a way around appearances and axioms. The twist was in a sort of referral fee we received from Vogel for putting him on to a borrower. In the event of the borrower's defaulting on the loan, we were given the option of assuming the debt at half the original rate. The arrangement allowed both of us to hedge our risk. Vogel would still make half his profit, which was likely better and faster than if he'd had to go to the borrower's debtors to redeem his claim.

Our end was even sweeter. It gave us the option to buy out our partners at big discounts to their original investments. There wasn't much they could do about it in the short term. They might bring suit in the long, but their spirits and more dependably, their money having been expended in the struggle to keep their heads out of water, they had all limped away muttering—until our recent reversal, that is. But this, Mickey was convinced, was temporary. The old order would be restored on appeal. Disclosure was the nub of the matter, and the evidence would show that he had concealed nothing. There was some truth in this. He hadn't hidden his arrangement with Vogel so much as misrepresented it, suggesting to the partner that we, McNeil, were informally backing the loan. Whatever its legality, we had incited the partner to borrow on bad terms and profited by his failure.

"You sent him to Vogel?" I slipped past him out the bathroom door. "This is your way of indulging him?"

"I negotiated for him. He's only got a hundred and change in receivables, but Vogel will lend him up to seventy-five. That's more than he could have gotten on his own."

"And probably more than he needs."

He followed me into the middle of the room. "No one says he has to take it all."

I opened a window. "And the terms?"

"Thirteen and a quarter for eight months. The mob would have charged him a hundred and thirteen. And if they couldn't get their money from him, they'd have come to us."

I drew the blind, threw back the covers, and looked on the bedside table for the book I was reading. I realized it was still in the dressing closet, in the overnight bag I'd taken upstate, and went in to get it. "He might have a friend," I said on the way out.

"If he had a friend like that, he'd already have lost him."

I got into bed and we said good night. He headed for the door. "When you went outside a few minutes ago, what'd you think about?" I asked after him.

He stopped in midstride. "Oh, nothing." He chuckled. "Just clearing my head. 'Be here now,' as Jeanette says."

"I didn't know we had any choice."

He was already shutting the door behind him. I couldn't tell whether he had heard me.

I set the alarm clock and picked up my book.

chapter nine

It was bad luck for Mickey that my orthopedist couldn't fit him in that next day, and for me too: the first available appointment was two days later. Mickey, mumbling about using the time to scout property, decided to wait around in Dunsinane.

I grumbled, but we hadn't come to the point where I could turn him away. He stayed on and I stayed away.

His presence in my house made me less than particular in my choice of amusement outside it. On the first night I sat down at a bridge table and started to lose. I changed partners, lost some more, changed and lost again. I stood up four hundred dollars poorer. But when I thought of the way Mickey and I had carried on the night before, I felt my money well spent.

Next evening I used a mild hangover to justify a stop after work at a bathhouse in lower midtown. Nothing went my way there either. The place had changed hands since my last visit. The old-country *schwitzbad* with the vaulted steam room over whose sweating tile the clientele shambled to banked seats, the echo of the newspapers they rustled till dampness quieted the pages, the icy plunge bath, the bearish masseurs, the refectory serving vodka and black bread—that place was gone. The white Bolshevik proprietor had sold to someone who fancied himself an improver. He installed a sauna, whirlpool baths and a weight room, carpeted the locker room, and proclaimed the establishment a spa.

The renovation was for the worse: the new masseurs had soft hands, the sauna was tepid, the whirlpool baths were loud, the locker reeked of camphor and mildew and the odor clung to my suit, the refectory had become a juice bar. Under different circumstances, I might have left in a huff. But it was late enough when I got home that Mickey went to bed soon after. He'd be gone the next day. Whatever its shortcomings, the spa had served its purpose.

I came home after work to find that Mickey had left me a few of his treasured Havanas. I thought I'd have one right away. I was battling a disappointment. Cecilia had walked out on me, or run. Vicky didn't appear to be around to distract me, and I didn't feel like having dinner alone. A late lunch had spoiled my appetite for the meal Magda had left on the stove.

I changed out of my office clothes, poured myself a drink, and led Frances onto the front porch, where she sat at my feet while I smoked. The early September evening was fine, the first hints of fall showing through summer fullness in the slant of the light and in the lengthening shadows. The cigar easily lived up to Mickey's billing. I had smoked it down to my knuckles when the specter of my neighbor rose through its guttering. Bud was on his way over.

I knew that he had seen Mickey. Maybe Mickey had asked him to brief me. He crossed the yew-hedge frontier and came up and over the hill overlooking the tennis court, his stride tapering on the ascent. Frances clambered into a sitting position, sounded her single-bark alert, and slid down again. The last wisps of smoke from my cigar drifted into the deepening blue.

I went to the head of the porch to meet him and saw that I was wrong. The young man in front of me wasn't Bud but his son Danny. He had grown up.

"Sure I remember you. Good to see you again," I said when he introduced himself.

"Good to see you, Mr. Fox. By the way, I don't go by Danny anymore. I use my full name, Daniel."

I could barely match the adolescent slouch I remembered to his new incarnation. He was broad instead of bony, looked me straight in the eye, didn't dither, had a certain polish. But then, personal transformations are hard to believe in. To see the squirt who had been Danny as the presentable Daniel was like seeing an acquaintance who's been on a crash diet. No matter how much weight he's lost, the original, swollen image sticks in the mind. Daniel was still Danny to me. I hoped he hadn't come as his father's emissary, or his mother's, to seek advice, or credit. "So, what can I do for you?"

"I was wondering, is Vicky around? I know she isn't due back at school right away. It happens that I'm not either. I thought I might take her out."

To ask a girl out, especially an older girl, takes nerve. But to ask her out through her father was audacity, or courage. I'd seen a similar quality in Bud, pushiness or boldness. The impossibility of deciding which it was made me impatient in the same way.

"That's a nice thought—courtly of you to run it by me. But frankly, I don't make a habit of helping Vicky choose her friends."

He snickered. "Oh, don't worry. I was telling you why I'd come. I wasn't asking your permission."

"Worry? I certainly wasn't worried. I was only noting a difference between you and Vicky in the matter of personal style.

The sort of boy she seems to . . . to run with wouldn't think it necessary to declare his intentions."

"Excuse me, Mr. Fox, but Vicky doesn't seem like the sort of person who judges people by their style. She has style herself but she doesn't care much about it in other people. She's open-minded."

I wondered how he knew her well enough to say so, or thought he did. Vicky open-minded?

She'd have to be open-minded to go out with him. Not that he wasn't handsome. He was, in the mode of another generation, his father's or mine even. He looked at home in his coat and tie. It was half-past seven on a summer evening, and he might have been a junior associate on Monday morning. This was fine by me. I wouldn't have minded his taking Vicky out—better an aspiring go-getter than an aspiring shaman—if I'd thought she might want to. But I didn't. He lacked the spirit of the time. There was none of the desperation to distinguish himself from the tyrannical elders, to proclaim his youth in aboriginal robes and apocalyptic chants, to look enlightened. That was so much the better for him as far as I was concerned. But it would disqualify him from Vicky's interest. Open-minded? She was open-minded with a capital—a cosmic—O, and that made him too square for her.

"So, is she here?" He nodded over his shoulder at the interior of the house.

"I'm afraid not," I replied. "I'll tell you, she's been keeping a full schedule lately, trying to fit everything in before she goes back to school." Now that the cigar was done, I felt myself sliding back into the shadow of the gloom I'd brought home with me. "But I suppose you'd know all about that."

"Things *have* been hectic, as a matter of fact. Nothing important, errands mostly. I'd have liked to make time for Vicky if she could have found some for me. She's someone I've been wanting to get to know for a while."

Again his directness reminded me of his father's: it had grown on me in Bud, but in his son it seemed uncouth. "I'll let her know you were here," I said.

He shuffled his feet and looked down at them to see what they might do next; coughed once, on the chance that his throat needed clearing; bent down to pet Frances, who showed no interest in his attention. He exhausted his excuses for lingering and lingered longer. The band of pink on the horizon shrank to a sliver.

"Well, nice to see you. Best of luck in school." I gave him my hand.

Frances's tail thumped against the stone floor of the porch and slapped the leg of the table as she got up. The screen door opened.

"Hello, Daddy. Daniel! I've been wondering about you. You look groovy."

"So do you, Vick."

"Why didn't you tell me he was here?" She held the door open and, still at the threshold, beckoned to him. He stepped around me into the house.

"I didn't think you were." She had already turned to go back in, and Danny followed. "I knocked on your door when I came in."

The screen door waffed on its spring and shut behind them. "You must have been wearing that headphone gadget again," I called after her. "You were, weren't you?"

She might still have had it on now, for all the notice she paid my question.

I sat back down on the porch with my drink and cigar stub and watched the blues blacken and the greens gray as evening fell, the crickets' first chirps as if synchronized with the ground lights switching on in the planting borders below the porch. Over the lawn, hedges, and driveway, light from new houses and their inhabitants dulled the night sky: streetlights, car lights, stoplights, lamplights, television screens. I tossed away the cigar stub between my fingers and went inside for a refill.

After I'd come back and sat down again, a brighter light streamed across my lap through the living-room window that gave onto the porch. The floor lamp beside the piano had been turned on and Danny, or Daniel, began to play—Vicky had given up playing piano. He played a piece I especially liked, one I'd wanted to put on the hi-fi a few nights earlier. He played it well. The overlay of distant melodies and suspended harmonies started to affect me. The gloom I'd been holding back advanced.

I got up, put down my glass and, with Frances at my heels, walked onto the grass, into the cold pocket of a swale. Fallen leaves bespoke the end of a summer that had slipped past me. I walked farther from the house, toward the road, but wherever I went the music seemed to follow. I couldn't tell what I heard from what I remembered. I knew it well enough that once it had been struck up, I could imagine the rest. I went back to the porch like a suspect turning himself in.

The words that kept coming back to me were *many times*. They stretched across the nine months that had passed since Cecilia had spoken them, when I'd told her that I'd make up for the interruption we'd suffered at the hands of the guard who kicked us off the beach in Puerto. I'd been kidding and thought that she had been too. But her words had proved to be slyer than I'd understood. She'd made them stick. *Many times,* she'd said, and in the first while anyway, seen to it. Thereafter she didn't so much have to; I saw to it too. Something had changed in the course of those many times, in the turning out of bedside lamps and sleeping off the diagonal and in the whole process of accommodation. We had made a pair.

Many times, she'd said. What it meant when she said it, in keeping with what I'd meant by *I'll make it up to you,* was *next time.* We were on vacation, and it was a vacation-type remark, to be left behind on the sand with our bottle of suntan oil. We'd been together casually before that trip, and there was nothing to make me think this casualness would change. Our encounters had the predictability of assignations, and the isolation from the rest of our lives. We'd meet for supper or drinks, have a dance or two at home or take a walk, starting far enough into the evening that bedtime wasn't far off. And no matter how late it got, we wouldn't spend the night together. If I was at her place, a walk-up off Union Square, I'd call a car. Her cat would make me sneeze if I stayed too long, and Frances needed to be let out. But there was no call for excuses. Cecilia went home from Dunsinane as readily. I supposed at the time that it was because she wouldn't have slept beside a stranger any better than I, later that she'd do it to suit me.

But why would she suit me? In a country that was strange to her, where novelty would presumably have been a pleasure, I showed her nothing and introduced her to no one. At first I didn't trouble myself about what she was in it for. A fling doesn't need explaining. Younger women went for older men all the time. They'd go for them after they'd been put off younger men. Simple gentleness and calm went a long way.

A generalization, I knew: in other moods, I'd wonder why she was taken with me. I'd wonder, then dismiss the thought as privately meddlesome. I'd always been married. I hadn't had to estimate my value in this way and wouldn't have known where to start.

Besides, why worry what she saw in me? Did I have to ask myself what I saw in her? She was lovely. What we were doing seemed straightforward. And to the extent it wasn't, well, the presumption of its temporariness rendered that quotient irrelevant and her loveliness paramount. She was away from home. It was only a matter of time before she'd go back.

After our return from Puerto, we picked up about where we'd left off. We might have started to see more of each other than before, might have been looser when we danced or more leisurely when we strolled. Our tenderness notwithstanding, what we had was a relationship of convenience. We had agreed implicitly to be agreeable. Neither of us, we must have known, would go too far out of the way for the other.

She went to Chicago to work Bud's booth at a trade show. While she was there his cargo had gotten held up in port, and he summoned her back to Aggregente. It was always a good idea to give her charm a chance to come into play; she might hold more sway over those customs agents than he could ever have. In any case he had had to run around managing the delay. On Mickey's advice, he'd established distribution lines across the northeast, and rushed in the thick of a late-winter blizzard to Baltimore, Philadelphia, and Cleveland to reassure his wholesalers, from whom he now needed payment up front. · They'd turned him down and he'd gone hat-in-hand to Mickey, who sent him on to Vogel.

"Did you miss me?" Cecilia asked when she was back. The question came at an odd time, neither at the start of a night nor at its height. I hadn't heard anything like it from her before. Even her way of asking was surprising: instead of softening, her eyes glinted, her hand tugged at her scarf, her head playfully rocked. I wondered what was in this look, self-consciousness or mockery.

The unexpected question came out of unexpected circumstances. I said that she and I never went anywhere together. That night was an exception, a kind of first date.

It happened by chance. I had an arrangement at the end of a workday to meet a senior accountant in my office—Kuvatz, his name was. I wanted to learn how an agreement to sell back my shares should be structured, and his command of the firm's manipulation of financial mechanisms made him the man to talk to on such matters.

They were the only matters to talk to Kuvatz about. No one in the office ever talked to him about anything else. Kuvatz himself knew this. You could see the insult in the protrusion of his uncloseable mouth and in the nervous tugs he gave his ears.

Others who'd been slighted as he had might have withheld information or worse, but Kuvatz was forthcoming. The chance to hold authoritatively forth on a subject was more than he could pass up. He must be lonely, you'd think, but later if not sooner you'd understand that you were mistaken, that the long-windedness was instead an expression of his resentment, an act of aggression, a means of capture. The one thing he had to tell me he told me over and again: that it would be advantageous both to me and to the firm if the redemption of the shares was funneled through a new venture, the acquisition of a property, for instance, or an investment in a business. This no doubt was sound advice, but I had known it going in. It wouldn't have hurt to hear him confirm it once. But after the third time I had numbed to it, and by the sixth I'd have been glad to do without it.

Luckily he'd given me an out. I hadn't seen it at first.

The firm had a pair of season tickets to professional basketball games at the new Madison Square Garden. Kuvatz dispensed them. They were to entertain clients with, but when there weren't any around they went to those in the office who requested them, mostly younger men who'd take their sons. Urgent work would sometimes fall late in the day into one of these men's laps and, lacking the seniority to pass the work on to somebody else, force him to send the tickets back to Kuvatz's secretary. She'd have left for the day, and the office boy would take them in to her boss, who, little interest as he might have had in basketball, had a bookkeeper's aversion to waste that made him like still less the tickets going unused.

On the evening I met with him, as we were about to go down to the corner bar, the tickets for that night's game came back. Kuvatz took them with a frown, and excused himself to dial a standby's extension. When he found that that man had already gone home, he began to work on me to go.

"They've fielded a strong team this year, I'm told."

"I'll pass," I said.

"I don't guess it's the kind of thing you do on your own, is it?"

"Not really."

"I'll tell you what. Basketball's hardly my cup of tea, but I haven't got anything doing. We could go together. For a lark, you know."

"I've got plans," I said. His jowly cheeks flushed.

I'd spoken half the truth. I did have plans. I had arranged to meet Cecilia, though not till later. "Maybe your plans will want to go."

"I don't think so." I took a half step back from the desk. "Why don't you go ahead?"

"Me?" He waved the suggestion away. He leaned across the

desk and thrust the tickets more or less under my nose. "I like to know I've gotten rid of them," he said.

"You know," I said after a long hour with him during which I ran my finger over a crack in the leather cover of the barroom bench I was sitting on till it gave me a paper cut, "maybe I will use those tickets." I looked at my watch. "I've missed the beginning, but I can still catch the better part of it."

"You'll need to change your plans."

To shore up my excuse, I went to the bar to make a call. I had no intention of going to the game but figured I'd leave a message with Cecilia's answering service, moving up our rendezvous. She probably wouldn't get it in time, but Kuvatz didn't know that.

I didn't get her service. I got Cecilia herself. Kuvatz tapped his swizzle stick on the table until I started speaking into the phone. "You don't happen to like basketball, do you?" I asked her.

"*Basketball!*" I couldn't tell whether the word meant nothing to her or everything. She said she'd be thrilled to see a game. I wasn't, but to perpetuate a fiction, I'd blundered into a possibly disagreeable reality.

While waiting to take the phone back from me, the bartender switched the television to the game, which was still in the early going.

Kuvatz stayed behind to finish his drink. "Enjoy yourself," he said. His forlornness nipped at my heels.

Cecilia and I had arranged to meet at a snug a few blocks from the arena. I got there before she did, and while settling in I found myself hoping that we might skip the game and go home to bed.

A leather pouch, then a light hand touched my shoulder and I swiveled around. Cecilia stood over me in a fur-trimmed leather jacket, miniskirt, and suede boots that came up almost to her knees and added to her height. I took her hand in mine and rose to greet her. She'd trimmed her hair. It didn't so much look shorter as narrower—her face looked wider against its frame. It had spilled over the corners of her eyebrows, but now I saw the delicate points they came to. A cream-colored chiffon scarf showed off her tan. It was fastened by a coral pin the same color as her lipstick. A flake from it clung to the edge of a bottom tooth. I brushed her lip, wiped it away, and gave her a kiss.

"Let's go," she said, putting her arm through mine and dashing my hope of skipping the game. "It'll be over before we get there."

"*Basketboll*," she said as we strode up Eighth Avenue. "Who knew you were so sporty!"

I didn't explain that the tickets had been forced on me. Her enthusiasm seemed to be based in part on her perception of my own. "Maybe I am sporty," I said. *Sporty*—what did that mean, anyway?

She still had her arm through mine and was hustling me along. "Hold on a sec," I said, and stopped for a bag of roasted chestnuts from a street vendor. This was something of an occasion in itself. I couldn't remember when I'd last eaten a chestnut.

Across the street from Madison Square Garden's rear entrance, on the monumental post office building's granite steps, a black man hawked plastic glow-in-the-dark hoops of various sizes. He himself modeled them, wearing them around his wrists and forearms, neck, waist, and ankles. "Never get lost in the dark," he cried. "You'll never get lost in the dark!"

"The home team is the Knicks," Cecilia said on our way in.

"I guess I knew that."

"Very sporty of you." She tightened her grip on my arm and gave it a tug.

The crowd's reactions echoed down the spiraling cinderblock

ramp we climbed to enter the arena. Cecilia had let go of me
and rushed ahead, the cheers and boos from inside spurring
her on. As I watched her striding along in her tall, high-heeled
boots and sheer stockings, it came to me that she might be
taken for a hired escort, and I, as soon as I appeared beside her,
for the man who'd hired her. I didn't mind if I was, but I didn't
like the thought.

At the top of the steps, I handed our tickets to an usher
who'd stopped Cecilia there. She took my arm again, and as he
led us down to our seats, five or six rows from the floor and a
couple of seats in from the aisle, I saw the absurdity of my self-
consciousness. No one paid us any notice. We'd have had to do
something outrageous in as vast a space. The thousands in it
seemed like scores of thousands. "Chestnut?" I asked Cecilia,
crinkling open the bag once we were seated.

The question was left hanging. She had bigger things than
chestnuts to worry about. The game was already into the second half, and we had catching up to do. The membrane that
we felt ourselves to have penetrated by entering the arena con-
tained hope and anxiety. We supposed that we had come to be
entertained, but we saw that by joining the home crowd, we
had become partisans, assumed a civic burden.

We were losing—the Bullets were ahead by five points.
Cecilia pointed at a couple of Knicks players who'd run back
too late to defend their basket. "How can they let them do
that?" she exclaimed.

I rustled the bag of chestnuts I was holding in front of her. I
seemed to want her to have the first. "Try one of these. They're
a local specialty."

"A local specialty?" She helped herself to one. It was the pre-
cise color of the hair on top of her head. The color lightened as
her hair fell toward her shoulders. "We have them at home."

"But they wouldn't be slow roasted like these. You've got to be careful not to burn yourself." She shook her hair from her face and was about to take a bite when I grabbed her hand. "They get very hot inside, like potatoes. If you peel off a bit of the skin you'll see that it's steaming."

She looked at me askance and bit into the chestnut. "Ouch," she said, flatly, and winked to make sure I knew that the chestnut hadn't burned her after all.

She held up the other half for my inspection. No steam rose from it. I touched the flesh. There was more heat in the change in my pocket.

The sounding of an amplified bullhorn to indicate substitutions caught me by surprise—I nearly jumped into Cecilia's lap. "So sporty!" she said again and pushed back the hair that had fallen into my eyes.

A player who came in for the Knicks was loudly cheered. His name sounded familiar even to me. "He had a marvelous college career at Michigan, marvelous," the man beside me replied when I wondered aloud about him. He pointed at a guard the Bullets were bringing in. "But it's him we've got to watch out for," he added. By *we*, he meant not only himself and me but Cecilia too. His glance moved from me to her.

The player he pointed at looked sleek. "He's called 'the Pearl.'"

"I'll keep an eye on him," I said. "Thanks."

"The name's Marion." I didn't ask whether this was his first or last name, or give him either of mine. Let him get started bending our ears, I thought, and I might as well have come with Kuvatz.

"He's giving us a hell of a time," this Marion told Cecilia. "He'll be dribbling one way and suddenly he changes direction, not by crossing over to the other hand like everyone else. Instead, he spins around his man. He's so quick with the ball that he can take a long step, pivot, and take another before his man can block his path."

The Pearl was indeed the one to watch, and for a while the Knicks watched him like the rest of us. They couldn't seem to find it in themselves to stop him. Their imperturbability made their helplessness seem intentional.

"They're testing us," Cecilia said to me. The Knicks' apparent nonchalance was uniting us. We found ourselves caring about the outcome more than they seemed to, trying to keep them afloat on our worry.

"I wonder about this bunch sometimes," Marion said. "They always think they can come back. But against a team like this I don't know that they can."

"They can," Cecilia replied.

"Look, mister," I said, and turned in my seat to face him and, behind him, his wife. "It's wonderful that you've got so much to teach my date. It must be hard for you to hear each other with the noise in here. Maybe you'd like to change places with me."

He was slow to catch my gist. He'd have liked to do it—the beginning of a smile and a start gave him away.

His wife saw this, and seeing that she had seen, he registered my sarcasm. "Just trying to help," he murmured.

I turned back. "What did you say to him?" Cecilia asked.

"Nothing much."

The Knicks brought in three new players. They played a trapping defense, chasing the ball the length of the court, double-teaming and jostling the Bullets, throwing them off their rhythm and tiring them out.

The substitutes' energy released the crowd's. Everything that went the Knicks' way gave them, us, an occasion to release the accumulated tension. Even their earlier failure to contain the Pearl was shown to be a part of their design. After a short rest he was brought back in.

The Knicks tried something new: they laid off him. The man guarding him hung back, challenging him to take uncontested jump shots from beyond the foul line. He missed. He needed someone breathing down his neck to keep him from thinking.

The Bullets were sunk without him. The Knicks pulled away.

It was then, the game in hand and Marion helping his wife on with her coat, that a light came into Cecilia's eyes. With a tug at her scarf and a tilt of her head that made her amber ear-rings swing, she asked, "Did you miss me?"

I wasn't sure at first that I'd heard her.

Had I missed her? Hadn't I been hoping to skip the game and go home to bed with her? I didn't know whether this was what she had in mind when she asked. I looked at her, at that amused expression with the hint of mockery.

"Well, sure," I said.

It went over poorly. Uncertainty about her motives came across as uncertainty about my feelings. I'd have done better to be more expansive. In a try at shoring up my answer, I put my arm around her, but she slipped out of my embrace. "Who made you like this?" she said. Though the gleam in her eye had hardened and she held her head still, the hint of mock-ery remained in the curl of her lip and in her voice. "Who scared you?"

The odor of the arena, of a hayloft inside a stale freezer, had started to get to me.

"I ask you a simple thing, a nice thing," she continued. "And it scares you. Your head starts to spin. If you didn't miss me, that's okay. But you're too scared to tell. You don't even know yourself."

Where was this coming from? She had always been so

agreeable. "I answered you," I told her after the moment it had taken me to collect myself. "I said that I had."

"Had what?"

First she had asked an awkward question. Now she insisted that I repeat my answer. "Missed you." I sighed.

"You can't stand to admit it." She turned back and faced the court, which I took to indicate the end of her attack, or at least a letup in it.

"It's not just me you're scared of," she added. "It's a lot of people. Like that man sitting next to us." She looked at the seat he had left. "There's always someone in your way, but really they're the people you're scared of."

"You're wrong about him." Now it was my turn to look at his seat. "He'd have made a nuisance of himself. And you're wrong about yourself. You, my dear—"

"—And Bud. You're afraid of Bud."

"Afraid of Bud? Did he say that?"

More fans were leaving. We had to stand to let a group in our row sidle past.

"*I'm* saying it."

"You're saying that that's what he thinks?"

"I don't know what he thinks."

Yet she thought she knew what I thought—or felt, a thing even harder to guess. "If that's what he thinks, he's got me wrong. You certainly have. I missed you. I'm sorry if you don't like the way I say it."

She took her jacket from the back of her chair and, as I helped her into it, said, "Take me home and show me." She turned to me and took my arm. The curl of her mouth had resolved into a smile, and her head rocked playfully once more.

To defuse with tacky flirtation the tension that her own

criticism had created struck me amiss. I started to point this out but thought better of it. What she proposed was no more than I'd wanted to do from the start of the evening.

But the very fact of our arguing was new. What marked that night as our first date wasn't only the outing, it was this argument. Criticism had been off-limits. It would have implied our having a stake in each other, difficulties to confront, a common future. Avoiding it was, I'd thought, an unstated rule. Now, for no reason I could fathom, by design or accident, Cecilia had broken it. What we'd had till then had been unearned. Now we quarreled as real lovers do.

I took her arm and led her back the way we'd come, along the spiraling ramps of the arena. Instead of going out onto the avenue we went below, to Penn Station.

A train had been held back to wait for those who'd stayed to watch the game till the end. The engineer sounded resentful in his announcement of the delay. Once we were off, he began trying to make up for lost time, racing through the tunnel to Queens. The train bounced on its springs and, as we rounded curves, wobbled, throwing Cecilia and me together. In fact we were pretty snug to begin with. She leaned against me and I leaned against a window. The scent of her hair mingled with my breath.

We talked about the basketball players. She had hunches about their characters: the Knicks' center was a prankster, their coach spent a lot of time walking his dog, one of their guards was a ladies' man. I asked her how she knew. The center's sleepy look gave him away and the coach was a dead ringer for an old family acquaintance who was always walking his dog. As for the guard—he had a beard and suede shoes—hadn't I seen him looking at her?

"He picked you out from that distance, in that crowd?"

"I could feel it."

The train slowed. The moon was big but louvered by cloud bars; tall weeds or their shadows waved beside the tracks. I listened for the wind but couldn't hear it. A row of floodlit billboards broke the darkness. Fab would clean my clothes with lemon-freshened borax, the brewers of Utica Club had drunk as much of their own beer as they could and were selling the rest, I could bring my wife and a few dollars to Ohrbach's and come back home with a new woman.

I turned to Cecilia and gently covered her eyes. "And how does this feel?" I asked.

"Your hand? It's cold."

"No, not my hand. My eyes. My look. If you felt that basketball player's look from fifty feet, you should be able to feel mine from a few inches."

She paused, crimping a corner of her mouth. I kept my hand over her eyes and noticed a gap in the fit of my middle and ring fingers below the knuckle. "It's hot. So hot it could burn your hand." She took my hand from her eyes, pursed her lips, and blew on it.

We'd had a lovers' quarrel. Back in Dunsinane, we had a lovers' reunion. Our quarrel had been just serious enough to jeopardize us. It gave us a distance to overcome.

She was familiar to me, but now she seemed to hold something back, something coincident with my pleasure but beyond it. Had I missed her more than I knew? Was it simply a reflection of intense desire for her, the glow of a body charged with my hunger for it that I sensed as a withholding, or was it a sign of the fear she had taxed me with? Our quarrel continued in my mind even as we made it up.

Later, in harder-headed states, I'd tell myself that at most it meant that I was in a little deeper than I'd realized, which after all was no deeper than she was in herself, as far as I could see. She was letting herself go, showing me how.

The lights in my bedroom were out but we weren't in the dark. A beam escaped through the crack in my dressing-closet door and cast itself like a clock's minute hand along the floor, toward the hassock at the foot of the bed. Near the head, a window let in more light, which gathered in the diamond panes and pooled along the band of turned-up sheet on the bed's far side.

In and out of this pool, like a bather washing one side of her body while keeping the other in the bath, Cecilia shifted and swayed. She lay across the bed, widthwise along the sheet, the light on the cleft of her back. I ran my fingertips along a notch on her spine and into a furrow where the light could not go. She turned—the light caught her flank and I caressed it, my hands clouding the pool. The feel of her conjured its own images, first, shapes at the back of my eyes corresponding to her contours and then, further along, lines in a wrinkled darkness. She drew me to her, illuminating a length of my side. The spur of my hip was like somebody else's, or something else, a gunwale or crook. I clasped her, rolled her back so that her side was in the pool, and ran my hand over her ribs; the spaces in the cage were no wider than the fingers that covered them. I rubbed the back of her neck and wanted to see that, too. With the sight of each part of her, I wanted to see more, or more clearly, and would look so long that the light appeared to radiate from her. What I saw I wanted to touch; what I touched, to taste.

"Listen to that," she said.

"Is it raining?" I moved to the edge of the bed, sat up far enough to kneel, and craned my head to look out the window. The sky was a marbled gray.

She kneeled beside me, her body forming an *s*, and inclined her head to the same angle. "Can't you hear it?"

I couldn't. I got up, took my glasses from the night table, and went to the window. It certainly felt like rain, the air warm and damp, the trees still. I lifted the screen, stuck my hand out, turned it upward, and waited. A night bird with a call like a broken rattle sang a few bars. Car tires hummed. A dog barked.

Cecilia came to the window, snuggling up to me as she leaned toward the ledge. With her arm around my body, the back of her hand brushing my lips, her knee buckled into the back of mine, my contentment deepened till it held intimations of love.

We watched the layers of darkness peel and the clouds churn overhead. At last I heard a raindrop fall and, a long moment later, felt another one on my palm, heavy as a drop of blood.

"How would you feel if I was still here when you came home from work tomorrow?" she asked. "Would you like it?" She leaned harder against me. Her hair spilled over my shoulder.

The question broke the moment. I wondered whether she was testing me. This wouldn't be like her. But it wouldn't be the first time tonight she had been unlike herself. She had accused me of being afraid of her, and if I told her now that I preferred to keep some distance, she could take it as proving her point. But was that my first concern? The fact that I was thinking along these lines could mean that she had me where she wanted me, or that she was right about my being afraid.

The rain let up. The drops that blew in on us were misty; a coppery flush was breaking through a corner of the sky. It seemed impossible that this was daylight—we'd just gotten in. On the night table on the other side of the bed, the alarm clock glowed but I couldn't make out the numbers.

We'd broken one rule by arguing and another by spending a full night together. Why not a third? I hadn't imagined coming home to her. But I did now.

"I believe I would like it," I said. The lateness of the hour, or the thought of it, might have sapped my energy for proper equivocation.

But when we were back under the covers with the curtains drawn, I added, "Don't you have to go to work in the morning?"

She didn't answer, but there was a catch in her silence, then a huskiness in her voice, her breath vibrating behind it. I thought there might be tears too. "Don't worry about it, Neil," she said. "If you don't want me to stay, I won't."

She threw back the covers but I kept an arm around her and pulled them back. "I told you to stick around."

"That's what you say, but it's not how you say it."

"How I say it? What would you say to giving my motives a rest for a while? I think they've stood enough looking into for one day."

She squirmed to put a little distance between us but made no second move to get up. "I'll be able to make more time for you if you want me to," she said at length. "I won't have to work every minute."

"Of course I want you to. Is the trouble with the shipments resolved?"

"The shipments?" This seemed to me to be an obvious question. She acted as if it was far afield. "Who knows? I'll find out more tomorrow."

"If Bud was still having that trouble, it'd be a funny time for a break."

"It's not exactly a break. He wants me to do some other things."

"And what are these other things he wants you to do?"

"Promotion, he told me. I'll find out more tomorrow when I see him."

"I didn't know he was around."

"How would you? With those big trees you have between you, it's hard to see anything at all."

He was there all right, and if I hadn't seen him yet it might almost have been because I hadn't talked about him. You had to mention Bud before he'd turn up. Then you'd see him all the time—until he'd vanish again. He was either out of the way or in it. It made him impossible to get used to. His appearances would jar me. There was a suddenness about them, and him.

As Cecilia and I began to spend more time together, Bud was in the background, going about his business behind the yews on the next acre. But in imagination he loomed larger, nearer, so that it sometimes seemed to me that he was between Cecilia and me. In light of how he'd thrown the two of us together at every opportunity, this idea didn't make any sense. It nagged at me all the same.

I left late the next morning for work, dozing after the alarm went off and—after rescheduling an appointment—taking my time getting ready to leave. I shaved and dressed more attentively than usual to make up in spruceness for what I lacked in rest, made toast and coffee while a squirrel tried to muscle his way into the bird feeder, and strolled with Frances down the walk to bring the paper in instead of picking it up on my way out. The rain had left a wintry mildness behind. A section of the sky was still gray. But the better part was washed in the gold of a baroque cathedral. The crooked trunk of the magnolia along the walk might have been a vaulted arch; the space between the bare branches, the panes of a stained-glass window.

Cecilia was fast asleep when I took breakfast up. She

wouldn't stir for love or money, not even after I'd ventured soft words and a caress, poured our coffee from a sterling pot, and pulled back the curtains. I stood by the window and watched her. The ambivalence of our last good night was gone. With the light pouring down on her and the dust motes around the dark drift of her hair, she made an exalted picture.

I started toward her and stopped. A couple of steps had changed everything. The dust swirling above her in her stillness was suddenly a morbid tableau. She was a corpse floating in murk. I had looked from too many angles—stare long enough at someone sleeping and you can't be sure whether you're cherishing them or anticipating their wake.

The clatter I made picking up the breakfast dishes finally disturbed her. She shifted positions, opened her eyes, and mumbled—hostile words, to judge by the sound of them. The light in her eyes and flush of the cheek that in shifting she turned up from her pillow and even the burnish of her hair looked angry. I asked her to repeat herself, but she shut her eyes again and went back to sleep, if she'd ever been awake. Her hostility, revealed in the tarnish and convexity of my reflection in the coffee pot as I carried the tray back down the stairs, rattled me. I tried to leave a note for her but ended up scratching out whatever I'd set down. It all seemed wrong, no matter how simple. Even "coffee in the pot" was no good—I'd drunk it all. There'd be plenty of time for her to make more for herself if she really meant to stay.

Magda's rust bucket pulled up the driveway while I was on my way out to the garage. She was slow to notice me, and gave a start when she did.

"Sorry to frighten you," I said.

She carried a small shopping bag from which a couple of bottle necks protruded at opposed angles. Her overcoat was unbuttoned, revealing the pointy collar of her dress and her bollardlike neck. "Hot today," she said with a glance over her shoulder at her car.

"It is." I realized that I hadn't left her a note either. The sight of Cecilia would have surprised her.

"I was almost all the way here when I remembered that I needed to pick up some things from the market, and when I turned back I got stuck," she added. She put down the bag and made a shuffling motion, wiggling her fingers to indicate creeping, and looked behind her again. "There are crews on every road. The men stand there with their arms crossed. It's steam shovels that do the work." She imitated them too.

I hadn't seen her so chatty. I'd known her to be stern, the kind of housekeeper who could infuse every part of the job with a spirit of correction. This lighter side didn't become her.

I peeked at my watch and drifted toward the garage. Rush hour would be winding down. I thought I'd drive the Giulietta in, the weather was so fine. "I left home at the normal time, eight o'clock, a few minutes after," she explained, stealing another glance over her shoulder.

If it had been my discovery of her late arrival that was embarrassing her, she wouldn't have needed to worry. I wasn't used to seeing her in the morning anyway and was about to say so when it occurred to me that she wasn't the type to let a day of lateness shame her. Maybe her worry was that I'd suspect that she came at this time every day. Maybe she did.

Frances had heard our voices and was scratching at the door. When I opened it for her she trotted out and greeted Magda, who grabbed her affectionately by the snout and inspected her face the way you'd inspect a child's before school.

A creaking followed a click, and the rear door on the passenger side of Magda's car swung open. But no one came out. Frances cowered behind me. I looked at Magda, who opened her hand, raised her shoulders, and scrunched her neck in a gesture of denial.

A little girl of four or five ran from the car toward Magda. I couldn't tell whether her brown eyes were big and her plump cheeks rosy with fear or delight, whether the edge of the tooth peeking from her pouty mouth was also the edge of her smile. The dark spirals of her hair and the hem of her white frock sailed behind her across the driveway. Her breathlessness from running had made her giggle, and her giggles, feeding on her breathlessness, turned to laughs. The world was her oyster. "Your granddaughter?"

"It's just for today," Magda said. "There was no one to watch her. She won't break nothing."

"I don't mind if she does. She's a beaut!"

I learned that her name was Juliette and told her that my car had almost the same name, a coincidence that she found priceless.

Our acquaintance was nothing short of famous. In a matter of minutes, I knotted her finger in my shoelace, chased her around the orchard, and taught her to pet Frances. I told her we'd play again soon.

"By the way, there's something else," I said on my way back out. I stood at the threshold, speaking to Magda through the open storm door while she stocked a cabinet. "There's a friend of mine upstairs—a lady friend." She moved to the other side of the doorway and rubbed a rag over a spot on the doorjamb. A light had come into her eyes. "I'd like her to feel at home."

Whether for my sake or because my embarrassment relieved her of her own at my discovering that she'd brought her granddaughter, the news pleased her. But I saw that my last words had led her to believe I'd meant more than I had. "She will!" Magda exclaimed, winking as at the hatching of a grand conspiracy, shutting the door and trundling inside before I could set her straight. In the glimpse of myself I caught as I backed out of the garage, I was blushing like a cub.

Next glance in the mirror it wasn't myself I saw. I'd accelerated around the bend past Bud's and seen a gardener trimming his front hedge. I didn't think it could be Bud himself, not at that hour on a weekday morning. But Cecilia had said he was around, and the glimpse I'd caught was enough to make me check the rearview. He had stepped into the road and was waving an oversized pair of garden shears at me. I was a good twenty-five yards off and his image had receded into indistinctness, but I recognized him. His wave was broad, yet with a hint of futility, the loppers cutting ribbons in the air.

I reversed, stopping beside him and lowering the window to the sour thaw of leaf mulch left over from the fall. He put the clippers down and came around to my side of the car, pulling off one of his work gloves to shake my hand. He was slightly out of breath. Though he was only in shirtsleeves, perspiration dotted his stubbly beard and ran down his neck to the chest hairs that poked out of his shirt like filings drawn by a magnet; his eyes almost pulsed. His expectancy had always struck me as a quality of his liveliness, a winning one. Now it looked like a sign of nerves, the consuming action of his worry.

I had to tilt my head back to look at him, and the convertible top pressed against the crown of my hat.

He asked after Vicky, and I asked after his children in turn. I revved the motor; exhaust fumes overwhelmed the tang of mulch.

I gave him my hand. "Good to run into you, Bud. I've got to make tracks."

"A little late for chasing the worm, isn't it?" A car came up behind us. He moved closer to my car to make room for it to pass. He wasn't about to step out of the road and let me go too.

He took a couple of cigarettes from a pack in his shirt pocket and without asking whether I'd like it lit up both and handed one to me.

The smoke seemed to compose him—it stilled the hands that had kept fluttering so near my head. "How about this sunshine," he said. The gray line of cloud was now out over the water, rimmed by the sunlight that appeared to be dissolving it. If Bud hadn't been standing over me, I'd have been looking straight into it. The only shadows to be seen were the ones beneath the branches he had cut and stacked. "Spring's here."

"It's a bluff." I could almost see the big-flaked, windless, dogwood-winter snowfall to come. "You don't sound like a man who's wintered in the islands."

"That's because I'm a man who for the last two weeks has been wintering in St. Louis and Cleveland and Chicago. Can sinuses get frostbitten?"

"I heard you'd been doing some traveling."

"I've been everywhere. There's plenty of interest, no doubt about it. So long as we can turn the corner."

Another car went around us, the driver giving me a dirty look in passing. Not so many years earlier it would have surprised me to see two cars go down my road in the course of a morning.

"You wouldn't happen to know a man named Vogel, by the way?"

"Not personally."

"But you've heard the name."

"I have. Yes."

He leaned forward to look me in the eye. This left me staring straight into the light and I shifted to have him shade my eyes again. But my new position must not have given him the view of me he wanted. Once I moved he did too, which led in turn to my moving once more to escape the glare. We swung our heads back and forth like fighting cocks looking for a point of attack. When we were finally in some sort of alignment, I saw that both his hands rested on the side panel in front of the door. "I'm supposed to see him today," he said, "and—"

"Excuse me, Bud, if you don't mind." I looked at his hands.

"I thought if you knew him . . ." He saw where I was looking and looked there too in perplexity.

"The finish, it smudges so easily."

He raised his hands as if at gunpoint.

"So I thought if you knew him, you might talk to him for me, remind him of our relationship."

"I'd have been glad to, if I knew him. I don't, unfortunately. I told you that."

"But you do know of him, and he must know of you through Mickey."

"I suppose, but that's hardly an acquaintance. If there's something you think he needs to hear from someone else, why don't you have Mickey speak to him?"

"Mickey?" He looked around. Again the daylight flooded my eyes. I lowered the brim of my hat against it. "That's another story, if you see what I mean."

"I don't know that I do. But it doesn't matter since I can't help you in any case."

"Just a thought," he said, exhaling a last puff of smoke and flicking away his cigarette. Another car was approaching, from the opposite direction this time. He slipped his hand over the crack above the lowered window and ducked his head closer to mine, which gave his talk a confidential air. "Things all right with Cecilia?" I thought I saw his glance shift toward my house and wondered whether he knew she was there. "She's doing you justice?"

He was set up like a target. His head filled the window frame, his face so near that I could feel the modulation of his breath. I could have cold cocked him. It was such a bad position to taunt me from that I decided he mustn't have meant it.

The car flew past, and Bud's hair fluttered in its current. Before I quite knew what I was doing, I had begun cranking up my window. He jumped when he felt it, yanking his hand away, and I took mine off the crank in equal surprise. "I hope you don't mind my asking," he added.

"Not at all, but I've really got to get a move on." I shifted into gear and eased off the clutch, leaving it for him to get out of the way. "Good to see you."

"And you," I heard him say as I set off, his voice sounding distant through my half-shut window.

It was true that winter didn't go without a last gasp. The snow a few days later was perfunctory, the fulfillment of an old quota. It had the sparseness of an undermanned siege, the flakes spiraling down like parachutists. No arctic gusts, no darkness came with the passing storm cloud. The accumulation might have amounted to an inch as the papers claimed, but within hours the sunshine was routing the patches of white even from the big stones besides the streets. The remaining snow squatted on the ledges like cats, till it had shrunk to lounging lizards camouflaged against the trail of their own dampness.

Cecilia started to stay over, three or four nights a week. The warm wet early spring was the season of our domestication, rain our background and also our stimulant. Coming through half-open windows, its sounds and scents carried us along—the smell of the new grass, of the laurels and lilacs, the patter of raindrops and the warbling of the newly returned birds were all the activity we needed. They set a mood in which our differences could be taken for granted.

In the house where I had lived with Joyce and which I was still accustomed to consider hers, I'd have expected the loyalty to cling. But amid tree peonies' black stalks and flaming buds, the money-colored apple shoots and rioting broom sedge, it was hard to feel shabby about having Cecilia around. She was part of the general bloom.

We were quieter and easier, but there was one topic on which she began to have more to say: Bud. At first I welcomed the change along with the rest. I hadn't wanted to hear about him, but I hadn't trusted her not talking about him either. She worked for him and with him. How could she have so little to say about him? Why should she be guarded when he himself was outspoken about having nothing to hide?

This nothing-to-hide was so much a part of Bud's style that I had had to distrust it, to suspect that his innocence was itself a deception. And to suspect him was, sooner or later, to suspect Cecilia. Her avoidance of the topic of Bud had come to seem like a dodge, and I was reassured when it stopped. Her talking about him might indicate some distance between them and bring us still closer. I thought it meant that I had become more to her than he was.

Even if I was right, I didn't enjoy these confirmations. They were a bore. I might have been able to summon interest in the kinds of things she had to tell me about Bud if my investment in his business had mattered more to me. But my stake was Mickey's too, which annulled whatever proprietary feeling I might have had about it. It was ours, hence not mine. And it was too little to worry about anyway. It wasn't real money, not to me.

What was I to say to Cecilia's reports on developments at

Bud's company? This was the kind of talking about Bud that she had gotten it into her head to do. By the fireside, I learned that a bus strike in Puerto that had been cutting into workers' hours was near to being settled; while I was listening to a ball game, that a proposed tariff on metals used in Bud's process would be defeated in the Aggregentine legislature; while we were dancing, how well the backup generator had worked during a power outage; as I was falling asleep at night I learned it again.

A motivated business partner would have appreciated these briefings, not only for the information they provided but also for the manner of their presentation, in which the overcoming of every adversity followed from its acknowledgment. Bud himself couldn't have been more upbeat. A motivated partner would have found it all gripping.

But I wasn't such a partner. It was an effort to keep my eyes from glazing over. I took whatever amusement was to be had from hearing her recite a publicist's lines. But this soon paled. When it had, all I could think was that she was robbing our moments of their charm.

We were in the car one evening, out for a bite. The access road was under construction. We waited for a temporary traffic light to change. The line of cars was so long that the signal might have been stuck. "There's great news," she said, turning the radio down.

She wouldn't be able to see me nod in the dark; more active signs of assent would be called for. "It turns out that Bud's cousin has a friend who's been hired to run a division at a big department store," she continued in a dramatic whisper. "Bud's already been in contact with him. They're talking about a big order, *gigantesco*. Isn't it exciting?"

"Wonderful."

We crawled a short way. A police car in the hazard lane passed with its lights flashing. A high tide of head- and tail-lights in the distance indicated a pileup on the highway entrance ramp, and possibly an accident. I turned the radio back up to find out.

We cleared the temporary light. Traffic toward the highway ramp was indeed blocked, but a newly constructed left lane was open. As I cut into it I realized that it was a turning lane and ended at the next crossing. But it was too late. The car behind me had already taken my place. "Do me a favor? Roll down the window and see if you can get someone to let us in."

One car after another passed us, and after a while she ducked her head in. "Sit back so I can see the side-view in case lightning strikes and someone stops for us."

"Why are you upset, Neil? You should be happy."

The clicking of the turn signal was getting to me. "What do you say we turn back? We could grab something in the village."

"It's still a secret by the way."

"What is?"

"The order Bud's setting up. You can tell your brother, but don't say anything to anybody else till it goes through."

"Don't say anything?" I turned off the radio, and after glancing into the side-view mirror looked at her profile. A car pulled up behind us. Its lights flashed on her earring and gathered in points on the hair above it. "To whom?"

"You know how talk can bubble over."

"And I may not be able to contain my ebullience."

She turned and looked at me as the driver behind flashed his brights. In those flashes, I saw her more clearly than I should have. The set of her eyes and nose, the heaviness of her eyelids, and the flanging of the nostrils from the septum had at that instant a crudeness about them, a stupidity. "Let me tell you something that you don't seem to have noticed: I'm not interested in the ins and outs of your business. It's nice that you have such enthusiasm for it. I'm happy for you. But do I have to hear every detail?"

She turned her head and looked out the window. I sped to the crossing and made a U-turn, shielding my eyes against the sea of opposing headlights. When I'd gotten clear of them she turned back. "It's not *my* business. It's yours. Yours and Bud's. You're partners."

"But I'm supposed to be a silent partner, silent and deaf. If I had had any idea when I agreed to go in with him—whenever that was—that I'd have to hear about it every day, do you think I'd have done it? I gave him a few sous. It isn't worth my time."

She put her hand on mine, which rested on the stick shift. When I changed gears she took it away. "But you need to know these things."

"Do I?"

"To know whether to put in a few more sous."

"That'd be a great way to get him out of my hair."

"But you and Bud are in it together. That's how he thinks about it. Did you know that he has a picture of you from the newspaper in his office?"

I tried to think what picture this could be, and remembered one that had appeared in the back pages of *Crain's*. In our flannel suits, I and the man shaking my hand across a desk couldn't have looked more ordinary, unless you happened to look closely at my mouth. I seemed to have chosen that moment to bite my lip. The incisor that was bared over it gave me a snaggletoothed look. Someone in the office had noticed it, and I caught wind of a remark to the effect that the crocodile had moved up from my shirt. "If it's the picture I'm thinking of,

I look like I'm about to bite someone's head off. He must have it for a joke."

"Maybe he has it because it's true to life."

We didn't get our supper that night. Though Cecilia wasn't generally particular, none of the places I took her to looked good to her. Eventually she said she wasn't hungry and we went home. The next day she went back to the city, and disappeared. The days in which I didn't hear from her stretched to weeks and months. I'd phoned her and buzzed at her door till the message was unmistakable.

The cause was bewildering. We'd established ourselves beyond the point at which a spat like the one we'd had should be fatal. On the scale of my wrangles with Joyce, it would hardly have registered. There'd been no shouting, no attempts to wound. It wasn't legitimate grounds for a break. And if it had been only a pretext for one, wouldn't I have noticed her looking for it? She'd given no hint. On the contrary, the impulse for our being together as much as we were had come from her.

Before the spring, I could have taken or left her. The end of it was the last time I'd seen her. And now, with summer stealing past, I was carrying a torch for her. My regret pushed everything else that happened to the background. Whether public or private, for better or worse, events were pretty much of a piece to me. And though I'd remind myself that regrets are costlier with age, I brooded nonetheless on what had gone wrong, which was itself another aspect of their going wrong.

The proceeds from the first lot of shares I sold back to the firm came in. Once I cashed in the remainder, I'd have a sum that only a plutocrat would sneeze at. The coming windfall might have given me some pleasure. But I hardly thought of it, and when I did it was only to reflect that I'd have traded it in for another chance with Cecilia. It was the kind of fantasy I was too old and sensible to have, and had all the same.

I went back inside and ran into Danny at the foot of the staircase. "You play well," I said.

"Oh. Well, thanks." He seemed unsure what I was talking about.

"I enjoyed your performance." I nodded at the piano behind me. "That's not an easy piece."

"Well, thanks," he repeated. The self-possession he'd arrived with had left him. Even his jacket seemed to hang less casually on his frame.

I showed him to the door. The ground lights caught the chalky clouds he kicked up in his march across the gravel.

They were dispersing when he came back a moment later. "I almost forgot," he said, handing me an envelope. "My father asked me to give this to you."

chapter ten

I couldn't have imagined myself hurrying to open an envelope from Bud. No message from him was likely to interest me much. It wasn't that he was lacking in goodwill; he overflowed with it. But his goodwill was the spontaneous kind. I couldn't see him setting it down and putting it in an envelope to send over with his son. He'd have been after something.

But that was then. Now *I* was after something: news of Cecilia. I'd have liked to know what she'd said to him about us, even to contact her, if only through him. Bud, who had always seemed to be the barrier to her, had become my connection.

I wasn't about to ask him about her, though. It would compromise my privacy that much further, and if he was hoping to deal with me on a quid pro quo basis, then it would be a capitulation to him. He thought of me as his partner, Cecilia had told me. He'd have welcomed this need of mine. He might have been waiting for it to arise. Cecilia's leaving me would have given it to him if I let it.

But I hadn't let it. I hadn't been given the chance. Without Cecilia around, I no longer knew what Bud was up to. Evidently, he was still scrambling. Whenever that summer I happened to notice, he was gone. Driving past or getting up from my desk on the third floor and looking out the window, I might see Charlie pushing the mower or Irene working in the flower beds. I'd see the rest of the Youngers, but not Bud. From here or there, I'd imagine I heard him coming. Because he seemed to feel comfortable dropping by whenever it suited him, it wasn't the wildest mistake, or wouldn't have been if made once or twice. I made it more often than that, however—too often not to see that at the same time that I was steering clear of him, I was also looking for him, hoping for a chance to find out what he could tell me.

The contents of Bud's envelope were less than I'd hoped but better than I'd feared. Our county executive was running for congress and Bud and Irene were hosting a fund-raiser for him. The personal touch Bud added to the invitation showed his customary tact. "NO EX WIVES THIS TIME, NEIL," he wrote, "NOT YOURS, ANYWAY! SEE YOU THERE."

The assurance of my ex-wife's absence and my liking for the candidate weren't enough to make me put myself on display. I had something on for that night anyway, a club banquet. I sent my regrets along with a contribution. I did feel a scruple or two about the possibility of Cecilia's being there. I was also sorry for my inhospitableness to Irene. Bud popped in whenever he thought of it, but Irene had always kept her distance. I'd have liked her to take on a bit of his forwardness. It'd have been better all around.

I ended up sending regrets to the banquet committee as well. My colleagues were making my exit as difficult as possible. Though I'd refused to take on as many of the assignments they threw at me as I could, there were a few that I couldn't turn down, a visit with a Swiss client's headquarters in Zurich among them. I was scheduled to get back an hour beforehand and wouldn't feel like carting myself off to another obligation.

I spent three short days in Zurich. There was little time between meetings to heed the regular procession of men in Tyrollean hats, women walking small dogs in sweaters, green shuttered trams that were almost as quiet as the swans listing in the canals' slow currents. But it is impossible when traveling so far so quickly just to pass through. The part of the mind that adjusts to new surroundings cannot immediately readjust.

A distinguished-looking man of about sixty began talking to me one morning in the hotel elevator. His hair had thinned on top and was brushed back tightly along the sides, where it was not quite long enough to curl. His beard was pointy, his serge jacket had brass buttons, his talk was mundane: Was I enjoying my stay? Had I been here before? How did I find the service? I assumed he was connected with the hotel management. I replied that everything was satisfactory. He was glad to hear it, he said. It was evident that he had the privilege of addressing a man of parts. To such a man he owed nothing less than the truth. The truth, he was bound to confide, was that complaints at the hotel were not the rarity they'd once been. But he was certain that this confidence would not by itself suffice to lead such a man as I to the conclusion that the service was wanting. Such a man would judge for himself. He had personally investigated the complaints he referred to and concluded that they were in nearly every instance unfounded. There had recently begun to appear at the hotel a type of guest who looked for opportunities for complaint as a means of establishing his credentials of worldliness and discernment. Of course, the phenomenon wasn't limited to the hotel's guests. At this moment a broad class of men had achieved a level of comfort unprecedented in the history of the species. Even the patricians of Rome were not so fully indulged; Lucullus himself had had to contend on a daily basis with greater hardship. But he could assure me that for their intolerance of even the slightest discomfort the current age's pampered class would reap a bitter harvest, one by one.

My room was on an upper floor of the building, a typical continental grand hotel of about twenty stories. While he talked, the man kept making the elevator stop, though no one got in and he didn't appear to have any intention of getting out. As soon as the door would open on one floor he would push the button for the floor below. If you don't mind, I interrupted him. We were on fifteen at the time. His finger hovered over the button for fourteen. You can finish testing the elevator once I'm out of it, I added. I've got somewhere to be. Oh you have, have you? he said. I was in this elevator before you were. I can stop whenever I want. It's my prerogative. I don't know what that's got to do with anything, I said. Aha, he said, a glint coming into his eye, I see you're one of them. You're not required to do anything to get where you're going. You don't have to lift a finger. All you have to do is stand and wait. But even that's too much for you. He punched every button down to the lobby and hopped out at the next floor. I'll see you below, he said. Don't forget to apprise the manager of your displeasure.

On my way out of the city, the cab to the airport was held up at a crowded junction. The driver happened to lower his window while an organ grinder on the corner was playing one of those Alpine folk melodies that in the shops of my boyhood were inescapable at Christmastime: *Min Vater isch en Appenzeller,* I think it was. We weren't stopped there for more than a minute, but in that life-size music box of a city, it was a minute too long. The tune stuck in my head. It and that music-box feeling for which it was the theme were with me on takeoff and touchdown.

At home, I responded to the news that the heating-oil delivery man had taken a look at Frances and refused to get out of his truck and that his counterpart at the lumberyard had stacked a cord of wood against the wrong wall in the garage by trying to nap. But after lying in a sleepless trance for what had seemed no more than a few minutes, I bolted upright. In one of those jet-lagged moments in which the obvious and the strange—the near at hand and far away—change places, the possibility of Cecilia's being at Bud's party struck me anew. I was tired of thinking about her. I'd see her if I could, if only to begin putting her out of my mind.

When I got up, I discovered that hours had passed. It was nearly ten. I dressed quickly, with the sense that everything that was right in front of me was as distant as Zurich. Wherever I might drag my body, the better part of my mind was behind in a world I had entered just long enough to be held over in it.

The night was dismal. The rain froze where it landed, and the frost kept the burrs in the weeds from catching in my coat. But it wasn't so much the rain and cold that made the night dismal. It was the low sky and the clammy wind blowing in from the water. As I made my way up the front walk, a shutter knocked against the bricks beside an upstairs window; freezing raindrops gleamed from a dangling hook and an empty eyelet on its corner.

"Hey, get in here! What are you, trying ta remember the password? Does this look like a speakeasy?" I was peering through the viewer in the front door when it flew open. The baboon who'd stained my sport jacket at the first party was on the other side. He whisked me in and a warm draft hit me, an interior wind created by the guests' collective breath. "It's him, the feisty neighbor! What took you so long, milord, trouble getting down from your curricle?" He raised his hand to his mouth. "Sir Norwich Beaufort Chalfont-Godspeed IV!" he trumpeted. "Where'd you park your batman? I'll send the coach boy around presently." He turned to the man beside him, who had a long strand of hair hanging to the side, like an orchestra conductor. "You don't want ta cross this guy. He runs hot under the collar. Almost walloped me last time." He turned back my way. "Hey, Champ, who're you gonna knock out tonight? See?" he said to the other man. "He's getting sore already." He put his arm around me as I was wiping my feet. I kicked an umbrella stand trying to create space between us.

"Look who's here!" he shouted. Quite a few of the faces that turned looked familiar, more than they should have considering how long it had been since I'd last seen them. For a moment I imagined that this was no fund-raiser but a costume party and they had come as their old selves—hostages to the celebration of their friend's upward mobility even while their feast exhausted his stores—and been here all this time.

Even Bud's son Charlie, taking my coat in the same way he had before, seemed to expect me. "You're awful late," he said. He was taller now; he'd grown at that frantic boy's pace the sight of which makes anyone, however fast he lives, reflect that time is slipping away. Charlie's voice was changing. Stray whiskers appeared on his chin like dust on polished furniture.

"'Awfully,' you mean."

"Yeah. You're the only man with a blue raincoat."

"I did it on purpose. Anyone who tries to make off with it will look conspicuous."

Again my attempts to kid him fell flat. "Oh, no one'll do that." He looked at me askance. "Who'd want a blue raincoat?"

"Exactly."

He stepped onto the landing. "The coats are in Danny's room. Danny's old room. It's mine now."

"Congratulations," I mumbled after him.

My eyes lit on Irene at the other end of the hallway. Guests surrounded her, but I could see the light in her hair and the shimmer of beads on the straps of her dress.

The living-room furniture had been pushed to the sides the way it would have been at a fraternity mixer. I worked my way into the back of a sprawling line for drinks.

"I know you," the man ahead of me said. He was chomping on a celery stick with cheese smeared in the groove. A lampshade's bright round shadow on the ceiling directly overhead gave him a high halo.

"You don't sound so sure of it," I answered, but I remembered him from the last party. His eyes drooped and his mustache wilted and his mouth frowned, and all the downward pressure seemed to fall on his bow tie, which sagged at the corners. He played his manner off against it; there was a hangdog congeniality about him. "You're, you're, don't tell me, your name starts with a *W*, right? I can see it." He rattled off a series of names beginning with *W*. "I know. It's Wolf," he added. "Right? No? All right. Don't tell me."

"Wolf's close enough. It's Fox."

"I said not to tell me. You didn't tell me, did you? It's not Fox. You're pulling my leg. It's something else . . . Frelinghuysen! Am I right?"

I gave him my name again. He tried to stop his ears but was too slow, and when he said "I'm Isadore," he spoke dismissively, drowning the last syllable in a sigh. In failing to remember my name, he seemed to have lost his esteem for his own.

We inched toward the bar. It was my turn to stand beneath the halo. "You were calling yourself Izzy when we met before."

"I was answering to it anyway."

"Where's the guest of honor?"

"Long gone. He left this guy behind." He pointed out a young man with rolled-up sleeves, a loosened necktie, a "Free Huey" button on his vest, eyeglass frames propped on bushy hair.

"Did the candidate speak?"

"It was lofty. The nation at a crossroads, Southeast Asia, the Chicago Seven, civil rights—you'd have thought he was running for president."

Izzy peeked over his shoulder at the entrance. "If you're looking for your friend," I said, "he's by the door."

"My friend?"

"The guy with us when we met before."

"I met quite a few people."

"You were standing with a skinny guy with big ears. Only an hors d'oeuvre could keep him quiet."

The man I was talking about came into partial view. Not much of him was visible to us, a section of the back of his head and the lobe of one of those big ears. I pointed that way. "He's over there. Hector, isn't it?"

Izzy shrugged. A man tried to cut between him and the bar. I tapped the man's shoulder, and when he turned I saw that it was my orthopedist. "Just checking your reflexes," he said, and we greeted each other and chatted while he poured our drinks. There was no bartender—unlike the last party, this had no service—and the orthopedist punished the whisky in his absence, holding the bottle at the base and letting it tip of its own weight until the liquor stopped spilling.

"Easy on mine. I'm just off a long flight," I said somewhat after the fact.

"So much the better." He handed me my glass. "A couple of these and you're anybody's."

I cleared away from the bar and turned back to Izzy. "Don't even mention that person to me," he said, picking up the subject he'd avoided. "That crook, I mean." Vengefulness pinched his expression, tensed its droopiness without lifting it. "He should be in jail. But where is he? Out on the town, trolling for the next rube."

The orthopedist lingered on the fringe. He was tall enough to hover discreetly. "Stole your money?" he asked.

"Of course he stole my money. A condo development deal. He was the trustee. Risk free, he said, an ideal shelter. In fact I think it was here he got me interested." He looked around for an ashtray, then emptied his glass and tipped his ash into it. "People are so disappointing. There's nothing they won't do for money. Absolutely nothing. Only children can have real friendships anymore."

I sipped my drink, seeking something in it: a return of a sense of dimension, a firming of the ground beneath my feet.

"I'll get him sometime," Izzy said.

"And how'll you get him?" I asked.

The orthopedist wandered off. "How? Oh, I don't know." Izzy gazed in his enemy's direction. I thought I felt a pair of eyes on me and glanced up. A curly haired redhead with sine-curve eyelashes and a brunette with a wooden-bead necklace were standing together. If they'd been looking at me, they weren't any longer. Each had her attractions, but neither was like Cecilia. I took a look around the room and saw how little anyone had in common with her. This wasn't her world. I was kidding myself if I expected to see her.

"By powder," Izzy said. He raised an imaginary pistol. "That's how I'll get him. Bang, bang."

A man came up from behind and, his back to me, put a hand on Izzy's shoulder. "I didn't realize you were armed," he said, his shoulders shaking beneath his white jacket and broad parti-colored collar, his thin hair shagging down the back of his neck. He looked like a barker or a balloon-twister.

"The times demand it," I heard Izzy say. I missed most of what followed between them. My eyes strayed to Bud at the far end of the room. The contrast between his suntan and the light checks of his jacket made him stand out, not only from everyone else but from the piano he was leaning against and the wall behind him. His image looked superimposed on its background.

I started toward him, thinking I'd ask him straight out about Cecilia, but changed my mind. There were more people between us than I cared to fight my way through, and Alan, an upstart junior partner from my firm, was one of them.

Izzy looked where I was looking. The man he'd been speaking to had fallen in with a woman in a vinyl jacket. His back was still to me. "Him too," Izzy said.

"Who? Him?"

"I hear Bud's been taken in. Swimming with the sharks." He took a bite of celery and laid his hand on the other man's shoulder. "He was just telling me about it. I don't know if you're acquainted."

The man turned. Thick eyebrows above wire-rimmed glasses and thicker sideburns framed his eyes and cheeks like smoke falling back on a smokestack. It was Garson, who had left the meeting with Mickey and me that Bud had brought him to. "We're acquainted," I said.

"Keep him covered," Garson said, taking a step back and

making his own imaginary pistol. Now there were two guns pointing at me.

The redhead I thought had been looking at me a moment earlier crossed the firing line. "Uh oh. Looks like I've walked in on a stickup. You'll have to shoot me to get to him," she said over her shoulder.

"That's very noble," Izzy said, his eyes darting over her buxom prow. "That's some bodyguard you've got," he said to me.

"I really must thank you, Neil," the redhead said. "I hadn't realized how close it was in here until I tried to pick up that glove myself. And for every person, two feet! When I bent down, shoe-polish fumes rushed up at me and the blood swam in my head. I thought I'd better stand up quick. It was so nice of you."

Before I could tell her that she had the wrong man, she spirited our glasses to the bar. A couple of other guests came along and the conversation moved on. I thought I'd caught a glimpse of Cecilia. I realized my mistake and my empty-handedness began to bother me. I'd fade if I didn't keep going. I looked around for the redhead and for the drink I'd expected her to bring back.

There were no clean glasses left at the bar. The man who always seemed to be on my train into town no matter which one I took was also trying to find a glass. His wife had big green eyes and a winning air that made me abandon the inference of his misery I'd drawn from his desolated look and inability to lose himself in a newspaper—assuming she *was* his wife.

He picked up a couple of the dirty glasses. "We could rinse them with gin," he said. "That's the practical solution."

"Why don't we look for some others?" she said.

I followed them toward the kitchen without intending to

go so far. I'd take a quick look around for Cecilia and go home to bed. I hadn't exactly searched high and low.

The redhead approached from the side, bearing two well-filled glasses aloft, out of harm's way. I stopped him and pointed at her. "One of those is mine," I added. "Special delivery."

"See you on the morning train."

"Here you are."

"Here I am? I didn't realize that I was the one who'd disappeared."

"You wouldn't believe what I went through to get this." She handed me the glass in triumph and awaited my approval. She'd been holding it for a while—the ice was melting and the side was fogged with the imprint of her palm. But the liquor looked dark. I took a drink. It was coarse and syrupy and made me shudder.

"What's the matter? Don't you like it?"

"It caught me by surprise."

"I can get you something else if you'd like."

"That's all right."

"I thought it was what you asked for."

"I don't remember that I asked for anything."

Melancholy descended on her. The lengths she'd gone to for me seemed in her mind to have created a contract between us. She'd brought me a drink and I was to drink it.

And so I did, quietly. To speak was now beside the point. To encourage me she smiled at my every sip, like a mother watching a child eat his supper. When I'd belted back the last of it she laughed. This laughter was odd, a sort of hissing that filled the silence we'd lapsed into while the party buzzed and clattered around us.

With the last drink I became aware of an exhilaration rising against my fatigue, flowing into it like a cold downdraft. My ears hummed. I was coming around, happily. I was already too old not to take accesses of vitality as they came.

Izzy stopped in passing. "Hey, what'd she say to you?" he asked me.

"Who?"

"Corky. That woman you were talking to." He pointed out the redhead.

"Her? She's got me confused with someone else."

"I'm sure Corky knows who you are."

"She thinks I'm someone who picked up a glove she dropped."

"But you are! She and her husband just split." He winked at me, and moved on.

"Everything all right in *die Schweiz?*" Alan clapped me on the shoulder, a cufflink peeking from his jacket sleeve, his Friar Tuck belly pressing against his tattersall shirt and peg-legged pants. "You know I covered for you while you were gone. That Edmonds—talk about a prickly client! But this isn't the place, is it? I'll brief you. Let's have lunch one day next week."

I'd as soon have lunched with an opossum. We both knew that there was no need for him to brief me. The meeting with Edmonds was discretionary, a slot we routinely left open in deference to the size of the account in case something were to come up. But nothing had come up. The only reason for Alan to have held the meeting was that he had his eye on the account, and if Edmonds was difficult, it was probably from not liking to have his bill padded. What Alan meant by saying that he'd covered for me was that he was on the way up and I was on the way out. That's what he wanted to remind me of.

Bud hustled past. He stopped when he saw us, changed his grip on an ice bucket, and stepped squarely on my toe.

I jumped back, nearly bumping Corky, who was hovering on the fringe. "Sorry, Neil!" Bud said.

"That's all right."

"It's your own fault, you know, for crossing me up. You're not supposed to be here. It's no wonder I tried to walk right through you." He shook my hand and turned to Alan. "Neil had the consideration to let me know weeks ago that he wasn't going to be able to make it here tonight. But that's Neil. He's awfully decisive for a man who can be counted on to change his mind. I should've known I'd be seeing him."

"Those are some feet he's got," Alan said. "What size are they—thirteen, fourteen? They must get stepped on all the time."

"Not really."

Corky reached past Bud without looking at him, took my empty glass from my hand, and headed off.

"Scotch!" I called after her. "Not bourbon!"

"That reminds me," Bud said, holding up the ice bucket. "I'd better go fill this. Thirsty crowd. See that guy pouting by the piano? He might be happier if he had some ice. Now that you're here, Neil, don't disappear on me. Great matters are at hand."

"They may have to wait. I don't know that I'll last here much longer. I'm just off a long flight."

Bud rested his hand on my shoulder and turned to Alan. "There's another thing about this man. He anticipates fatigue. He's never actually tired. He doesn't let things get to that point. Have you ever known him to yawn?" A jewel in the middle of a ceramic tile on a cabinet caught my notice—a rooster's eye. The rooster stood on one leg, surrounded by a cornucopia, maybe to signify that he'd soon be someone's dinner; the berries were blood-colored. "Tell you what, Neil. Stan's going to knock out a few tunes at the piano. We cleared space in case people want to dance. I should be able to get away then. I'll meet you at the bottom of the stairs when he sits down, and we'll go up and hold our little conclave. It shouldn't be long."

"It's nearly six in the morning for me." To make my point I flashed my watch at him. "I haven't reset it yet."

Bud took hold of my wrist and looked at my watch. "You don't want to reset it. It's perfect. The dial says 'Switzerland' and you've got the time there." His grip tightened a notch. "What we have to discuss can't wait."

It was only a matter of time before I'd hit the wall. I'd be talking in my sleep. "Look," I said, "I'll stick around if I can, but I ought to have been in bed a long time ago. I'm only here because—"

"Neil, you made it after all," Irene said, stopping between Bud and me. "I've been waiting for a chance to say hello ever since you came in. I kept being waylaid. I didn't think I knew so many people."

"That's the beauty and the bane of being at your own party," Alan said.

"True," she replied and turned to engage me, leaving Alan and Bud to themselves.

Our chat, Irene's and mine, was desultory, pleasant, neighborly. Its predictability allowed us to think of other things. It allowed me to think of them, at least. I'd forgotten how much of herself Irene kept hidden beneath the baggy blouses and sweaters she went around in. The fitted velveteen cocktail dress she now wore reminded me. It revealed not only abundance but delicacy in the contour of her shoulder and the line of her collarbone, which ran under the beaded strap of her dress. It seemed to cry out for tracing your fingertips along. Against these lines and lights, the green of her eyes and the pink of her cheeks, and even that beauty mark like a fractured constellation of the bone beneath it, made you feel that she had no special claim on her own attractiveness, that if she was modest she was also generous.

Corky came back with my drink, three fingers of scotch over a single ice cube. She hovered beside Irene and me again, making us self-conscious.

I lit a cigarette that Irene began to share with me. I offered her one of her own. She puffed the more deeply on mine and said that she didn't smoke. This was plain from her unpracticed manner. But as she leaned toward me to take the cigarette and bowed her arm to smoke it, I caught her scent, a sweet musk of perfume and perspiration.

"It makes sense for him to diversify," I heard Alan say to Bud. "He can't hide a chunk of change like that under the mattress."

"Bud," Irene said, with a nod toward the kitchen. "I could use a hand in there."

"On my way," Bud said and shook the empty ice bucket. "Anyone seen Stan?" He looked at me. "Alan and I have been talking about Revtex."

"I was complimenting him on his choice of backers." Alan's glance took in all of us—Irene, Corky, and me. He had assumed the testimonial manner he'd have picked up at business dinners. "Neil's leaving our firm, but I wouldn't say he'll be out in the cold. The writing on the checks we'll be cutting him will have to be cramped to fit all the zeros, from what I hear. Those double-digit returns pile up over twenty-five years."

"Is it any of your business?" I said.

The point of his chin retreated into his collar. "Take it easy, Neil. I was just ribbing you."

Corky, who seemed to think I needed steadying and that she was the one to do it, laid a hand on the back of my shoulder.

"He made out," the man behind her said. "Since when is that something to be ashamed of?"

"That's not Neil's style," Irene said.

"He doesn't flaunt it," Bud said. "He doesn't go out of his way to hide it either. He is what he is."

I swallowed some scotch and glanced over my shoulder, at Corky, who took her hand off me, and at the man who'd come up behind her. I knew him by his unruly eyebrows. He'd cornered me while I was picking up my coat at the end of the last party. He was in better shape now. Seeing me looking him over, he held up his glass and said, "I'm on this stuff tonight."

"Club soda?"

"Voilà."

"Catch up with you in a few minutes," Bud said as he and Irene moved off. Alan had already stolen away.

The man behind Corky still held his glass aloft. "Good for you," I told him.

"Good for me? You're the one whose garden's growing. I'd drink to you, but you know what they say."

"What's that?"

"That only a cuckold toasts with water."

"I'll have to remember that," I said, and when the man lowered his glass and said, "Hello, Red!" to Corky in a put-on voice, I left them. I was halfway up the stairs before I realized that it was Cary Grant he was imitating.

There were a few guests milling about in the coatroom—Danny's room. Charlie hadn't finished putting his stamp on it. Posters of professional athletes covered one of the walls. The rest were bare, except for a framed diploma and a small autographed still of a classical pianist. As before, the coats were piled on the bed. And also as before, Charlie had fallen asleep on the coats. But being bigger now, and longer, he covered more of them and slept more heavily.

The effort to rouse him was timid. A woman patted his hand, while the man beside her said, "Wake up, son" in a voice that would have been too quiet for conversation downstairs.

Charlie rolled over and started to snore.

"Wake up, son," the man said, gently shaking him.

The boy sat up in a daze.

"Look at that," said the woman. "He was faking. I'll bet he was awake the whole time." She nudged him out of the way, sifted through the coats, and found her own and her husband's.

Charlie had taken special care of mine. It was hanging squarely from the rails of a wooden valet beside a television with the picture on but the sound off. The paint was chipping from a window sash behind it; mist licked the storm glass.

I saw the coat, and stared. It was an everyday but pathetic effigy, an emblem of my disappointment that night and in the months leading to it.

"So, is this your secret?" a woman in the doorway asked me while I was putting on my coat and draining my glass. The room was too dim for me to make her out at first and, though there was no one else she could have been talking to, I didn't answer. I didn't feel like talking anymore. I was wearing down—the leitmotif of my jet lag, the tune of *Min Vater isch en Appenzeller,* had come back into my head. I'd already imagined myself down the stairs and out the door.

It was Corky. I told her hello and good-bye.

Instead of getting out of my way, she got in it more fully, and when I asked to be excused, tried to push me back into the bedroom.

I held my ground. "I'm all in," I said. "See you next time."

I tried to push past her again. She tightened her grip on my arm.

"Are you out of your mind or just very pushy?"

The cuneiform slashes of Corky's eyes widened. "You flash your brights on certain women—our hostess, for instance—and the rest of us are caught in the glare."

I was backed against a column facing the door where the bedroom gave onto a walk-in closet, yet she was leaning away from me as though I was the one bearing down on her. "You've got me confused with someone else, I'm afraid—you did earlier, you know. I haven't had any lights to flash all night, let alone high beams."

"I have a message for you," she said. "It's from Cecilia Bernal. You were seeing a lot of each other for a while."

I turned and faced her. She was scratching one of her ankles with the other, roughing up the yarns of her stockings.

"So?"

"I was kind of confirming that. It's not the message."

"I didn't think it was."

She glanced at the far corner of the room. "The television's on—I hadn't noticed."

I crossed the room to shut it off.

"She says to tell you that you were very special to her and that she thinks of you often."

I twisted the knob and watched the image vanish into the screen's obsidian void. "That's it?" I asked her. "That's all?" She nodded that it was. "What the hell does that mean?" I felt like shaking her. "Why didn't you tell me sooner?"

"I didn't have a chance."

"It's one sentence. How much of a chance do you need? We've been together for the better part of the last two hours."

"There were always people around. It's a funny message. At least, I felt funny about it. It's not exactly . . . I thought you might prefer to hear it in private. If she was important to you."

I saw why she'd been eager to get my drinks. They were for washing down her message. "And where is it that she thinks of me often from? Where is she, Uruguay?"

"I don't know. The letter—she didn't say much about herself except for what she asked me to tell you. There's a return address, but I think it's in Pennsylvania. I barely glanced at it. It could say Paraguay, I guess. I doubt it, though. I'd have noticed the foreign stamps. Anyway, I've got the envelope. I can give you the address if you want to call me."

Two men came in one after another for their coats. The first nodded and looked away. The second seemed not to see us at all. "I thought he was pretty sharp," he said to the first man.

Corky didn't have much more to tell me. The telephone number she gave me ended in zeros and was followed by a room number. "You're in a hotel?" I asked her, twice. She missed it the first time. Stan was going heavy on the sustenato.

He'd lightened up by the time we were back downstairs. When I'd asked again, she cast a wide glance, murmured, "That's another story," and gave me a moistly ardent goodnight kiss. A scent of wax and rose petals hung about me after I'd wiped off her lipstick.

This scent was like a materialization of the cloud I'd been under since she'd passed along Cecilia's message. The calm I'd received it with left me as it sunk in; gratitude for any message yielded to a sense of this message's uselessness. Cecilia said she thought of me often: how often would she have had to think of me for her to recognize that she owed me an explanation? She'd kept her disappearance mysterious, but wasn't this mystery gratuitous now, and cruel? I could think of plenty of practical reasons for her to break with me. I'd have liked to know only which had swayed her.

Head down, hands clutching my gloves in my coat pockets,

I was making for the front door when I heard a voice behind me exclaim "There he is!"—Bud's voice.

Though I didn't see him right away, I felt him coming, and as I waited for him to close in, I looked back over the party like a man awaiting capture. Regret for my liberty distorted my vision before I'd lost it. In imagination, I had already gone out and headed home, seen the clouds above the layers of darkness, shadow spilling into shadow—verdigris, umber, coal—without realizing what I'd been thinking of until, surveying the scene in the living room, I found in the drift of cigarette smoke, reflection on the coffee table's glass top, and the sway of a dancing couple the light and motion of the clouds and the salt pond and the trees that I'd seen myself walking beneath and past. I'd brought the outside in. It took only the fall of a hand on my shoulder to put it back out again, to remind me that my wild realm was settled and subdivided. The hand fell on my shoulder, and as I turned around my own hands in my pockets squeezed the pigskin of my gloves like deflated footballs.

"There you are," Bud said. His congenial look—hooked mouth, twinkling eyes, arched brow—could have been a look askance, with a flash of understanding that you'd only confirm by refusing to grant. The corners of his handkerchief peeked from his breast pocket, where they might have mingled with his motives.

"Now, listen—"

"I know, Neil, I know. You were on your way out. I'll keep it short." He started to steer me toward the stairs, but when I saw a crowd on the landing I let him lead me—maybe even led him myself—toward the back of the house, through a swinging door into the dining room.

It was quiet. You could no longer hear the piano well enough to follow the tune. There was dried statice in a basket between candlesticks on the table, a figurine on the sideboard, a tapestry on the wall behind it, and house plants in a window bay. Some of these plants climbed up the arms of the wrought-iron stand that held them. Others hung to the floor.

Bud pulled a chair away from the table for me, splashed some brandy into snifters he'd taken from a cabinet in the corner, lit the candles, which were short with long wicks, and a cigarette. All this to-ing and fro-ing made his curl dangle over his forehead however he brushed it back, until he took the seat opposite mine, pulling the chair back from the table and crossing his legs.

The candlelight bathed only the upper portion of his face and not even all of this; but wherever it shone, his tanned skin glowed. "Instant ambiance," he said.

"What happened to Cecilia?"

"Cecilia? Did you think you'd see her here?"

"I heard she was out of town."

"Let's not go into that now. I know you're eager to turn in, and I haven't got much time myself. I can't desert the party for long. The proposition I have to put to you is pretty simple. You'll probably tell me to go ahead without batting an eye. But I'll need to act quickly. I'd better run it by you now."

"I'd like to know what she's doing out of town."

"I'd appreciate it if you'd let me come to the point."

"Does she still work for you?"

"She's left the company."

"I see." I tried to imagine her in an unknown part of a state that was probably bigger than the unknown country on the unknown continent where I'd tried so many times to imagine her. "Was it her choice?"

"I had to let her go."

"When?"

"A few months ago."

It'd have been about the time she had disappeared. Could she have been too embarrassed about losing her job to tell me? Then a darker thought—of a piece with the candlelight and climbing plants—crossed my mind. "For what reason?"

"I was about to tell you that things have been getting a bit tighter, Neil."

"I understand. You've had to prune nonessential staff."

"Sure, if you want to put it like that." The swinging door opened halfway. I couldn't see the woman behind it who had come to say good night. Bud told her to wait, that he'd see her out in a minute. When she'd shut the door, he said, "We've got a cash-flow problem. It's temporary. No, less than that—momentary."

"There was a while when you seemed to rely on her to do quite a few things."

"Hear me out, would you please?"

"Though I must say, when she came back last spring she didn't seem all that busy. Didn't she fulfill her responsibilities here?"

He took a slow sip from the snifter, holding it to his mouth like an oxygen mask. The candlelight pooled around the cognac and was reflected in a band onto his eyes, which looked at and past me, from a sea of fact to the great headland of an idea.

He tipped his ash on an hors d'oeuvres plate with olive pits on it, sat back, and said, "You'd know as well as I."

I lit a cigarette and let this sink in. Of course, I said to myself. But to Bud I said nothing. His tolerance for my silence was even less than usual. He was in a hurry after all: anxiety to dispense with the topic had led him to tell me what he had kept to himself all along. "Now come on, Neil. Don't act surprised. It was an open secret, more or less. . . ." His voice trailed off.

"You don't say," I said despite myself. "And what makes you think so?"

"Well, Mickey, for one thing. He said—what did he say?— that 'you're no stranger to that category of diversion.' Or something along those lines."

"Mickey? He had a hand in this?"

"You're making it sound like some sort of conspiracy. It wasn't that way. Sure, Cecilia might have had encouragement at first, but she came to really like you."

"She took off as soon as you stopped servicing my account with her. Maybe you'll tell me that that's a sign of affection."

"Did she split as fast as all that? I wouldn't be so sure I had anything to do with her timing. It isn't as if you were stuck on her. That wasn't the impression she got. She wasn't even sure you thought her worth the trouble."

"What about Mickey? Did he—"

"He thought it was a good idea to have someone on the payroll with Cecilia's versatility. Versatile, that was a word he'd use about her. Magnetic was another. He was sure that once we'd ramped up production and raised our profile, she'd be a real magnet."

"And put me back in the hunt in the meantime. What versatility!" I'd risen halfway from my chair, whether to reach across the table and grab him by the throat or just to walk out I didn't know.

"Take it easy, Neil. You don't understand." He flashed a grin meant, I suppose, to reassure me. It seemed to work. When he waved me back into my chair, I obeyed. "Everyone could see you were taking your breakup awfully hard. I was doing you a good turn—God knows you've done them for me. But I wasn't going to toot my own horn. I didn't think I needed to. You're not the kind who won't see what's in front of him."

He splashed some more brandy into my glass. I'd propped an elbow on the table and was peeling wax from the base of a candlestick. The sound of slammed car doors, then of querulous voices, reached us from outside. "I'm just glad I can see a way out of this squeeze," he continued. "It requires a small stopgap. Small and short-term. A few weeks' turnaround." He pointed at the bay windows. "What a house this is! I love how the night presses in over there, the way it comes right up to the glass. It can't always get so close, you know. Most places I've lived it wouldn't come past the edge of the sidewalk."

For how much longer would I have listened to that salesman's blend of insinuated appeal and bluff familiar aside? To be decisive was apparently beyond me. The night was too far along; I was too far along. I sipped my cognac and peered through the bowl of the glass, imagining the distortion to be corrective.

The door swung back and Irene came in. "There you are," she said to Bud. "There's a commotion outside."

"Oh?"

"People are upset."

"People are always upset. Neil and I are working a few things out."

"Nate's up in arms—there might have been an accident. You need to go out there."

"I'll be right back," he said to me, springing up and grasping my elbow. "Why not treat the old girl to a dance, Neil? It's the least you can do."

He whispered to Irene on the way out.

I picked at the molten wax on the candlesticks and stared at the climbing plants. I may have strung a few thoughts together about what I'd just heard, might have tried to mull it over. But if I did I hardly knew what those thoughts were. Jet lag, drink, the overlay in my head of the Swiss folk tune on the strains from the piano in the living room: it all combined to stupefy me. I might have known I wasn't thinking straight, but I wasn't looking forward to waking to a new day when I would be.

"Are you all right, Neil?"

I'd forgotten Irene was there. Maybe I'd expected her to follow Bud out. I jumped to my feet. "Me? Why, sure. Never better."

"Sorry to interrupt you. I'm sure Bud will be right back."

She'd stepped away from the door and leaned on the sideboard. I polished off my cognac and went over to her. "Thanks for having me. I'm glad I was able to come. It was a great party."

"This party? You're too kind. We threw it together for John Nickelson. If I had known how busy Bud would be, I'd never have done it. Not that I did much of anything. I hope you had dinner beforehand."

I was caught up in the play of the candlelight in her eyes. When she tilted her head back, I realized I was standing too close to her and backed off. "I'd be happy to fix you something if you're hungry," she said.

"Thanks, but I'm okay."

We waited there. She might have been searching for something else to say. I myself wasn't bothering. Just to be near her was exhilarating and, in the half-light that let me take her in more or less discreetly, intimate. Her scent quickened all the corners of my brain that the long day had dulled.

A couple came in to say good night to her. She led them to the door and I followed. "I'll catch up to Bud on the way out," I said, lowering my lips to her ear to make myself heard over the piano. The party had thinned out but under lowered lights Stan was still going strong.

Garson came up behind Irene and put his arm around her waist to lead her into the living room for a dance.

She resisted. "You're a moment too late," she told him. "Neil beat you to it."

He retreated without looking at me.

I tossed my coat over a wing chair pushed with the rest of the living-room furniture along a far wall. "I hope you don't mind," she said.

"It's my pleasure. Besides, you've given me a taste of revenge. I had a run-in with that guy."

"Really? I'd thought that harmony reigned here. We're all behind the same candidate."

"You didn't want to dance with him."

"It wasn't that. I saw my chance to dance with you. To hear Bud tell it, you're a master. I won't be able to keep up with you, but I'll do my best. I'm in your hands."

Roughly half a dozen couples danced beside the piano, the women—Corky among them—holding themselves close to the men in a throwback to halcyon days. To keep clear of a pair of freeform dancers who were hopping around with their glasses in their hands, I staked out a territory apart from the rest, away from the piano and the light of a lamp on a hi-fi console in a corner.

If Irene wasn't the dancer that Cecilia was, she had her charms. Her manner was more complementary. She'd meant it when she said she was in my hands. Though she held me as close as the other women held their partners, she was languorous, even abstracted. After the stress of the party, which was winding down, this dance gave her a chance to relax, to float. The current we drifted on was more than musical. It seemed to flow from the field of paisley on the rug at our feet, the light in the trees I saw out the windows, the shadows we danced through. And from her: from the curve of the small of her back, the pivot of her waist, the swell of her breasts, the curl of her eyelashes.

I dipped her. It caught her by surprise. My knee pressed the inside of her thigh, and her breath caught. The gasp was faint but unmistakable. I looked at her, but she didn't look back. "You're making this difficult," she said.

"And you're making it easy." I meant that she was making it easy by her dancing. But my lips happened to brush her earlobe in the reply, and I lingered there to catch the scent from the cleft of her shoulder. "I wish you'd drop by sometime," I added.

"Let's move over," she said, and led us back among the other dancers.

The move rattled me. I hadn't meant to be forward. But isn't this how Bud would have had it? What was his treatment of me if not a series of liberties? He'd wanted me to loosen up, and when I had, his wife had seen me as a ballroom lothario. She wouldn't be alone—others would see it this way too. While Stan was breaking into "Little White Lies" from "You'll Never Know," I caught them grinning at me.

We ought to have stopped; our bubble had burst. Irene seemed to keep dancing only to be a good sport. Distrust had made her rigid, and, to make matters worse, the new tempo was too fast for her. She couldn't keep up. By the second chorus we were lost. We'd been floating; now we pitched and yawed. Other couples got in our way, and we got in theirs.

I paused for us to start over. Irene continued to veer and lurch. I drew her closer, meaning to slow her down. This wasn't how she took it, though. She wrenched herself away, into the path of a free-form dancer, a woman whose quick reaction enabled her to avoid a direct collision with Irene. It was an artful dodge, a swivel of the hips and a sidestep, but it cost her her drink. It spilled, grounding a few of the flying paisleys at her feet and, if the Orient's rugs are its maps, defiling the city that had produced it—not the market square or the harbor, to judge from the spot, but a significant tract on the outskirts, capped by an ice cube.

Irene rushed off, but as nothing had cracked or banged or smashed, the hush was slow to descend. Stan didn't so much stop playing as wind down. The dancers stood wide-eyed along the edge of the rug. Someone turned up the lights. "What happened?" a man whose feet were still dancing asked.

The reply, from a woman with lavender-tinted eyeglass lenses, was too low for me to catch. I shut my eyes and covered the lids with my fingertips. As I was opening them, Corky came up and kissed me half on the lips. "Itchy fingers and busy hands," she declared. "Who'd have guessed? G'night, darling."

"Volatile's not the half of it," someone said behind me. "He's a one-man wrecking crew." The speaker came nearer, clapping me on the back with a malign hand. "Looks like you've fixed their wagon this time, champ."

I turned to give it a swat. "Lighten up," Hector said. "I'm just busting your chops."

"I know what you were doing. It's what you do."

Irene returned with a bottle of soda water and a rag with which she began dabbing at the spot on the rug.

Bud stepped between Hector and me. Bud's jacket was off and his sleeves were rolled up. I wondered how long he'd been back inside. "Hector's just razzing you," he said. "Besides, it's nothing. Coming right up, isn't it, Irene?"

"All gone," she said. "Just about."

"No hard feelings, all right?" Hector reached around Bud and offered me his hand.

I was hit by a new wave of fatigue. It seemed again that I

was walking home: the cloudbank, the wind in the trees, and the light on the salt pond were as real to me as if I was really outside.

I snapped awake and said, "All right."

"Looks like it's time to turn in, champ. Keep that fly zipped, wherever you may roam."

In the lamplit corner, smoke washed over the shade as it drifted toward the piano case. The back and forth of departures reflected in boomeranging glimmers on the glass-topped coffee table.

It took a moment to remember where I'd left my coat. Something about putting it on once I had, the feel of the lining on the back of my hands or its weight against me, recalled the identical sensation of the same action that morning in the hotel lobby in Zurich. It seemed to me that I might still be there, that what was remembered might be before my eyes and what was before my eyes might be behind them. This may have been to the good. With only insult and embarrassment to keep me awake, it may have been better not to know where I stood.

I headed down Bud's walk beneath a lifting sky—moonlight was finding its way between the clouds and glistening on the wet bricks at the edge of the driveway—when I heard the door I'd come through open behind me and footsteps approach. The footfall grew louder. I walked faster, and my toe clipped a planter beside a drainpipe. I might have stumbled into a flower bed if the man I was hurrying from hadn't caught me. "Easy there. Did you think a mugger was stalking you?"

I straightened my coat and kept walking. Bud marched along with me in only his shirtsleeves. Our feet crunched gravel. "Your urban instincts coming out," he added.

"I haven't got any urban instincts."

As we walked along the driveway, he shifted from my right

flank to my left, putting himself between me and a couple of cars—his Giulietta and a big sedan—that were parked at odd angles as if on a showroom floor. He brushed back his curl and let his hand rest on his head for a moment. "Here's the—"

"Hey, Bud!" a man standing beside the cars called. "Hey! Bud!"

Bud sighed and turned to the man. I kept going. "Hold up, Neil, would you?" he told me, starting toward the man.

"I should be able to find my way without a guide," I said behind him, more quietly than I'd intended.

"I wanted to say sorry again," the man told Bud. He was hatless and had turned up his collar.

I took a step in their direction, and a few more, over to Bud's Giulietta. The panel above the rear wheel on the passenger side had been gashed. The jagged mesh looked like the outcome of a shark attack.

"That's all right," Bud replied, pawing the gravel. "We'll get it straightened out."

"I know we will."

A woman got out of the sedan. "The main thing is no one got hurt," she said. "Has anyone seen my shoe?"

"That's the main thing," the man agreed.

"I'm sorry too," I mumbled in Bud's direction—he was a few yards off and was turned the other way—and started again for home over the wet ankle-high grass.

I didn't get far before Bud had caught up to me. He didn't say anything this time. To keep quiet must have been a struggle for him. I could all but hear his gears clicking. As we waded through the draft onto a rise where there were more grada-tions of darkness than the eye could stitch, I thought I'd better break the silence. "I'll be all right from here," I said.

He didn't reply, didn't turn around or even hesitate. "I'll see about setting some time aside for you next week. We can ride in together," I added.

Nothing I said made any difference. He stuck with me. We'd come through the gap in the yews and had the lights from my house to guide us. Beside the ash stump, near the top of the orchard, he stepped on one end of a hefty stick, causing the other end to shoot up to his waist, where he snatched it out of the air. "How about that?" he said. "Practically leapt into my hand."

On the orchard ground, the underside of apple leaves glistened beneath the fallen fruit's spotted peels. Mist sprayed us from the trees, and the limbs appeared to shiver in the light behind them. Oil wrinkled the surface of a puddle at the base of Peter's memorial dogwood.

Rotten apple scraps gummed our soles as we followed the flagstones to the lighted porch. Each window in the row on the garage door appeared in another shade of black. Frances barked her perplexed alarm from inside, bringing the hum of car tires on the boulevard to my notice by momentarily drowning it out. I reached into my pocket for my keys and had another mental flash of the hotel lobby in Zurich that morning, when I'd handed in my room key; again *Min Vater isch en Appenzeller* chimed in my head, its rhythm broken by the tapping of Bud's stick. Droplets rimed his hair and collar, but his temple throbbed and his eyes glowed: *he* certainly knew where he was.

He started to follow me in but maidenlike I headed him off in the doorway. "Thanks for the escort. I can put you on to a body shop that does good work. Looks like you'll need it."

He lifted his eyes to mine. "It's your help I need, Neil."

"My money, you mean."

"That's right."

I leaned against the doorjamb. Warm air hissing from a duct behind the open door drifted under the back of my coat.

He intoned a figure, softly as if to rarefy it. I scraped with my toe at a moth wing that was stuck to the side of the milk box. A foil bottle top lay on a step below.

"I can make do with slightly less," he added.

"You're dickering? I never asked the price."

"No, of course not. You're right. My mistake. The point is, whatever figure we hit on . . . Say, would you mind stepping down from there? I'm getting a stiff neck. . . . The point is—that's some news, by the way, about your being bought out: congratulations!—the point is, you're right about the figure, whether we decide on a few thousand more or less, it's small beer for you."

I'd have stayed where I was, watching the mist gather like some byproduct of calculation in his hair, if Frances hadn't squeezed past me out the door. She wouldn't wander far, especially not in a cold drizzle, but I went to the edge of the walk to keep an eye on her. Bud followed.

"You're jumping to conclusions," I said.

"It's no jump, not when you get your money back before you've missed it. The payments I've got coming in the next week or two will cover your loan twice over."

"Aren't they already mortgaged?"

"Some are. That's why I need you to tide me over. You'd think that with the terms I gave him, that pest Vogel might be a little forgiving. But I wouldn't put it past him to move against me first chance he gets. I don't get the sense that patience is in his line. I shouldn't have let myself get talked into dealing with him."

"Frances!" I cried at the sound of cracking twigs, "get out

of there!" Seeking privacy in which to do her business, she was trying to wedge herself in a gap in the boxwood hedge below the porch. She backed out like a truck at the bottom of a cul-de-sac.

"You were saying?" Bud said.

"I wasn't saying anything."

"I know it's been a bumpy ride. I could have been more careful about the people I got involved with. When that engineer wasn't drunk, he was in a caffeine fever. And my cousin's friend—his outfit's threatening to come after me."

"For what?"

"For next to nothing. It's taking a bit longer than I'd expected to fill their order. It's only been a few weeks. Can you believe it? An enormous operation like that."

"I can."

"Exactly. I tell my cousin to ask his friend to cool his jets, and he jumps down my throat. Such a sweet, helpful guy, I thought. I hadn't seen the other side. There's one thing, though. These desertions make you tremendously grateful to the few people you can count on. And that's you, Neil. You're the straight shooter in the bunch. I'm sorry to have to lean on you."

Frances trotted toward another set of shrubs and disappeared beneath a buckeye canopy. I trailed her, keeping to the garden path, hands in my pockets, Bud at my side. He didn't have *his* hands in his pockets. One wagged his new walking stick, the other hewed the wind with gesture: he was making his stand, exuberantly, but also with a show of disinterest, as if a principle were at stake instead of his livelihood.

And I? I was just walking my dog, checking for stars behind the scudding clouds.

"It is unfortunate," I agreed.

"These are growing pains. We've got to take the long view."

Frances emerged from the bush, shook herself, and trotted back to the front door.

I tried to walk back up the path, but now it was his turn to block my way. "How much are we talking about here—these are not great sums! And for two, three weeks tops. It can't hurt you."

A pair of chimney swifts swooped and fluttered around the turret on the third floor. As they darted past my office, I caught a glimpse, fast as their flight, of a figure in the window behind them, oblique to the glass, veiled by the curtain, identifiable as myself by the rough edges of his front teeth and the tiny screws at the corners of his eyeglass frames. I blinked and he was gone.

I stepped around Bud onto the lawn. "What would you know about that?"

He stopped, and so did I. He grabbed my arm and knit his brow, or so it seemed from a series of smudges in the darkness. Maybe my eyeglasses needed a wipe. "Look, it wasn't . . . She wasn't—"

"You misunderstand me." I freed myself from his grip and marched on, rejoining the path.

He hurried alongside me. "Well, you might feel this way now. I'll check back with you tomorrow."

"I wouldn't bother."

"For Chrissake, Neil, you know how these things go! If Vogel moves on me, the banks will get nervous and try to grab what they can too. There'll be a feeding frenzy. They might even come after you."

"They wouldn't get far."

I stopped and faced him near the top of the path, in the delta of the porch light spilling down the front steps. A dimmer light from an upstairs window turned his shirt buttons a pale green.

He cleared his throat but before he could speak I cut him off. "There's nothing more I can do for you, Bud."

His shirt was soaked through—he caught his breath against a shiver. His high color had sallowed. His forelock, wet and straightened, was glued to his cheek. "Nothing?"

I nodded.

He drummed the stick on the flagstone a few times and shuffled his feet. "Then I've got bupkes."

I looked over his shoulder toward the gap in the hedge where the glow from my house converged with the fainter one from his, the title deed to which nestled among the ribbed and cabled weaves of the dress socks in my drawer. That house, his house, was about to be mine. The foreclosure would be straightforward. The balance of the mortgage wouldn't amount to much—I'd pay it off in a few strokes of the pen, tear down the house, remove the hedge, and plant an alley of sycamores from the head of his front path to the chimney in back. "If that," I mumbled, and tried to blot the image of my renovated landscape out.

Frances scratched the door and I inched toward it myself. "Fine, Neil, have it your way. But do me one favor, will you? It won't cost you a dime. Don't say I couldn't read the writing on the wall. I read it all right."

"Hmm?"

"You don't know what I'm talking about, do you?"

"No." The admission seemed to prove his point. He snickered, and his shivering might have been as much from excitement as from cold.

Then I remembered. "On your wall, you mean? At your last party?"

"That's right."

"They were shadows."

"Exactly. And all you had to do was pass your hand over them to make the words say what you wanted them to. When you became my partner, I thought that's what you'd do."

"You're not making sense, Bud."

"I wasn't wrong about the writing. I was wrong about the partner."

I was about to go in when a glimmer from a spur halfway down the length of his stick filled me with menace. He was still handling that stick, twisting and knocking and appraising it. I was about to turn my back to him but thought again.

He saw it right away. "What ever gave me the idea that he was my friend?" he asked in a negligent undertone. "What was it?" he repeated—maybe to me this time, though I didn't have an answer—and, with Frances scratching at the door again, gave the stick a short wave. "If it had been you holding this, I'd have been a fool to turn *my* back." He lifted the stick and threw it downhill; it seemed to fly for a while before crashing in the apple trees. "I'd have done it, though."

Would he have been a fool? I might have liked to tell him he wouldn't have been. But I didn't have it in me then. And anyway, I wouldn't have had the chance. I was looking toward the orchard, wondering about the damage from the stick he'd thrown. When I turned back he was already walking away fast, as at the beginning of a larger transit.

When was it that I thought I saw him again—three years later, or four? It must have been about a year before I left Dunsinane for my house here in Key West, so less than two before the onset of the emphysema that, though it makes for strangled days and long nights, can't keep me from enjoying a good smoke every so often. The specific date eludes me. It was a bright fall day—I'm sure of that much—bright and warm, and I was by myself. Mickey had prevailed on me to go down to Merrick Bay, on the South Shore, to look into a new process for seeding oyster beds in contaminated waters.

He saw an opportunity in those waters. What I saw, peering down from the jetty, was slime. The dredge and netting were an algae-colored green, the ropes gray. The oysterman, when I passed on offers to sample his product, turned a shade of red. It was bad form of me to refuse, but I wasn't in an obliging mood. I'd learned that a developer—P. T. Barnum's grandson, as it happens—had been granted a permit to parcel the estate that lay between me and the shore into half-acre residential lots. He would grace the development with the family name. If the bottleneck on the parkway I'd taken irritated me less than usual, this was because the looks I cast at the landscape had the sweetness of parting glances.

Sullen at my refusal, the oysterman had left me on my own. I had no idea what to look for in an oyster bed and was on my way in a quarter of an hour. I didn't feel like driving back right away, not on an afternoon like that. I put down the top—I was in a Mercedes coupe by then; the Giulietta's fickleness had worn me out—and followed the road signs to Jones Beach. I had never been there. The complex of parking lots, water towers, way stations, embankments, walks, outbuildings, and drinking fountains and the thought of the stocks of concrete and asphalt that had gone into them and of the piles of limestone and sand beneath them astonished me.

I had the whole expanse more or less to myself and walked until my wonder at the scale of the building was lost in the grating of stones in the surf, in the shimmer and salt. Then it was time to think of turning back.

But I couldn't turn around just anywhere. On the beach I

need a milestone. I set my sights on a tide pool winking on the sand.

I marched toward it, on and on. It receded and disappeared. Even then I kept after it, till it dawned on me in a maze of reflections—from flagpoles, trash cans, loudspeakers, spigots, seaweed, stones on a breakwater—that the pool had been a mirage.

Another objective loomed up on the spot, one that, though I couldn't exactly make it out, was too big to be an illusion: a biplane. What it was doing there I never found out. Some distance shy of it at the edge of the water, a man with binoculars strapped around his neck and a gut hanging over his bathing trunks stopped me. "Hey, mister," he said. "Are you a strong swimmer?"

"Depends what I've had for lunch," I replied with sunny-day congeniality. "Why?"

"That guy out there. He's in trouble. I'd try to help him myself if I could."

The swimmer was out beyond the breakwater. But he wasn't all that far out and didn't seem to be panicking. "What makes you think he's in trouble?"

"He's stuck. He's been swimming like that for ages, but he keeps getting pulled farther out." He glanced at his binoculars. "Brand new. He's lucky I was messing around with them and noticed him."

"Mind if I take a look?"

He lifted the strap off his neck and handed me the binoculars. "My wife ran up to the phones and called for help. Should of been here by now."

The crawl in which the swimmer's hands thrashed the water and his elbows barely broke its surface and his legs dragged him down revealed his exhaustion. But from the pace of the flow going past him, you'd have thought he was carving the waters—if, that is, you hadn't seen the like of it. "I'm not going out into a riptide like that," I said.

I lowered the binoculars and, when I looked through them again, thought I could make out the lines of the eddy. It was narrow. Forty or fifty feet to either side of the swimmer, the whitecaps rolled in; but where he swam the surface was calmer. By swimming across the tide, parallel to the shore, he might have been able to free himself. Instead he thrashed away, four strokes and a breath, four strokes and a breath.

He lifted his head out of the water between strokes to peek shoreward. I blinked. Was that Bud? The resemblance wasn't so strong. The swimmer's features were less firm, deeper set, puffier. But then, why did I think of it? What had I recognized? It wasn't impossible—Bud had to have gone somewhere. The change might be an effect of the soak and of the years. I kept the lenses trained on him, watched his head bob on the water, waited for him to take another look.

"If you don't mind," the man beside me said, tapping the side of the binoculars.

"Just another minute." The swimmer was losing more ground. He was bound to look up again, to wave or shout.

I waited, but he kept paddling. When the man's wife joined us and asked to look through the binoculars, I gave them to her. Stocky and gavel-kneed like her husband, she'd raised the binoculars to her eyes when he snatched them from her.

"For Pete's sake," she said, "give me a chance."

"Doesn't look good," he said. "Doesn't look good at all." The swimmer was a vanishing speck.

"What's keeping the rescue boat?" his wife asked.

We heard a churning on the water and saw the launch scudding toward the swimmer, its bow high.

"Lucky guy," said the man beside me. The boat circled, the motor droning at idle.

"He nearly drowned," his wife said. "You call that luck?"

They hoisted the swimmer up and in. I pointed at the binoculars. "Would you mind letting me take another look?" I asked. "I think it might be someone I used to know."

"That'd be some coincidence," the man said. "All right, but be quick about it."

It took me a moment to sight the boat in the lenses. By then the pilot had started to swing it around, and the swimmer, hunched in the stern with a towel draped over him, faced away from me. The skin on his neck and ear was lobster-colored.

"Seen enough?" the man asked me. The prow cut a long arc through the swell.

I held on to the binoculars. At the end of the turn, the swimmer looked over his shoulder at the shore, straight into my sights. His hair was thin, his eyes beady, his mouth turned down at the corners without a hint of gratitude, let alone the elation that Bud would have felt to be still kicking. It wasn't Bud.

But walking back up the beach through an azure broken only by a cloud whose fish shape, imitating the form of the land below, suggested a parallel life elsewhere, I was less sure that I *had* seen enough. It wasn't Bud, but it might have been.

acknowledgments

This book could not have been written without help from Nick and Maura Balaban, Marilyn Berger, Jeremy Berlin, Andy Cohn, Frederick Crews, Shelagh Eldon, Jeffrey Fleisher, Don Hewitt, Brigid Hughes, Diane Johnson, Ferrell Mackey, Sara Michas-Martin, the Sewanee Writers' Conference, Simona Sawhney, Frank Steinfield, Christopher Tilghman, the Virginia Center for the Creative Arts, David Wallenstein, Joanne Wallenstein, Stephen Wallenstein, and Ted Weissberg. It would not have been begun or persevered in or completed without Ginger Strand's encouragement and savoir-faire. My debt to the extraordinary reader and editor Kathleen White for her ingenuity in shaping early drafts is greater still. Jeff Hantman, Alan King, Bud and Patricia Miller, Howard Pashman, Mike Pressman, Lou Wechsler, Fred Wilpon, and Howell Woltz replied generously to all the questions I could think to ask. My dog Orlando lay at my feet through much of the writing and led me on daily walks through woods where the characters' moods and motives were conceived. Would that I could walk with her still. The commitment and acumen that Ben Barnhart brought to refining the manuscript from the moment he took it on are in themselves an inspiration to produce another. Publicist is supposed to be a results-oriented job, but the fun I've had dealing with Ethan Rutherford trumps numerical consideration. To the extent that this novel may be said to be about failed partnerships, the experience of writing it ran counter to the theme: *The Arriviste*'s existence rests on acts of kindness for which I can hardly be grateful enough.

James Wallenstein's work has appeared in *GQ, The Believer, Antioch Review, Boston Review, Hudson Review, Jacket Magazine,* and elsewhere. He lives in New York. *The Arriviste* is his first novel.

Milkweed Editions

Founded as a nonprofit organization in 1980, Milkweed Editions is an independent publisher. Our mission is to identify, nurture, and publish transformative literature, and build an engaged community around it.

Join Us

In addition to revenue generated by the sales of books we publish, Milkweed Editions depends on the generosity of institutions and individuals like you. In an increasingly consolidated and bottom-line-driven publishing world, your support allows us to select and publish books on the basis of their literary quality and transformative potential. Please visit our Web site (www.milkweed.org) or contact us at (800) 520-6455 to learn more.

Milkweed Editions, a nonprofit publisher, gratefully acknowledges sustaining support from Amazon.com; Emilie and Henry Buchwald; the Bush Foundation; the Patrick and Aimee Butler Foundation; Timothy and Tara Clark; the Dougherty Family Foundation; Friesens; the General Mills Foundation; John and Joanne Gordon; Ellen Grace; William and Jeanne Grandy; the Jerome Foundation; the Lerner Foundation; Sanders and Tasha Marvin; the McKnight Foundation; Mid-Continent Engineering; the Minnesota State Arts Board, through an appropriation by the Minnesota State Legislature and a grant from the National Endowment for the Arts; Kelly Morrison and John Willoughby; the National Endowment for the Arts; the Navarre Corporation; Ann and Doug Ness; Jörg and Angie Pierach; the Carl and Eloise Pohlad Family Foundation; the RBC Foundation USA; the Target Foundation; the Travelers Foundation; Moira and John Turner; and Edward and Jenny Wahl.

Interior design by Ann Sudmeier
Typeset in Dante MT Pro
by BookMobile Design and Publishing Services, Minneapolis
Printed on acid-free 100% post consumer waste paper
by Friesens Corporation

ENVIRONMENTAL BENEFITS STATEMENT

Milkweed Editions saved the following resources by printing the pages of this book on chlorine free paper made with 100% post-consumer waste.

TREES	WATER	SOLID WASTE	GREENHOUSE GASES
41 FULLY GROWN	18,754 GALLONS	1,139 POUNDS	3,894 POUNDS

Calculations based on research by Environmental Defense and the Paper Task Force. Manufactured at Friesens Corporation